The River of Silver

"Much, in the end, like the world of Daevabad itself. And if this is the last we see of Chakraborty's wildly unique magical world, it is certainly a gleaming and precious gift."

—*Paste Magazine*

"This story compilation is a must-have . . . as it showcases her amazing characters and lush world one more time."

—*Library Journal*

The Empire of Gold

"Chakraborty's writing continues to impress and it flows beautifully once again in this book."

—The Speculative Shelf

"A feat of masterful story craft, exploding out the world while also never losing sight of the intimate moments driving its main characters. Simply excellent."

—The Library Ladies

"The perfect end to a must-read series!"

—Novel Knight

"If lush world-building and political intrigue is what draws you into a fantasy story, this one has plenty to offer."

—Novels and Nebulas

The Kingdom of Copper

"The second installment of Chakraborty's stunningly rendered Middle Eastern fantasy trilogy. . . . As good or better than its predecessor: promise impressively fulfilled."

—*Kirkus Reviews* (starred review)

THE

River
OF *Silver*

Tales from the
Daevabad Trilogy

S. A. CHAKRABORTY

HARPER Voyager
An Imprint of HarperCollins*Publishers*

THE RIVER OF SILVER. Copyright © 2022 by Shannon Chakraborty. Excerpt from THE ADVENTURES OF AMINA AL-SIRAFI © 2023 by Shannon Chakraborty. All rights reserved. Printed in the United States of America. No part of this book may be used or reproduced in any manner whatsoever without written permission except in the case of brief quotations embodied in critical articles and reviews. For information, address HarperCollins Publishers, 195 Broadway, New York, NY 10007.

HarperCollins books may be purchased for educational, business, or sales promotional use. For information, please email the Special Markets Department at SPsales@harpercollins.com.

Harper Voyager and design are trademarks of HarperCollins Publishers LLC.

A hardcover edition of this book was published in 2022 by Harper Voyager, an imprint of HarperCollins Publishers.

FIRST HARPER VOYAGER PAPERBACK EDITION PUBLISHED 2023.

Designed by Paula Russell Szafranski
Interior ornaments © Fine Art Studio / Shutterstock.com

Library of Congress Cataloging-in-Publication Data has been applied for.

ISBN 978-0-06-323391-1

23 24 25 26 27 LBC 5 4 3 2 1

CONTENTS

For my readers.

This would have never been possible without you.

AUTHOR'S NOTE

Though it was more than a decade ago, I can still remember the day I first shared what would become *The City of Brass* with my writing group back in Brooklyn. New to the group, new to writing, and *extremely* new to sitting on a stranger's couch while presenting my heart's work, I shared the kind of manuscript I thought epic fantasy was supposed to be: one including at least a dozen character viewpoints, multiple cross-country treks, and scores of different cities, villages, and expansive magical vistas, all with pages upon pages of detailed backstory, convoluted histories, and exhaustive descriptions.

You might say they disagreed.

There are certainly epic fantasy stories that require that kind of exploration, they argued, but at its heart, *The City of Brass* was about Nahri's and Ali's journeys. About a young woman ripped away from everything she knows, forced to rebuild her life again and again—and yet who finds in that survival a fierce determination to fight for her people and her happiness. About a young man who struggles to reconcile his faith and his ideals of justice with the reality that the city he loves is built on oppression—and that dismantling it will mean bringing down his own family's rule. And while I wanted to set them in a fully realized world among a rich constellation of friends and family, lovers and enemies, all with their own histories, quirks, and agendas, I did decide early on that *this* particular story would focus on Nahri and Ali, and later Dara.

I have a great affection for my side characters, however, and a firm belief that writing things out is the most organic way to let stories grow and breathe. So in the course of working on the trilogy, I've gone on parallel quests with unnamed scouts and charted Muntadhir and Jamshid's relationship in their own words, seen Zaynab rise as a rebel leader, and dived into Dara's youth in a far more ancient Daevabad. I've written scenes that informed my own understanding of the books, even if all I took from them was a line or a sentiment. They were my own form of research notes, but not ones that I intended to share.

Then came the pandemic. Without diving too deeply into my personal experience of a crisis that still isn't over, suffice to say that for the first few months of lockdown, I couldn't write a thing. The world was on fire, my family needed me, and I was supposed to *create*? In a desperate attempt to get literally any words down, I found myself returning to my old Daevabad scenes. Working on something familiar and already partially drafted, in a world I loved and knew intimately, proved much less intimidating than the blank page of a new project. Slowly the words began to return so I went further, envisioning the lives of my characters beyond the conclusion of *The Empire of Gold* and the tales of people long gone before *The City of Brass* begins.

I share some of those tales with you now. The stories are arranged chronologically, with a short introduction to let you place them in the context of the trilogy. I hope that you enjoy this brief return to Daevabad as much as I did and know that I am forever grateful you decided to give my books a chance.

May the fires burn brightly for you,
Shannon Chakraborty

THE RIVER OF SILVER

Manizheh

This scene takes place a few decades before *The City of Brass* and contains spoilers for the first two books.

Her son was glorious.

Manizheh traced one of Jamshid's tiny ears, drinking in the sight of his perfect little face. Though he was barely a week old, the black of his eyes was still tempered by a fiery-hued haze. His small body was warm and soft, tucked safe in the cradle of her arms. Even so, Manizheh held him closer as she made her way out of the tent. It might be spring, but it was still early in the season and Zariaspa clung to its chilly mornings.

The valley before her was glowing in the dawn light, flashes of pink and purple clover twinkling with dew against the long grass. She stepped carefully over scattered stones and broken bricks. She and Kaveh had pitched their tent in one of the many forgotten human ruins that dotted this land, and little was left now to distinguish those remnants from the rocky hillside, save a few archways and one squat column decorated with a pattern of diamonds. Yet as she walked, Manizheh wondered what this place might have once been. Could it have been a castle, a royal home walked by other anxious new parents terrified of the world into which they'd brought a child with noble blood?

Manizheh glanced down again at her son. Her Jamshid. His was a regal name, taken from the humans long ago like so many of their names—a borrowing most Daevas would deny, but Manizheh had been educated as a Nahid, learning things the rest of her people were not permitted. Jamshid was a name of legend and kingship. An optimistic name, spiraling from the last shred of hope in her soul.

"This is my favorite place in the world," she said softly as Jamshid's eyelids fluttered, the baby sleepy and milk-drunk. She laid his head against her shoulder, breathing in the sweet scent of his neck. "You are going to have so many adventures here. Your baba will get you a pony and teach you to ride, and you can explore to your heart's content. I want you to explore, my love," she whispered. "I want you to explore and dream and get lost in a place where no one will watch you. Where no one will cage you."

Where Ghassan will not hurt you. Where he will never, ever learn of you.

For if there was one thing about her baby's future she was sure of, it was that Ghassan couldn't learn of Jamshid. The very prospect made Manizheh sick with fear, and she was not a woman easily frightened. Ghassan would kill Kaveh, of that she had no doubt, in the longest, most excruciating manner he could devise. He would punish Rustam, breaking what was left of her traumatized brother's spirit.

And Jamshid . . . her mind would not let her contemplate the ways Ghassan would use him. If Jamshid was lucky, Ghassan would settle for inflicting on him the same life of terror she and Rustam had been subjected to: enslaved in the palace infirmary and reminded every day that if it were not for the usefulness of their Nahid blood, their family would have been exterminated long ago.

But she didn't think her son would be lucky. Manizheh had watched the years harden Ghassan into a reflection of his tyrannical father. Maybe Manizheh had been a proud fool to deny Ghassan what his heart had wanted most; maybe it would have been best to unite their families and tribes: to force a smile to her face in a royal wedding and close her eyes in the darkness of his bed. Maybe her people would be breathing easier and her brother wouldn't jump when someone closed a door too loudly. Was that not the best choice for so very many women, the most they could hope for?

But Manizheh hadn't chosen that. Instead she had betrayed

Ghassan in the most personal way she could, and Manizheh knew if she and Kaveh were caught, she'd pay for that in kind.

She pressed a kiss to the soft downy hair lying in a messy pouf around Jamshid's head. "I'll come back for you, little one, I promise. And when I do . . . I pray you can forgive me."

Jamshid stirred in his sleep, making a tiny sound that drove a knife of grief through her chest. Manizheh closed her eyes, trying to memorize every detail of this moment. His weight in her arms and his sweet scent. The breeze whispering through the grasses and the chill in the air. She wanted to remember holding her son before she took everything away from him.

"Manu?"

Manizheh stilled at Kaveh's hesitant voice, her emotions free-falling again. Kaveh. Her partner and conspirator since they were children sneaking out to steal horses and wander the countryside. Her closest friend, and then her lover when their curiosity and teen-age pinings turned to fumbling touches and stolen moments.

Another person she was about to lose. Manizheh had overstayed her visit to Zariaspa by three months, ignoring Ghassan's letters ordering her return. She'd be surprised if the king wasn't already mustering soldiers to retrieve her. One thing was certain: there would be no leaving Daevabad again. Not while Ghassan ruled anyway.

The ring, she tried to remind herself. *While you still have the ring, there is hope.* But her childhood fantasy of breaking free the sleeping Afshin warrior from the slave ring she and Rustam had found so long ago seemed just that right now: a fantasy.

Kaveh spoke again. "I prepared everything you asked. Are you . . . are you all right?"

Manizheh wanted to laugh. She wanted to cry. No, she was not all right. She clutched her baby closer. It seemed impossible that she would have to let him go. She wanted to scream at her Creator. She wanted to collapse in Kaveh's arms. For once she wanted someone to tell *her* that everything was going to be okay. She wanted to stop being the Banu Nahida, the goddess who was allowed no weakness.

But hers was not a role one could escape. Even with Kaveh, she would always be his Nahid before his lover and friend, and she would not shake his faith now. She made sure her voice was steady and her eyes were dry before she turned around.

Heartbreak was writ across his face. "You look beautiful with him," Kaveh whispered, reverence and pain edging his voice. He drew closer, gazing at their sleeping son. "Are you sure about this?"

Manizheh rubbed Jamshid's back. "It's the only way to hide who he is. Nahid magic is strong when we're children. If we don't do this now, he'll otherwise be healing his wet nurses and having skinned knees close up."

Kaveh gave her an uncertain glance. "And if one day he should need such abilities?"

It was a justified question. In her arms, Jamshid seemed so tiny and fragile. There were illnesses and curses he could catch. He could tumble off a horse and break his neck. Drink from one of the many iron-poisoned streams that coursed through Zariaspa's thick forests.

And yet those risks were still less than getting caught out as a Nahid.

Amazing, how death might be more preferable to life in Daevabad.

"I don't know what else to do, Kaveh," she confessed as they returned to the tent. Their fire altar smoldered in the eastern corner. "I'm hoping a day will come when I can remove the mark, but that day is not today. Honestly, it's a magic so old and understudied that I just hope I can make it work."

"How will we know if it does?"

Manizheh stared at her son, stroking a finger down his tiny scrunched face. She tried to imagine how Jamshid would look when he was three months old. Three years. Thirteen. She did not want to contemplate beyond that. She did not want to contemplate entirely missing him grow up.

"If it works, I won't be able to control his pain," she answered. "And he will start to scream."

THREE WEEKS AFTER HOLDING HER BABY FOR THE LAST time, Manizheh stood in Daevabad's throne room.

"So you see . . . ," she said, finishing her fictional, fumbling excuse for the monthslong delay in Zariaspa, "my experiments at the time were far too promising to abandon. I needed to stay and see them through."

For a long, tense moment the room was so silent one could hear a pin drop. Then Ghassan drew up on his throne, fury scorching his expression.

"Your experiments?" he repeated. "You stayed in Zariaspa, ignoring my pleas and messengers, to tend to your experiments? My wife, your queen, is dead because of your *experiments*?"

Saffiyeh was never my queen. But Manizheh did not dare say that. Instead, she fought not to sway on her feet. Nahid magic be damned, she was utterly drained. Her legs and back ached from riding, and her breasts were swollen with milk that would not stop, the slightest pressure of the pads and cabbage leaves stuffed beneath her shirt to conceal her condition bringing stinging tears to her eyes.

Pushing past all that, she said, "I did not receive your messages in time." Manizheh was too weary and heartbroken to make her response sound sincere; even she could hear how devoid of caring her words came out. "If I had, I would have returned sooner."

Ghassan stared at her, looking betrayed. There was genuine grief in his expression, an emotion Manizheh had not seen in his face for a very long time. With each decade as Daevabad's tyrant, he expressed less sentiment, as though ruling the city was sucking the warmth from his heart.

She had no sympathy. Ghassan had had her seized—well, no, not seized, because not even the king was terrifying enough to make people touch her—but she'd been surrounded by soldiers and forced off her horse at the Daeva Gate, made to walk the entirety of the main boulevard through her tribe's quarter to the palace. Manizheh had done so, trying to keep her head held high and hide the fact that she struggled for breath as the road switchbacked up Daevabad's hills. Her people had been watching, their frightened faces visible behind windows and cracked doors, and Manizheh could not let the Daevas see her falter. She was their Banu Nahida, their light. It was her duty.

But by the time she'd arrived at the palace her ancestors had built, its stones singing to her, she was a mess. Her clothes were filthy, her dress torn and streaked with mud. Her chador had slipped to her shoulders, revealing her wild hair and ash-dotted brow. All this before they'd even taken her to the throne room, the sacred place where the Nahid Council had once deliberated.

She wondered what her ancestors would think to see her now, disheveled and dirty at the foot of her family's stolen throne, meant to grovel before the descendants of the djinn who had slaughtered them.

If she was wise, she'd apologize. That's what Ghassan wanted, Manizheh knew. She had humiliated him. Daevabad's court was vicious, and its rulers were not spared the gossip of courtiers. Manizheh had made him look weak. Was Daevabad's fearsome king really all that mighty if his own Nahid could defy him? If that defiance had killed his wife? And truthfully, for Saffiyeh's death, Manizheh was sorry. She had never borne any ill will toward Saffiyeh; if anything, she had hoped Ghassan's marriage meant he'd finally given up his designs on her. It would cost Manizheh nothing but pride to apologize, and perhaps a good healer would, chastened by the unnecessary loss of life.

Manizheh held Ghassan's gaze, aware of the court staring at her. His Qaid, Wajed, another Geziri djinn. His Ayaanle grand wazir. For all Ghassan's chirping about improving relations between the Daeva and djinn tribes, there was not a single Daeva face among those staring down at her. And these djinn didn't look like they were grieving. They looked eager. Hungry. Everyone enjoyed seeing an uppity "fire worshipper" shoved back into place.

We are better than you. I am better than you. Not for the first time, Manizheh was tempted to give in to the rage that roared inside her. She could probably break the bones of half the men sneering at her, urge the ceiling to collapse and bury them all.

But she was outnumbered, and for such an act, Manizheh knew every Daeva in the city would die. She would be run through with the weapons of any man left alive here, and then Rustam would be executed, as would Nisreen, her most loyal friend and assistant. The priests in the temple and the children at school would follow. Their Quarter would run black with innocent blood.

So Manizheh lowered her gaze. But she did not apologize. "Are we done?" she asked instead, her voice cold.

She could hear the rage in Ghassan's. "No. But you are no doubt needed in the infirmary by the other patients you abandoned. Go."

Go. The command scorched through her, humiliating. Manizheh spun on her heel.

But he wasn't done. "You will not leave this palace again," Ghassan declared to her back. "We would not wish for something to happen to you."

Her hands were burning with magic. A snap of her fingers. Would it be enough to shatter the bones at the base of his skull?

She squared her shoulders and relaxed her hands. "Understood."

Gossip rose in waves as she strode through the crowd toward the door. The djinn's metal-toned gazes were hostile and accusing. A heartless witch, she heard. Jealous and cruel. A snob. A bitch.

A fire worshipper.

Manizheh held her head high and swept through the door.

But outside the throne room was no easier. It was the middle of the day, and the palace was bustling with secretaries and ministers, nobles and scholars. Her filthy chador still dropped to her shoulders, Manizheh was instantly recognizable, and she could only imagine how tarnished she looked, dirty and without escort after being punished by their rightful, believing king. The noise of the corridor died with people stopping to stare.

A pair of Daevas across the hall, looking worried, moved for her. Manizheh met their eyes and slightly shook her head. They couldn't help and she wouldn't put any of her people at further risk. Instead, she faced the whispers alone. She was cold, it was hissed. She was evil. She'd all but murdered Saffiyeh, the sweetest of queens, to get back into Ghassan's bed.

The burning had spread up her arms, her neck. A haze swam before Manizheh's eyes. She could sense every stone, every drop of

Nahid blood that had been spilled in this place. Was everyone else aware how much she and her people had sacrificed for them to be standing there, judging her now?

Of course not.

Aware that the palace magic was going to simply *take* her rage and do something regrettable with it if she didn't get herself under control, Manizheh headed toward the first entrance to the garden she saw, breathing fast. She seemed to startle the guard, who jumped at the sight of her, but recovered in time to slam the door and throw the latch lock once she was through.

Manizheh fell back against the stone wall and covered her face with her hands. Her entire body hurt. Her soul hurt. She felt empty and burned out, a husk. All she could see in the darkness of her mind's eye was Jamshid and Kaveh where she last left them—the man she loved holding their forbidden child in his arms among the ruins and spring flowers. She could still hear Jamshid's wails as she tattooed the mark on his shoulder, severing him from his heritage. The sound had been ringing in her ears since she left. Hiccupping screams and muffled sobs, again and again.

Then Manizheh stilled. It wasn't just the memory of Jamshid's cries she heard; she heard another child, weeping somewhere beyond the tangled web of greenery.

She hesitated. This was the wildest corner of the garden, neglected for centuries and now essentially a feral jungle. Its towering trees soared beyond the palace walls, thorny vines choked the paths, and the undergrowth was so thick that the forest floor was dark and slippery with rotting leaves and moss. Here the canal that ran through the palace was silent and unfathomably deep, its black water claiming at least one life a year. Of course because this was Daevabad, it wasn't merely nature that was dangerous. The palace magic that flowed through her veins had always seemed most ruthless among these silent trees. As if something ancient and wounded had buried itself beneath the ground, fed on the blood and suffering of millennia.

Accordingly, this part of the garden was avoided by anyone with

sense. Things happened in these woods that djinn didn't understand. A once-scrawny cat had emerged as a tiger with glass teeth and
a serpentine tail. The shadows were said to peel from the ground
and swallow the unwary. A mix of gossip and genuine magic, the line
between stories told to frighten children and servants who actually
did go missing hard to parse out.

Stories that hadn't frightened Manizheh. Until now. Yes, she
was a Nahid and the palace's magic had never harmed her. But she
couldn't imagine what would have lured a child out here, and for a
moment, she wondered if the sound might be a trick, a cruelly personal goad.

The wet, hiccupping sobs didn't stop, trick or not. Growing concerned, she followed them, half expecting to find some monstrously
large bird making mimic calls.

But it wasn't a bird she stumbled upon. Beneath a massive cedar,
swathed in roots so tangled that one would have to be very small to
slip through, was a young boy. He lay curled on the mossy ground,
hugging his knees to his chest as his entire body shook with sobs.
The finery of his clothes stood out in the gloom. Where it wasn't
streaked with leaves and dirt, his cotton dishdasha was so white it
gleamed. The sash at his waist was silk; bronze and indigo patterned
against a rich copper. Gold ringed his wrists and ears, pearls loop-
ing his neck. They weren't the garments most little boys playing outdoors would wear—certainly not her own son, who would dress in
homespun wool and patched hats as he shivered during Zariaspa's
winters.

Then again, the little boy before her wasn't like most. He was the
next djinn king.

He was also very foolish. For a glance revealed young Muntadhir
al Qahtani appeared to be alone and unarmed, one mistake com-
pounded with another. She couldn't imagine what had led to the cos-
seted little prince being out here by himself, weeping in the jungle.

Can't you? After all, Manizheh had been a royal child and had
learned early to mask her emotions. They were weaknesses in the palace, liabilities others would seize upon to hurt you. And Muntadhir

was not just the son of the king—he came from a family of warriors, from a people who prized themselves on their hardiness. He was clearly old enough to know the price of grieving where he could be observed.

He was also going to get eaten by a shadow creature if he kept carrying on out here, for which the Nahid siblings would likely get blamed, and so Manizheh stepped forward. "Peace be upon you, little prince."

Muntadhir started, his head jerking up. His wet eyes had no sooner locked on hers than they went wide with fear. He scrambled to his feet, backing into the tree trunk.

Manizheh raised her hands. "I do not mean you any harm," she said softly. "But this is not a safe place."

The prince only blinked. He was a beautiful child, with big bright gray eyes framed by long dark lashes. A hint of russet gleamed in the black locks that fell in perfect curls past his chin. Closer now, Manizheh could see that tiny amulets of sand-blasted glass had been pinned to his clothes. A necklace of similar materials wound around his neck, the pale glass beads interspersed with those of wood and shell framing a pendant of hammered copper. The pendent was likely filled with holy verses written on minuscule scripts of paper. Village superstitions to protect the young royal from all manner of evil. His mother had been from a small coastal settlement, and if Manizheh had found Saffiyeh meek and quiet, she could not help but note how she had still tried to protect her son with what she knew.

Now she was gone. Muntadhir had frozen, like a rabbit in the presence of a hawk.

Manizheh knelt, hoping to appear less threatening. Despite what the djinn believed, she would never hurt a child. "I am very sorry about your mother, little one."

"Then why did you kill her?" Muntadhir burst out. He wiped his running nose on his sleeve, starting to cry again. "She never did anything to you. She was good and kind . . . She was my amma," he wept. "I need her."

"I know, and I'm sorry. I lost my mother too when I was young."

Lost was a cruelly accurate word, because Manizheh's mother had been among the many Daevas who disappeared under Khader's, Ghassan's father, brutal reign. "And I know it seems impossible now, but you will survive her. She would want you to. You have people here who love you, and they'll take care of you." The last part seemed like a lie, or at least not the full truth. The fact of the matter was that people would indeed be flocking to the motherless young prince, but they'd have their own schemes.

Muntadhir just stared at her. He looked completely lost. "Why did you kill her?" he whispered again.

"I didn't," Manizheh replied, keeping her voice gentle but her words firm. "Your amma was extremely sick. I didn't get your father's message in time, but I didn't mean to hurt her. I never would."

Muntadhir stepped closer. He was gripping one of the mossy branches that separated them so hard that his knuckles had paled. "They said you would say that. They said you would lie. That all the Daevas *do* is lie. They said you killed her so you could marry my father."

Hearing such bigotry muttered by adult courtiers was one thing; out of the mouth of a mourning child was so much worse. Manizheh found herself struck speechless by the accusation in his eyes. Muntadhir was standing tall now, every bit the future emir.

"I will see you dead one day." The Qahtani princeling trembled as he said the words, but he said them, as though testing out a new skill he had not yet mastered. And then, before she could respond, he fled deeper into the woods.

Manizheh watched his retreating back. Muntadhir looked so very small against the fog-shrouded undergrowth. For a fleeting moment, she wanted the prince to be consumed by the jungle, nature taking care of a threat she knew was going to fester.

And that is why you left Jamshid behind. Abandoning her son might have broken her heart, but at least he wouldn't be raised in this awful place.

Manizheh forced herself to keep walking, but she was soon exhausted, the wet heat sapping what little strength she had left. Her legs were shaky, and there was a new slickness where they joined. Though it had been weeks since Jamshid's birth, she was still bleeding off and on. Manizheh had no idea if that was normal, no idea if Nahid bodies reacted differently to birthing. By the time she was old enough to ask such questions, there were no Nahid women left who could tell her.

But her pain didn't matter. Because the closer she got to the infirmary, the clearer it was that another Nahid needed her.

If the palace magic had claimed Manizheh, its overgrown jungle interior was Rustam's. Her little brother had never been the healer she was—no one was the healer she was—but he was a genuine savant when it came to plants, and the garden was as attuned to him as a loyal, adoring dog to its master.

Now it had gone wild. New vines of ivy and gigantic trumpet-like flowers spread everywhere, the bright green of fresh growth stark. Long before it was visible, Manizheh could smell Rustam's beloved orange grove, the too-sweet aroma of overripe citrus and rot thick in the air.

Her breath caught when she came around the bend. The infirmary garden looked like it had taken a dozen doses of growth potion. Waist-tall silver-mint bushes were now the height of trees alongside platter-size roses whose thorns could serve as daggers. Rustam's orchard, his joy and point of pride, had gone savage, hulking over the rest of the garden like a looming spider. Its explosion of fruit must have been too much even for the volunteers who collected the extras for the Temple food pantries, for oranges lay rotting on the ground.

Manizheh picked her way through the weeds as fast as she could—which was not very. Her head was pounding, and a layer of ash coated her skin. Her chador was gone now, snagged by a tree, and her dirty hair hung loose around her shoulders. She'd barely made it to the pavilion when a sharp pain tore through her pelvis. She bowed over, stifling a cry.

"My lady!"

Manizheh glanced up to see Nisreen dropping the medical instruments she'd been laying out in the sun. She rushed to Manizheh's side.

"Banu Nahida . . ." Nisreen stopped, her wide worried eyes staring at Manizheh with open shock.

Manizheh gritted her teeth as the ache came again in her womb. *Breathe. Just breathe.* "Where is Rustam?" she managed.

"He's in the middle of a procedure. He'd already started when word came you were back."

"Is he all right?"

Nisreen opened and closed her mouth, looking lost for a response. "He is alive."

That was not a reassuring answer. Manizheh knew he'd be alive. Ghassan could not risk killing his only Nahid while she was still gone. But there were a very great number of other things he could do to Rustam.

"My lady, you need help," Nisreen insisted. "Let me take you to the hammam."

Manizheh pressed a fist harder against her belly. Right now she wasn't sure she could make it to the hammam, let alone clean herself up without passing out. But the signs on her body would be obvious the moment she undressed.

She met Nisreen's eyes. Her assistant, the closest thing Manizheh had to a friend. Perhaps more important, a woman who would go to her death before betraying a Nahid. She hesitated only a moment longer before taking Nisreen's outstretched arm and leaning heavily onto it.

"No one else can see me," Manizheh murmured. "When we get to the hammam, make sure there is no one there. And barricade the door behind us."

"Barricade the door?"

"Yes. I'm going to need your help, dear one. But I'll need your silence even more."

MANIZHEH DIDN'T END UP PASSING OUT IN THE BATH, though she was so dazed that she might as well have. Time moved in a blur of steam and hot water, the smells of rose soap and old blood. Nisreen was gentle and quiet. There had been a moment of hesitation when she first peeled off Manizheh's dusty clothes, but then she got to work, reliable as always. As she was bathed and scrubbed, the water turning an ugly gray, Manizheh might have wept, tears running with the soap down her face. She wasn't sure. She didn't care.

Once in her familiar bed, however, she did fall asleep and slept hard. By the time she stirred awake, her room was dark save for the light of her fire altar and of a small oil lamp that had been placed next to her bed.

She wasn't alone; her Nahid senses picked up the heartbeat and breath of another as easily as her eyes would have spotted them in better light. Disoriented, Manizheh tried to sit up and succeeded only in provoking another pain in her belly.

"It's all right," a soft voice assured. "It's just me."

"Rustam?" Manizheh blinked. Her brother came to her in blurry pieces—the black eyes they shared and the bright white of his veil.

"Baga Nahid right now." Rustam eased another pillow under her head and put a foul-smelling cup to her lips. "Drink."

Manizheh obeyed. When Rustam e-Nahid personally brewed you a potion, you drank it without question. The relief came so fast that Manizheh choked; her aches, the swelling all over her body, and her pounding head immediately eased.

"Creator bless you," she said hoarsely.

"You should eat," he said in response. "And take some water."

She drank from the new cup he offered, but shook her head when he offered up a small platter of cut fruit and plain bread. "I am not hungry."

"You need to eat, Manu. Your body's weak." Rustam reached for her hand.

Manizheh jerked her hand back before he could touch her. "I said I'm not hungry."

There was a moment of silence. She still couldn't see him well. His gaze was downcast as it usually was. Rustam rarely made eye contact with people anymore, and when he did, he struggled to maintain it.

He spoke again. "I may not have your talents, sister, but I am as Nahid as you. I do not need to touch your hand to know what has happened."

Fresh tears burned in her eyes. Manizheh hadn't cried in years before Jamshid was born. "Nothing happened. I'm fine. It was simply a rough journey."

"Manizheh—"

"*It was a rough journey,*" she repeated, her voice fierce. "Do you understand? There is nothing to talk about. Nothing to know. You can't be blamed for what you don't know."

"You and I both know that's not true." Rustam snapped his fingers and the oil lamp burned brighter, throwing wild illumination and shadows across the room. "Do not carry this burden alone. You can't. Not this."

"There is nothing to tell."

"There is! You cannot vanish for a year and come back after having a—"

The entire room shook. There was a blast of heat, and the flames in the fire altar soared, scorching the ceiling and making Rustam's effect look like child's play.

"If you continue that sentence, you will never speak again," she warned. "Do you understand?"

Rustam grabbed the empty cup from her hands, but he was trembling. His hands shook when he was afraid, an affliction he couldn't control and one that had only gotten worse over the years. He could barely hold an object without it rattling in Ghassan's presence, and when they had to attend public functions, he and Manizheh had taken to putting binders on his wrists with knotted rags he could grip to control himself.

And now Manizheh had made him tremble. She had no choice— he was foolish to speak openly when Ghassan had hidden eyes and ears everywhere—but regret immediately washed over her.

"Rustam, I'm sorry. I just—"

"I understand," he said harshly. "That you would threaten me is answer enough." He opened and closed his fists and then pressed his hands to his knees, fighting for control. "I hate this," he whispered. "I hate them. That I cannot even ask you if . . ."

"I know." Now she did take his hand. "Can I ask *you* something?"

"Of course."

"Would you add that which I cannot tell you to your prayers?"

Rustam lifted his gaze to her again. "Every day, sister."

The sincerity in his eyes only made Manizheh feel worse. She wanted to tell him. She wanted to huddle together under her blanket as they did when they were children and weep. She wanted another Nahid to tell her that it was going to be okay. That Ghassan would fall and she'd see her son again. That they would reverse the spell she'd done and return to Daevabad to rule together as their family deserved.

But her little brother looked awful. Rustam was shivering slightly, his skin pale with a sick yellow tinge. The shadows under his eyes were so pronounced, it looked like he'd been punched, and he'd lost weight. She couldn't see the rest of his face. Rustam removed his veil so rarely that she sometimes had to remind him that he could when they were alone, and Manizheh knew it wasn't just piety. He'd turned inward to survive their lives in Daevabad, retreating behind every wall he could to a place where no one could touch him.

It was enough to paint a picture of the way her brother must have suffered in the year she'd been gone. There would be no other signs. There never were. Rustam's bones healed when Ghassan's thugs broke them, as did the gashes left by whips and the burns left by acid. Ghassan had never raised a hand to Manizheh; he didn't have to. He'd learned long ago that beating her brother made her submit faster than anything else. However, not all his invisible marks had been put there by Ghassan. On Rustam's wrists was a different story. Her brother had tried to kill himself more than once, but doing so successfully was difficult for a Nahid. His last attempt—a poisoning—had been years ago, and Manizheh had been the one to bring him back. He had begged her to let him die. She had fallen to her knees and begged *him* not to leave her.

It was the last time she'd wept before Jamshid's birth.

She would not lean on Rustam further. Instead Manizheh tried to bring a steadier expression to her face. "Could you have the kitchens bring me some ginger tea?" she asked. "I think it will settle my stomach enough that I can eat."

Relief swept over his face. Ah yes, she knew the look of a healer pleased to have a solid task. "Of course." Rustam rose to his feet and then fumbled in the pockets of his robe. "I brought you something. I know you like to keep it hidden away, but I thought . . . I thought it might give you some comfort." He placed a small, hard object in her hand, closing her fingers over it before stepping back. "May the fires burn brightly for you, Manu."

Manizheh's heart twisted. She knew what was in her hand. "For you as well, beloved."

He left with a bow and Manizheh settled back into bed, curling in on herself. Only when she heard the door close did she command the flames to constrict, returning the room to darkness.

Then she slipped the ancient ring he'd given her onto her finger. The band was badly battered. Manizheh was familiar with every single one of its dents and scratches—for there was no object she had devoted more attention to than the ring containing her people's only hope at salvation.

"Please come back," she whispered. "Please save us."

Duriya

This scene takes place a year or so after the previous one and contains spoilers for all three books.

The djinn woman picked up one of the freshly washed bandages by its very edge, as if dangling a spider. She sneered. "Is this a joke?"

Duriya glanced at the bandage. It looked perfectly respectable to her, scrubbed in water so hot it had left Duriya's hands cracked, and then bleached dry by the sun.

"I don't understand, ma'am," she said, making herself sound as cowed as possible. She hated acting like this, but had long ago learned to school her tone around these demons. There was little a djinn enjoyed more than an opportunity to put a "dirt-blood" back in their place.

"They're still *damp*. Can you not tell the difference between dry and wet cloth? If I put the bandages away like this, they'll get musty. And unless *you'd* like to explain to Banu Manizheh why there's mold growing in her supplies, you'll go wash them again."

The woman threw the rag back at Duriya. Duriya caught it, staring in despair at the laundry she'd just brought in. It was to have been her *last* basket before she was allowed to go home.

"Perhaps I could let them dry in the sun a bit longer," Duriya offered. "I just took them off the line, I swear. They haven't been—"

With a single kick, the djinn woman knocked the basket of bandages over. They spilled across the supply room floor. Not that the floor was dirty—nothing attached to the infirmary or its terrifying inhabitants was allowed to be unclean. The small army of shafit servants to which Duriya belonged spent all day and night sweeping floors, scrubbing laundry, and mopping up spills. The magical patients inside—to say nothing of the ebony-eyed bone-breakers who treated them—could not possibly be subjected to unsanitary conditions, not for a moment.

I wonder if they have any idea that the servants they rely on to keep their rooms so clean have to wade through wastewater in the shafit district every time it rains. I wonder if they'd care. None of that mattered, though. The rules of the infirmary were inviolate.

Duriya bowed her head. "Yes, ma'am." Then she gathered her laundry and left.

It was an achingly gorgeous day, the sky bright and blue with jewel-toned songbirds warbling dreamy notes up in the trees. But Duriya pulled her scarf lower over her face as she left the infirmary wing and made her way along the isolated paths that led to the canal. It was best not to attract attention while alone in the palace: very few djinn came to the aid of a shafit maid. Such danger was one of the many risks of working here, the bargain one had to strike for the comparatively decent wages a palace position offered.

Risks that Duriya feared had grown more numerous. When she'd first taken a job at the palace, it had been serving Queen Saffiyeh and her little son, the heir to the djinn throne. The queen had been soft-spoken but kind, one of the few djinn who bothered to learn the names and see to the well-being of their shafit servants. Duriya had felt safe; no one touched a maid wearing the queen's colors.

Now the queen was dead, and Duriya doubted her new Nahid masters had even noticed another face among their shafit washerwomen, let alone cared about her safety. Or even her life. Shafit were warned of many things upon being dragged to Daevabad, but there was one warning given above all others:

Avoid the black-eyed djinn, the ones who called themselves Daevas.

Gruesome stories circulated about these Daevas, who were said to live apart from the other djinn and worship flames instead of God. Duriya had been cautioned never to meet the gaze of a Daeva, never to speak in their presence unless spoken to, and never, ever to touch one—shafit had lost a hand for less. And her new Nahid masters were not only Daevas—they were the *leaders* of the Daevas. The last of an ancient dynasty said to have presided over a war to exterminate the shafit, fought by an army of magically enhanced warriors who could shoot sixty arrows at a time and bury entire cities alive.

Duriya wasn't sure she believed all the rumors: this was a city of liars, after all. But the constant presence of armed soldiers in the infirmary—soldiers who didn't take their hostile gazes off either of the Nahid siblings while they worked on djinn patients—was enough to make her wonder if perhaps it was time to start looking for another job.

The bank of the canal where they did laundry was empty. Duriya dunked the basket in the water and then set to laying out the wet bandages on a line of twine stretched across a sunny break in the trees. Despite her show of obsequiousness, she had little intention of actually scrubbing these damn rags a second time. Maybe musty bandages would help the djinn with their foul dispositions.

She worked fast. The canal had become a grim reminder of just how trapped she was in Daevabad, and she didn't like to linger here. When Duriya had first started working in the palace, she had nearly wept upon seeing the rushing dark water that coursed through the garden. There were no rivers or streams in the shafit district, but here, at last, a chance presented itself.

For contrary to what she let most people believe, Daevabad and its djinn had not been Duriya's first introduction to magic.

That introduction had come much earlier, on the banks of the Nile where a lonely little girl had made a most unusual lifelong friend. And so the first opportunity she had, Duriya had raced back to the canal. She called that friend the only way she knew, a way that had never failed her: biting her finger until it bled and plunging her hand into the cold water.

"Sobek!" she'd begged. "Please . . . please hear me, old friend. I need you!"

But if Sobek had been able to hear her cry in these foreign waters, he hadn't followed it. Nor had he come any of the other times she'd tried to summon him. Perhaps he could not. He was the lord of the Nile, after all, and she was on the other side of the world from their Egypt. And yet that hadn't stopped such a rescue from haunting her dreams. Dreams of the lake turning the rich brown of the Nile at flood and devouring the djinn city. Dreams of standing at Sobek's side as he ripped apart the bounty hunter who'd captured her, his crocodile teeth stained with blood.

"Are there any djinn who can become animals?" Duriya had once asked Sister Fatumai. She and her father had met Hui Fatumai their first week of being dumped in the shafit district by the bounty hunter who'd kidnapped them. The Daevabad-born woman was an organizer among the shafit and made a point of helping new arrivals settle in. It had been Sister Fatumai who explained to them the ways of the magical city and put them in the care of the small Egyptian community who'd taken the pair into their homes.

When it came to Sobek and the question of magical creatures, however, Sister Fatumai had not been encouraging.

"I have heard the stories your people tell of djinn," she'd replied. "Of their taking residence in cats and winged serpents, of hot breezes that sigh through trees and haunting cries that lure human victims to riverbanks. These are not those djinn. These ones are more like us; they believe they are the descendants of the great djinn that the Prophet Suleiman—peace be upon him—once punished. They are supposedly the weakest of the creatures of fire."

Duriya had remembered the way the bounty hunter had whisked them away to Daevabad on a boat that flew across sand and sea and her first sight of the awe-inspiring city with its floating glass minarets, markets of shimmering cloth and dragon-scale ornaments.

"These djinn are the *weakest*?" she had repeated.

"Puts things in perspective, does it not?" Sister Fatumai had remarked. "Of the other creatures, I can tell you little. Much is a mystery even to the so-called pureblooded scholars of this city. It may be a mystery for God alone."

There had been a quiet warning in those words, a diplomatic effort to change the subject. But desperate to find a way out of her situation, Duriya had pressed on. "I have met one of them."

Sister Fatumai had dropped the basket of food she was unpacking. "You've *what*?"

"I've met one of them," Duriya had insisted. "Back home. I've had a companion since I was a child, a spirit in the form of one of the crocodiles of the Nile. If I could summon him, I know he would bring my father and me home. He owes me a fav—"

Sister Fatumai's hand had shot out to cover Duriya's mouth, her brown eyes wide with alarm. "Daughter, if you want to survive this place, you need to forget you ever said such a thing. By the Most High . . . if a djinn heard you speak of summoning a river spirit, you and your father would be executed by the next morning—if you were lucky enough to live that long. Do you understand?"

Duriya did understand. She just hadn't listened. She had still tried to summon Sobek. But as her years in this miserable city ground on, her hopes had died a slow, ugly death.

"Your face hasn't changed since we arrived here," her father had said softly the other week, touching her cheek. He always spoke softly now, the things that had happened during the long nights on their journey to Daevabad scarring them both. "Maybe you will age as the djinn do. Maybe God will grant you a long life like theirs."

Just what I need—more centuries of scrubbing bloody rags in the canal. Duriya knew shafit did make lives for themselves here. They had no choice. They married and had children and made the most of things, believing in a justice that came in the next world.

But that wasn't what Duriya wanted.

She stepped closer to the canal now and knelt on the damp bank. Her reflection came back to her in ripples on the surface. Would Sobek hear her if she gave more than a fistful of blood? If she cut deeper, deep enough to turn the water red? Would she fall into a sleep below the canal and be whisked home?

A sleep that would break your father's heart, you mean?

Duriya shuddered. No, that was not an option. She took a few steps back, trying to shake off the despair that seemed to weigh upon her shoulders heavier each day. Her laundry wouldn't be dry for some time, but she needed to get away from the canal.

So she headed for one of the few places that brought her pleasure.

THE MOLOKHIA SEEDS HAD COST TWO MONTHS OF DURIYA'S salary, a sum she carefully stashed away each week until she had enough to visit the shrewd vegetable vendor at the market who made a business of smuggling seeds in from the human world with which to price-gouge his homesick shafit customers. Upon hearing her accent, he'd actually tried to charge her more—a trick he'd given up on the moment she threatened him with the curved razor-sharp knife she'd bought to mince the leaves once the plants had grown.

In truth, she would have paid even more. She and her father had lost so much: the jokes of their village, the thatched home that had housed generations of their family, the shawls and tapestries her late mother had weaved, and the raucous music of the festivals of saints. Duriya couldn't bring any of that back, but she could make her father's favorite dish. He was a far better cook than she was—so talented that he'd earned a spot in the palace kitchen—but the soup was simple enough that given the ingredients, Duriya could pull it off. And while a meal from back home might seem a small thing, she knew how much it would mean to him.

Having spent a fortune on the seeds, Duriya had been extra judicious in deciding where to plant them. Hers was a careful eye—she'd been raised in a farming village and under the tutelage of the lord of the Nile himself. And she'd found a great spot . . . well, sort of. There was one place in the garden that everyone seemed to avoid: the monstrously oversize orange grove that dominated the outer boundary of the infirmary grounds. The grove grew so thick that the fruit-laden boughs and enormous white blossoms formed an impenetrable wall. But on its eastern edge, the canal darted close, forming a narrow hidden triangle near the menacing jungle that offered her the perfect conditions of sun, moisture, and discretion. It was close enough to the infirmary that Duriya could easily sneak away to tend to her plants even if she had to take care to avoid the Daeva gardeners; they were the only ones permitted to touch the Nahid healing herbs grown nearby.

Absorbed in her thoughts and briefly dazzled by the bright sunshine as she left the shadow of a towering cedar, Duriya was nearly upon her bed of covert plants before she realized she was not alone. A gardener—dressed in a dirt-streaked tunic with the sleeves rolled up to reveal pale golden arms—was on his hands and knees on the rich patch of soil that until recently had hosted molokhia plants tall enough to brush her waist. Plants that had cost her weeks of wages and which she had tenderly coaxed from the ground, inhaling the scent that reminded her of home and praying that the gift she would prepare for her father might make him finally smile again.

The plants had been violently ripped out by the roots. Her hard work and lost wages now lay discarded on a pile of weeds. Only a single molokhia plant remained rooted in the ground, and as she watched, the gardener, his back still to her, reached for it.

Duriya's good sense—the wisdom that led her to lower her head before her dry-linen-obsessed mistress and shut her mouth about Sobek—vanished.

"Don't touch that!" She lunged for the gardener's hand. He jumped and turned around in surprise . . . which meant that instead of wrenching his wrist away, Duriya struck him hard across the mouth. He yelped and fell back, landing flat on his ass in the dirt.

Wide, astonished black eyes met hers. She'd hit the man hard enough to tear the white veil from his face and draw blood from his lip. He stared at her, completely speechless.

Then the gash in his lip began to heal. The skin knotted together, scabbed over, and then the wound was gone, leaving nothing but a few drops of ebony blood on his ruined veil.

The veil . . . oh, God. There was only one man in the palace who wore a white face veil and whose injuries healed in moments.

Duriya had just punched the Baga Nahid himself in the face. Over *molokhia*.

Her hand flew to her own mouth in horror. By the Most High, what had she just done? Should she run? The shafit were all the same to these people; surely if she fled, Baga Rustam would never be able to pick her out of the crowd of part humans who tended to his needs.

But if he did? If they came for her father?

Duriya dropped to her knees. "Forgive me, my lord!" she cried in halting Djinnistani. She had always struggled with the language and did so even more when she was anxious. "If I . . ."—oh, for God's sake, how did she express *had known*?—"I do not hit you, the Nahid."

Confusion knit his brows together. Duriya was clearly not saying that correctly.

She tried again. "I do not . . . see?" *Is that the word?* "Aware—"

"Speak your tongue." The Baga Nahid's Djinnistani was clear and slow. "Your language."

"*My* language?" she repeated, torn between uncertainty and fear. But when he only nodded, she switched to Arabic, figuring it was worth the slim chance of avoiding execution. "Forgive me," she said again, far more smoothly. "I did not realize who you were. If I had, I would never have dared touch you. Or interrupt you," Duriya added in a rush, remembering this was technically his patch of dirt she was commandeering to grow her plants.

The Baga Nahid had been watching her face while she spoke, his gaze moving between her mouth and her eyes as though studying her response. "So you would have hit another person?"

He asked the question in Egyptian Arabic so flawless Duriya jumped. "How did you . . . I mean, no," she said quickly. This was not the time to question how some fire doctor from another realm spoke Egyptian Arabic. "It's only that . . . these plants are precious to me. When I saw you about to pull the last, I reacted without thinking."

His eyes narrowed. By the Most High, they were unsettling,

blacker than coal, blacker than any that could be construed as human. She shivered, and once she started, it was impossible to stop. Oh, God, this was it. He was going to kill her. To break her neck with a snap of his fingers or, worse, give her to his sister. People said Banu Manizheh liked to experiment on shafit, that if she caught you, she'd force poisons down your throat that would melt your organs from the inside out and grind your bones to dust for her potions.

"I'm sorry," Duriya whispered again. She stayed on her knees and dropped her gaze. That was how djinn liked shafit. "Please don't hurt me."

"*Hurt* you? Creator, no." Now it was the Baga Nahid who sounded flustered. "You just surprised me. I get lost in my thoughts when I garden and was not quite expecting to get set upon by a mysterious woman bursting out of the jungle." From the corner of her eye, she saw him rise to his feet and brush the dirt from his clothes. "Let me help you."

Baga Rustam reached for her hand, and Duriya was too astonished by his doing so to do anything but let him pull her to her feet. Once she was standing, she promptly stepped back and snatched her hand away.

The Daeva healer didn't seem to notice—or perhaps if he did, he was simply accustomed to such a reaction. "Why do you say they're precious?" he asked.

Duriya stared at him. "What?" She was still trying to wrap her mind around the fact that she had attacked one of the most dangerous men in Daevabad. Having a conversation with him about molokhia seemed too far into the world of the bizarre.

"The plants I was weeding." His Arabic had gone from Egyptian to the exact dialect and accent of her village, and the effect was thoroughly disconcerting. She did now recall hearing the Nahids had some sort of sorcery with language, but this went beyond her wildest imaginings. "Why did you say they're precious?" he pressed.

There seemed little harm in answering honestly. "They're not weeds. They're a vegetable called molokhia. I bought the seeds at the market."

"And decided to grow them in my garden?"

Duriya flushed. "You have good soil. But I'm sorry. I know I shouldn't have. It's just—my father has been so homesick. I thought if I made his favorite dish . . ."

His expression immediately softened. "I see. Well. I would not wish to thwart the hard work of a kindhearted daughter."

Rustam knelt back on the ground. He slid his fingers into the dark earth, and it burst into life.

Seedlings shot up and around his hands in pale green swarming tendrils. They rose as if time itself had sped up, unfurling leaves and stalks that soon dwarfed the Baga Nahid's hunched form. Duriya's mouth fell open in astonishment as a bed of molokhia even lusher than her own grew tall around them. The emerald leaves tickled her arms.

"There," the Baga Nahid said. He had to beat back some of the plants to escape; the leaves were grasping and clinging to his arms and legs like needy children. "I pray that makes up for my indiscriminate weeding."

"How did you . . . why did you?" she breathed.

"There were enough roots remaining." Rustam wiped his hands on his knees and then shrugged as if he hadn't just performed a miracle. "I feel like I should be asking you how. It's not the average person who can get a new plant to take root in my garden."

Pride warmed in her. "Well, like I said, you do have good soil. It didn't take much else besides the usual methods."

"The usual methods?"

Was she really discussing gardening with the Baga Nahid? Duriya was starting to wonder if perhaps she'd hit her head during their tussle and this was all a dream. "Back home, we use a blend of ash and rotting water lily to encourage the seeds to grow. And of course we mix manure in with the dirt."

Rustam frowned. "Manure?"

Surely a gardener as skilled as himself knew what manure was. Maybe his language abilities weren't as adept as they seemed. "Animal droppings."

His eyes went wide. "*Animal droppings*?" he repeated. "You used animal droppings—next to my orange grove—to grow your seeds?"

"It's what we do back home," she protested. "I swear! I meant no disrespect. It's a genuine technique, honestly, something even a child would know. I would never—"

Rustam laughed. It was an almost strangled sound, as though he didn't laugh often, but it matched the bright mirth shining in his too-dark eyes. A smile flitted across his face, and Duriya found herself blushing deeper.

"Animal droppings . . . ," Rustam marveled. "I suppose the Creator has yet some mysteries in store for me." He met her gaze again. "Who *are* you?"

She hesitated, considering and disregarding a fake name. Perhaps it would have been best to remain anonymous, but she found herself wanting to tell him. "Duriya."

"Duriya. I am Rustam, though I suspect you know that." There was a hint of self-deprecation in the curve of his lips. "And where is your land of molokhia grown in this manure?"

Duriya could not help but return his smile. "Egypt."

"Duriya of Egypt." Rustam said her name as though it were a title, and though the effect might have been mocking from another djinn, there was nothing but warmth in his voice. "I have seen you before. You are a washerwoman in the infirmary, yes?"

"I am, but I'd be surprised if you've noticed me. We try to stay out of the way."

"I've seen you doing laundry at the canal with the other women. You—you have a rather memorable smile." He colored slightly as he said it and faltered. "Do you . . . ah, do you like your work?"

Did she like washing rags for vicious djinn? Was he asking in truth? "The wages are acceptable," she said evenly.

He chuckled. "A diplomatic response." He hesitated, dropping his gaze. "Would you perhaps like to work here instead? In the garden, I mean. For me."

"You want *me* to work in your garden?"

"What can I say? I find myself intrigued by these human methods of which I am so ignorant and a human child so informed. Who knows what else you may teach me?"

Duriya was wary. The Baga Nahid seemed friendly enough—far kinder than the stories had made him out to be—but Duriya had learned the hard way not to trust djinn. "Is that an invitation you often extend to women who leave you bloody?"

Rustam met her eyes. "It's an invitation I've never extended to anyone."

Oh. Duriya's heart beat a bit faster. She wondered if he heard it. People said the Nahids could do that.

People said the Nahids could do so much worse. These were the holy men and women of the black-eyed Daevas she'd been told to never, ever get involved with. The ones under guard day and night because they were considered so dangerous. And now she was flirting— she might as well admit they'd moved into that—with the Baga Nahid himself in his garden.

People said so much, and she wondered just how many had actually met a Nahid.

Her courage returned. "I've heard your people don't like mine," she said bluntly. "You'd have someone with human blood working in your garden? Is that even allowed?"

"Deciding who works in my garden is one of the few freedoms I have left." His mouth twisted in a bitter expression, but then it was gone and Rustam merely looked nervous. He reached for his veil, fumbling with the ties. "But only if you're interested. Truly. I would not fault you a rejection."

A rejection was probably the wise choice. Duriya was neither young nor a fool, and even as he veiled his face once again, she did not miss the redness in Rustam's cheeks. Washing rags for vicious djinn could be insufferable, but catching the eye of the Baga Nahid seemed dangerous on an entirely different level.

And is that how you'll spend your decades here? Your centuries? Feeling a bit bolder, Duriya studied his hands, his long fingers stained with the dirt from which he'd regrown her molokhia, and then looked into the darkness of his gentle eyes.

She took a deep breath. "Do you like soup, Baga Rustam?"

He blinked. "What?"

Duriya ran a hand through the molokhia plants. "You've grown them to maturity. Perhaps I can make the soup I attacked you over and we can discuss a fair salary?"

Rustam's eyes crinkled in a smile. "That sounds delightful."

Hatset

This scene takes place a couple decades before *The City of Brass* and contains no spoilers.

Seif Shefali seemed determined to end her marriage before it began.

"He looks old," her father commented, loud enough to be overheard. "Older than they said."

"Baba, he is barely a blur," Hatset retorted. Their ship had yet to dock upon the ghostly promenade outside Daevabad's walls, and her future husband was a little more than a small figure in a black robe. "You cannot judge his appearance from here."

"I have excellent eyes. A blessing wasted in this miserable den of fog." Seif sniffed. "They might have at least spruced up the docks for your arrival."

Hatset wished she could have disagreed, but the city to which she had tied her fate had not put on a very welcoming face this morning. She had been to Daevabad once as a girl and still remembered the awe of sailing through the veil that hid the island. Its brass walls had gleamed in the bright sunshine, the verdant mountains a backdrop to the stunning cityscape of a thousand towers and temples. Back then, Daevabad had seemed the very definition of magic.

Now Daevabad was so shrouded with fog that Hatset could see nothing of the city and only a bare hint of its walls. The empty docks protruded from the mists, broken pilings jutting from the water or lying crumpled on the shore like abandoned corpses. Not exactly a hospitable sight. Their sandship silently coursed through the motionless water of the lake, and Hatset could only imagine how alien their colorful vessel must have looked against the featureless gray. Her people had decked it out for a celebration, for a proud declaration of Ayaanle wealth and power. Its surfaces had been painted in a gilt that would have shimmered in the sun, but now looked more like the pale yellow of fallen leaves. The absurdly expensive silk sails had dropped flat in the still air, concealing her people's emblem.

Everything felt wrong. Hatset tightened her grip on the ship's railing. "You're not doing much to put me at ease."

"I'm not *trying* to put you at ease. I'm trying to make you turn back from the ridiculous scheme." Her father turned to face her, the mischief in his golden eyes replaced by worry. "You do not belong in this place, daughter, and it is going to kill me to leave you here. It is Shefala you should rule, not this Daeva rock."

I want more than Shefala. But Hatset did not say that. "Turning back isn't possible, and you know it. If I changed my mind now, we would insult the Geziris so terribly that it would be three centuries before our people had any influence here again." Hatset squeezed his hand, trying to bring a confident expression to her face. "And you might remember this was *my* choice."

"Children should not be permitted to make choices."

"Baba, I am a hundred years old."

They both fell silent as the Sahrayn crew drew nearer and began preparations for docking. Hatset's stomach fluttered as the ship landed with a jolt, and she had to force herself not to jump. A new city and a new husband. A new future upon an entirely different political chessboard. The moment Hatset stepped off this ship, she was no longer representing herself alone. She was Ta Ntry itself, the first non-Geziri woman to wed a Qahtani king in a thousand years, and her people's fate would rise and fall alongside hers.

And now that king *was* close enough to be observed. Hatset did so carefully. She'd taken measures to learn all she could of Ghassan al Qahtani in the months leading up to her departure and discovered his background was a study in contrasts. He'd spent his youth as a warrior nomad in Am Gezira's harsh mountains and then as a general in his father Khader's bloody war to put down revolts in Qart Sahar—before being launched into a life of untold opulence as Daevabad's king, in a luxurious palace he was said to rarely leave. From brutal war to brutal politics: Khader had been notoriously sectarian, elevating only Geziri officials and banning Daeva religious festivals.

As far as Hatset could uncover, Ghassan had quietly complied with his father's policies, only to reverse many as king. He spoke of bringing the tribes together, putting those words into action when he decided to take a foreign wife. He, indeed, was said to be going a bit *further* toward the Daevas than most djinn were comfortable with. He sat upon the shedu throne as several generations of Qahtani kings had now, but also forbade shafit from guilds and trade work, and cloistered his women and family in the custom of Nahid royalty. There were even rumors Ghassan planned to choose his next grand wazir, a position that had been held by the Ayaanle since the war, from the Daeva tribe when the current man retired.

We shall see about that. But Hatset put future scheming aside to properly consider the king before her. Though an edge of silver streaked his black beard, Ghassan did not look old—or at least not much more aged than she was. He was a broadly built man, one who appeared eminently capable of still jumping on a horse and chasing down rebels despite his elegant black robe and rich clothes. He looked . . . confident, in a way Hatset suspected could easily edge into intimidating. Indeed, she did not miss that most of the courtiers surrounding him—save for his Qaid, grinning in a crimson turban—were a careful few paces away, their gazes lowered.

And yet when Ghassan met her eyes, catching Hatset studying him despite her care to avoid detection, the smile that lit his face surprised her. It was a kind, albeit slightly mischievous grin, as though they were co-conspirators and not strangers, and it made her heart skip in a way that was embarrassingly unbecoming for a woman of her experience and station. Hatset was very nearly tempted to draw her shayla over her face.

"Peace and blessings upon you," Ghassan al Qahtani greeted as he strode toward them, reaching for her father's hands and kissing his cheeks as though they were old friends rather than king and extremely disgruntled subject. "Welcome to Daevabad. May your light shine upon my home and your ease be found in its walls."

"This haunted Daeva rock could use some light," Seif said gruffly in Ntaran.

Hatset kicked her father's foot beneath her gown. "Upon you peace, my king," she said warmly in Djinnistani. "It is wonderful to finally arrive."

"I trust your journey was not too arduous?" Ghassan gave an admiring glance at their sandship. "Aye, that looks like a castle itself."

"We nearly ran into a convoy of human pilgrims crossing the Sea of Reeds, but it made for an interesting adventure for us and presumably a terrifying tale for them."

"I am certain," Ghassan chuckled. He beckoned toward the knot of waiting officials. "Muntadhir, come. Join us."

The group of men parted, and Hatset got her first look at the boy she knew so many of her kinsmen were hoping her own children would one day replace. Muntadhir was a handsome youth, his appearance a mirror image of his father's from his brilliantly colored turban to his gold-edged robe. Gone were the protective talismans Hatset knew Geziri children often wore around their neck, replaced by a prince's collar of pearl and ruby ornaments. He couldn't have been more than eleven or twelve: young enough that he might have played up his youth and come to her as a prospective stepson, a child in need of a mother.

That he hadn't seemed a deliberate choice and perhaps not his own—he seemed too young for such machinations.

"Lady Hatset, Lord Seif." Muntadhir's eyes darted to his father. Closer now, Hatset could see that the emir was on the thin side and quite pale, as though he didn't get outdoors enough. "Peace be upon you both."

"And upon you peace, Emir Muntadhir," Hatset returned. "It is lovely to meet you."

Seif's gaze had settled on Muntadhir with a mixture of parental worry, sadness, and the sort of brash judgment that Hatset knew all too well meant he was about to say something regrettable. "Your son looks as though he'd be better off playing in the sunshine than getting dragged out in the cold to meet visiting dignitaries."

There were breaches of protocol and then there was directly criticizing the parenting decisions of the king of Daevabad. Hatset closed her eyes, momentarily wishing a hole might open beneath her father's feet and whisk him back to Shefala.

Instead the sky opened up, the rain that had been a bare drizzle becoming a deluge.

"Alas, but there is no sunshine," Ghassan replied, his voice flat. Hatset opened her eyes to find him gripping Muntadhir's shoulder. "Please, come. My emir and I would not leave our guests in the rain a moment longer than necessary."

BY THE TIME THEY ARRIVED AT THE PALACE, THE RAIN WAS pouring down with a strength to rival Ta Ntry's monsoons and Hatset found herself grateful for the excuse to go directly to the hammam—even if the time apart would give her father only that many more minutes to craft additional insults in the hopes of getting them both tossed out of Daevabad. The bath servants were kind, if much quieter than the women back home, who would have been teasing her about her upcoming nuptials. Hatset made sure to treat them with warmth and tip them in gold. She didn't intend to be the kind of queen who equated fear with power.

She had just finished dressing when there was a knock on the door and a page entered. "My lady, the king requests your presence."

Hatset was surprised. "Already? I thought we were to meet again at dinner?"

The woman bowed her head. "He is waiting just outside."

He was? Outside *here*? Her nerves fluttered. Was this somehow related to her father's rudeness? Hatset was suddenly aware of the servants watching her, the gazes only some of the many that would trail her every move until the day she died. Perhaps the summons meant something to them.

I will need to make allies here and soon. Hatset would need to figure out which of these servants she could trust. Which courtiers and which secretaries. Which guards and which ministers. Any political success she hoped to find in Daevabad would depend on how wide her network of information could spread.

She smiled graciously at the page as she draped her shayla over her head. "Of course."

The king was waiting upon a small covered pavilion. His royal robe was gone, but the richly embroidered gold sash at his waist and the cut of his midnight-colored dishdasha were equally sumptuous, with opals ringing the collar.

"Lady Hatset . . ." Ghassan touched his heart. "I trust you are feeling a bit more rested? I can return later if you're still tired from the journey."

"I am feeling much recovered, God be praised," she replied. "Yours is a very welcoming home, my king. And I must say whatever coffee it is your kitchens brew is quite powerful."

"I am glad to hear my 'haunted Daeva rock' has some pleasures."

He repeated her father's words in flawless Ntaran with only the trace of an accent, and it was all Hatset could do not to wince. "I apologize for my father's rudeness. He is not eager to see his only child leave, but what he said about your son was cruel and unfair."

An emotion she couldn't read flickered in his gray gaze. "It was calculated, I will grant him that. I can give Muntadhir many things, but a carefree childhood in the sun is not one of them." Ghassan met her eyes. "I would not be able to give any child of mine such a blessing."

It was a warning, and Hatset took it in stride. "I would imagine not. Though I would also hope that a warm home could be created anywhere, as long as the people in it are willing."

"Perhaps, Lady Hatset." He was still speaking in Ntaran, and Hatset found comfort in that. She was fluent in Djinnistani, but it was the language of business. Of commerce and government and speaking with strangers. Ntaran was for home—as surely the king knew. But Hatset had been in politics long enough that she could enjoy such a gesture without forgetting there was a reason behind it.

Ghassan motioned toward a wide set of stairs that curved out of sight, shadowed by a trellis of hanging yellow blossoms. "I was actually hoping to speak to you on that very subject—without your father, if you would permit me. Are you up for a walk?"

She was cautious—and intrigued. In truth, there was very little reason for them to speak before the wedding—entire teams of diplomats, political advisors, treasury secretaries, lawyers, and clerics from both their tribes had already hashed out every detail of their marriage, from the ceremony to the contract that would bind their peoples together. What could the king wish to know that he would prefer kept between the two of them alone?

"Of course," Hatset said politely, keeping her tone pleasantly unconcerned.

They set off toward the stairs. The king nodded at a guard, but the man didn't follow, and in moments, they were alone. Hatset admired the palace as they walked. Her family's castle had been built upon human ruins centuries ago, but Daevabad was already ancient when Shefala was settled, and everything in the palace seemed to sing of its magical past. She felt as though she could close her eyes and hear the whispers of the legendary Nahids as they passed remnants of wall paintings and trace the steps of the earliest Qahtanis—not to mention her own ancestors—who'd strode these corridors and remade the world.

The view beyond the stairs didn't disappoint, either. From the palace walls, Hatset could see Daevabad stretched below, the city dazzling in miniature. The tribal boundaries sprawled across it all like a web, ensnaring the lives of tens of thousands.

"It's breathtaking," she said.

"It is," Ghassan agreed. "I try to take in this view at least once a day. Though when you realize you're *responsible* for it all, the way it takes your breath is far less pleasant."

She sneaked a glance at him. Ghassan was not what she would consider a handsome man, though Hatset suspected decades ago one of his winks would have sent noblewomen blushing. Instead he had a sturdiness, a sort of classical grace. His profile was strong, and his hands, heavy with jeweled rings, were still calloused, reminders of his decades as a soldier.

He spoke again. "I have heard a great many tales of your Shefala. An architect brought me drawings, and I have likely irritated countless Ayaanle travelers in the past few months harassing them for anything they could tell me of your home or person."

Hatset wouldn't judge his prying—she'd been doing the same. "Have you learned anything interesting?"

"Plenty. But I struggle to make sense of it. For everything I hear paints a picture of an intelligent, measured noblewoman with a promising future in a stable, idyllic land." Ghassan waved a hand toward the city below them. "We may be pretty, but despite my efforts, *idyllic* and *stable* are not words I would use to describe my Daevabad. So I suppose, Lady Hatset . . ." He turned to look her full in the face. "I am wondering why you're here?"

Hatset leaned against the low wall. "Perhaps I was won over by the stories I'd hunted down about *you*."

Ghassan laughed, a rich sound. "An old widower with a child, a fractious city, and a political life that will never give you a second of peace . . . is that what young women dream of these days?"

"I am hardly a young woman, and surely you know I've had husbands before you." *Husbands* wasn't perhaps the best word. *Consorts* probably worked better, men with whom she'd exchanged simple vows on the understanding they were temporary and discreet. Many women of her station did the same. A proper husband, one with the correct political connections and with whom she might spend a century of her life, was a choice no djinn rushed into. Companionship and desire could be fleeting, and though she had enjoyed the men she'd been connected to, their partings had all been amicable.

"I do know," he mused. "Though that still doesn't explain why you would accept my proposal. I thought perhaps you were being pressured by your tribe or your father, but I can see that's not the case—he seems halfway to stealing you back home, and you don't strike me as a woman pressured to do anything. So what is it then?"

Hatset stared at him. Of the hundred scenarios she had pre-pared for—a hostile stepson, an interfering politician, her father *ac-tually* stealing her home—being asked so bluntly by the king himself why she had chosen this path wasn't one of them. Why would he? He was a powerful, confident man, and in Hatset's experience, most such men assumed any woman would be lucky to have them. Why would the king of the djinn question her desire to be queen?

It was what every woman wanted, wasn't it?

Yet he had, and for that . . . Hatset found herself wanting to respond with something less trite. She was enjoying his clever ways with words more than she should have—for she could tell even back at the docks that this was a man who could spin the truth so beauti-fully the sky itself might doubt its hue.

And that was exactly it, was it not? Because Hatset *liked* that she had to stay on her toes in this exchange. Ghassan was not like her consorts, placid and so eager to please that she could never have a genuine conversation with them, never confide in them. Her days in Shefala would have passed like all the rest, handling family squab-bles and dealing with the same merchants and nobles her father and grandmother and great-grandparents before them had dealt with. It was hard work—worthy work—making sure that the marketplace ran smoothly and her people were fed if the monsoon arrived late, but Shefala was a town.

Daevabad was *Daevabad*. There was no other city like it in the world. Hatset could make decisions here that changed the lives of tens of thousands, not just in the city itself, but throughout the land. Decisions that cemented *her* people's power and security, like seeing that an Ayaanle djinn stayed on as grand wazir. Decisions that were righteous, such as pushing to restore the protections for the shafit that had been the very reason their ancestors had taken this city in the first place.

"Ambition," she finally said.

The surprise on his face thoroughly pleased her. "Ambition?" he repeated.

"Indeed. Your stories are accurate, my king. Ta Ntry is an idyl-lic land, and I suspect I would have been happy ruling there. I never contemplated another path. But then the merchant council brought your proposal to me, and it was all I thought of for a week. I love Shefala, but it is not . . . this," she said, nodding at the vast city spread before them. "It is not the heart of our world, with all the excitement and terror that suggests. I will have opportunities here to make a difference, to meet people and experience things I could not even imagine back home. It sounded like an adventure—a challenge—that I couldn't pass up."

Ghassan seemed to regard that. "And perhaps a chance to strengthen Ayaanle power as well?"

Hatset smiled sweetly. "The offer was *your* idea. You must have known how we would receive it."

He returned her grin. "I like you. I told my Qaid you were rumored to have a clever tongue, and he told me I'd be blessed to have a wife who would be unafraid to call me out on my nonsense. I am pleased you chose to come here despite your father's determination to be a thorn in my side."

"He will be a sharp one. But yes . . . ," she added cautiously. "I am also pleased to be here."

Ghassan paused and when he spoke again, the flirtation had gone out of his voice. "There is one more thing I would have you understand before you agree to our marriage. One far more personal."

"And that would be?"

"For me, Daevabad's well-being will always come first. I am a king before I am anything else. And after that? I am a *father* before I am a husband. Muntadhir is my emir, and that will not change. Not even if we have a son." There was that flicker of emotion again in his eyes, and when he spoke, his voice was softer. "I owe him that for the life that he lives here."

Hatset schooled her reaction, not missing the firm set of Ghassan's mouth. This was a battle she'd prepared for and one she knew would be a long, complicated war—if it even amounted to that. After all, their people did not conceive easily. She had hopes, of course, but right now they were just that.

She put the sad eyes of the boy emir on the docks out of her mind. "I understand. Just as long as any children we have together were given equal protection, wealth, and a secure future."

"But of course. They would be Qahtanis."

They would be Qahtanis.

That seemed a fate that could carry as many curses as it did privileges. But she looked around, and the curses—such as they were—seemed lessened by the blessings and opportunities. She drew herself up.

"Then I am agreed, my king." Her heart skipped as she said it, but she was. Hatset wouldn't have left Ta Ntry if she wasn't certain. That Ghassan had held this conversation and offered her a way out had only solidified her conviction.

"I am delighted, truly. And if I may . . ." Ghassan reached for her arm, and Hatset allowed him to take it. "I would like to show you a better view."

Hatset arched a brow at his words.

He choked out a laugh, his cheeks briefly darkening. "I swear those words sounded more innocent in my head."

"Perhaps my father is right to distrust you," she teased. But she let herself lean into his warmth as they walked.

"The royal apartments are on the top levels of the ziggurat," Ghassan explained as they climbed even higher. "It is either an excellent way to stay in shape or an act of penitence depending on your day."

Hatset glanced down at the green spread of jungle that made up the heart of the palace. "Does no one like the gardens? They look so beautiful, and it would seem a more central location."

"I have never known a Qahtani to feel comfortable there." Ghassan shrugged. "You will come to learn that the palace magic can have a mind of its own . . . one that does not always approve of djinn. The garden is captivating and lovely during the day, but I would not enter its depths at night, even with Wajed at my side. And that is to say nothing of the silly tales the servants spin about its canal being haunted by marid."

Hatset tensed. Back home, the tales her people told of marid were not silly: they were accounts of weeping families who woke to find loved ones lured into rivers and drowned, their blank-eyed bodies left riddled with bloody marks. They were rare tragedies, thank God, but had happened enough that the Ayaanle had a very, *very* different understanding of the marid—to them, the marid were more than a vanished myth.

An understanding they kept to themselves—no one needed foreigners finding reason to go sniffing about Ta Ntry. "The upper level of the ziggurat it is," she said simply.

The sun had finally started to peek past the clouds when they came upon a large expanse of terraced land. It looked as though there might have been royal apartments there once—centuries ago. Ruined walls and crumbling arches dotted the weed-strewn plaza like jutting fingers of stone. Or rather . . . not stone, Hatset realized. It was coral, like the human castles back home.

"Wait for it," Ghassan whispered, his breath warm against her ear.

There was a swirl of smoke in the air, as though glittering black sand had been tossed to dance in the misty shafts of sunlight. A smell like seared wood, the aroma of magic.

The plaza rearranged itself. Coral walls shot up to rise over an elegant complex of buildings surrounding a pavilion that overlooked the city. The buildings were instantly familiar, the architecture of stout towers topped by stepped battlements aside a dizzying wonder of archways and small domes a perfect imitation of the human ruins back in Shefala that her ancestors had enchanted and transformed into djinn homes. The weeds and rotting leaves clogging the moldy stone planters were gone, replaced by green grasses and delicate Nile lilies floating upon mirrored basins. A whole baobab tree held court over a suspended garden that looked plucked from Paradise . . . if Paradise held plants and flowers exclusive to Ta Ntry.

Hatset was wandering through before she realized she'd taken a step. Shimmering linen cloth in purple and gold draped the entranceways, behind smoldering braziers of myrrh. It was a homage to her homeland as designed by an artist, and whether it was the long journey or her own uncertainties about her path, she felt tears spring to her eyes as she glanced back at Ghassan.

"You did not have to do this," she said in a rush.

Her response likely sounded rude in comparison to her earlier crafted words, but Ghassan appeared more bemused than anything.

"I wanted you to have a place to call your own here, a place that reminded you of home." He hesitated and then added more quietly, "I wish I had thought to do the same for my first wife. Saffiyeh always seemed so lost, and it wasn't until after she died that I realized it was the shores of Am Gezira she longed for, not the jewels and perfumes of Daevabad."

Hatset knew Ghassan was a talented politician, but the regret that peppered his voice seemed genuine, a mirror of his emotional insistence that Muntadhir would remain his successor. And though such devotion to his first wife and son were not necessarily promising signs for the political machinations *her* people hoped to put in place, they spoke well of the man she was shortly to be wedded to, the one whose life she would share.

He didn't have to do this. Hatset came from a family of merchant nobles, raised with the belief that while both gold and a family name were essential to power, only one could buy it. She could judge with a glance the exorbitant wealth needed to create such an enchanting place and knew equally well that Daevabad and financial stability were not synonymous—she was actually wealthier than her husband. Ghassan could easily have outfitted a wing of the palace with the accumulated royal treasures he already had, yet instead he had paid to make something new. A home uniquely designed for her.

And he hadn't shown it to her until *after* she'd agreed. Hatset gave him a tilted smile. "What would you have done if our discussion had led to me getting back on my father's ship?"

"Gotten on my knees before the Treasury and begged for forgiveness?"

"Then I will spare you such humiliation. It's beautiful," she said, taking his arm again. "Truly. This means more to me than I can express."

He covered her fingers with his own. "Then it was worth it. I hope to see you happy here, Lady Hatset. I do not doubt you will face pressure from the court and the noble families who have been here since 'the time of Anahid,'" he said, affecting a lofty Divasti accent. "But you have my blessing to incorporate whatever traditions bring you comfort. I hope in time we may hear the laughter of a child here, and that they shall be a source of comfort for us both."

They would be Qahtanis. His words—his warning?—played through Hatset's mind again. She tried to push it away. "May I show my father this place?" she asked instead. "I think it would give *him* some comfort."

"Please do. But first . . . I have one more of Daevabad's attractions." Ghassan gave her a conspiratorial wink. "Ever met a Nahid?"

FAINT LAUGHTER GREETED THEM AS THEY ROUNDED THE winding garden paths toward the infirmary. It echoed the growing warmth in Hatset's chest; Ghassan had spent their meandering walk making her laugh, so aggressively charming in his compliments and self-effacing childhood anecdotes that she'd teased him for it. The sky was now completely cloudless, the sunshine illuminating the leafy path and making the harem garden seem harmless in its beauty. Sure, the monkeys that had been swinging in the branches bore fangs and jewel-sharp claws, and yes . . . a root had made a swipe for Ghassan's ankles that he neatly sidestepped, but Hatset was a djinn. It took more than that to frighten her.

As they passed a gargantuan orange grove, the laughter grew louder, accompanied by chatter in what sounded like a variant of Arabic to Hatset's limited ear; she'd never mastered the human holy tongue beyond what she needed for prayers. Perhaps a pair of shafit gardeners were nearby . . . though the overly flirtatious tone to their voices—one that needed *no* translation—did not suggest much work was getting accomplished. Hatset was about to delicately suggest to Ghassan that they take another path, but then they came upon a sunlit glen, bursting with flowers in what seemed every color in creation. Silver and pale pink rosebushes rose in columns taller than her head and saffron coneflowers grew in manicured clumps aside purple irises, yellow narcissus, and bright red poppies.

The glen was not empty. But the man Hatset spotted first, sitting comfortably with a sketchpad on his lap, wasn't the Arabic-speaking shafit gardener she might have expected. The cut of his trousers and the black eyes that widened in a pale face were *Daeva*. He shot to his feet when he saw them, dropping the sketchpad to cover his face with a white silk veil that had been hanging from one ear.

Hatset blinked in surprise. The white veil—surely this couldn't be . . . She glanced at his giggling conversation partner. This woman clearly *was* shafit, her rounded ears and earth dull skin obvious signs of human heritage. She sat poised on the ground, a basket of gathered herbs and leafy greens in her arms. The young woman had been grinning when they entered the glen, but the expression died on her lips at the sight of the royal couple.

"Baga Rustam . . ." Ghassan sounded amused. "Taking a break?"

"My king." The Baga Nahid quickly stepped between Ghassan and the shafit woman. "Forgive me, I did not hear you."

"There's nothing to forgive," Ghassan replied magnanimously. He bent to retrieve the sketchpad Rustam had dropped. "A very pretty subject," he remarked, barely glancing at the woman half hidden behind the Baga Nahid. "It pleases me to see you enjoying yourself on such a beautiful day instead of hiding in your rooms."

He gave Rustam what appeared to be a friendly pat on the shoulder, and Hatset did not miss the flinch of the Daeva man.

"Y-yes," Rustam replied in a shaking voice.

"Come, meet our next queen." Ghassan led him forward and Hatset smiled, trying to put the trembling Nahid at ease. She'd heard the healers were peculiar. "Lady Hatset, this is Baga Rustam e-Nahid."

Rustam's gaze didn't leave his feet. "May the fires burn brightly for you."

Hatset glanced questioningly at Ghassan, who merely shrugged. "It's the way he is," he said in Ntaran.

"It is a pleasure to meet you, Baga Rustam," she returned kindly. "I hope we didn't interrupt you and your . . ." Hatset glanced up, but the shafit woman had vanished. "Companion."

Rustam's eyes shot to hers, so dark and flat Hatset nearly stepped back. "She is not my companion."

"Right," Ghassan replied flippantly, clearly accustomed to the Baga Nahid's eccentricities. He nudged the other man's shoulder. "Do you have a scalpel on you?"

Rustam's expression shuttered. "No," he said, his voice going hoarse.

Ghassan pulled free the khanjar at his waist. "Then use this. Show her what you can do." Ghassan grinned at Hatset. "Just wait. You've never seen anything like this."

Hatset stared at the pair, bewildered and uneasy. Rustam's fingers had closed around the dagger's hilt. He stared at the weapon for a long moment, and then with a single jerk, he ripped open his wrist.

Hatset cried out, moving instantly to help him. Black blood poured from the gash, dripping through Rustam's fingers and onto the flowers. But as Hatset looked for something to stanch the wound, she realized it was already healing. As she watched, his skin surged back together, stitching itself shut without a scar in seconds.

"Isn't it incredible?" Ghassan gushed.

"What's going on here?" a woman's voice demanded from behind them.

Rendered speechless by what she had just seen, Hatset started as another woman stormed into the glen. She was Daeva, likely about Hatset's age but far more petite, with premature silver in her frizzy hair and tired lines around her raptor-like eyes. Her rumpled clothes were streaked with ash and blood.

There should have been nothing intimidating about the disheveled Daeva woman. But when she glanced at Baga Rustam, still holding Ghassan's khanjar wet with his blood, the very air in the garden went still, like the eerie calm before a tropical storm.

"Banu Manizheh," Ghassan greeted, his voice taking on a chill. "How astonishing your timing can be when you wish it so."

Manizheh ignored the king's sarcastic response, looking only to her brother. "Rustam, Sayyida Kuslovi's fever isn't responding to treatment. I need you to brew her a stronger tonic."

Rustam's gaze darted to Ghassan, and the king waved a hand. "Go."

The Baga Nahid was gone so fast that he might have blinked out of view. His sister's assessing stare turned to Hatset, and Hatset forced herself to hold it.

So this is the legendary Banu Manizheh. The Banu Nahida who Hatset had heard so many stories about, so many warnings. Warnings that had been easy to dismiss as gossip or fearmongering when Hatset wasn't standing before a woman who radiated power like no one she had ever met. She'd seen dead sharks with more emotion in their eyes than Manizheh's currently held.

But Hatset was a diplomat. "Peace be upon you, Banu Nahida," she greeted politely. "It is an hon—"

The other woman cut her off. "Do you have any illnesses?"

Hatset was taken aback by the abrupt question. "No?"

"Good. If you are ill or beset with childbirth, please come to me immediately. I'd rather not risk you dying and me getting blamed. Again." Manizheh cut a contemptuous glance at Ghassan as anger blossomed in the king's face. "I received your invitation to tonight's . . . event."

"My betrothal dinner," he corrected. "A feast to welcome your future queen."

"Right," Manizheh dismissed. "I will not be there. My brother and I have patients." Without another word, Manizheh turned on her heel and left.

Hatset's mouth was dry. Well. There went any rumors she'd heard regarding an affair between these two. Or jealousy. Or the Banu Nahida having *any* romantic interest in Ghassan. She'd seen love turn sour. This wasn't that. Wine could become vinegar, sure.

This was acid. This was *hate*, pure and unadulterated. And given whatever the hell that business had been with Ghassan goading Rustam into injuring himself, Hatset wasn't sure she could blame Manizheh.

"My esteemed Nahids," Ghassan said caustically to no one in particular. "Do not fret. Should you need their services, I assure you their actual bedside manner is far improved. Muntadhir's birth was quite difficult, and neither of the Nahids were anything but professional. They stayed by Saffiyeh's side the entire time."

Hatset tried to imagine having that viperous woman at her side during childbirth and quickly decided against it. Should she get pregnant, she would write to Shefala and request a midwife from back home.

Except, of course, the danger wouldn't end for her children at their birth. It would only be beginning. Hatset suddenly remembered something her father had said back in Ta Ntry when he was begging her to reconsider Ghassan's proposal:

Do not put yourself in a war that is not yours, daughter. You do not understand the kind of violence Daevabad has witnessed. You do not understand the enmity that runs between the Qahtanis and the Nahids.

And as Ghassan had promised, as he had warned?

Their children would be Qahtanis. And Hatset had already said yes.

Muntadhir

This scene takes place about seven years before the events in *The City of Brass* and contains spoilers for that book only.

D hiru." A hand shook his shoulder. "*Dhiru.*"

Muntadhir al Qahtani groaned, burying his face in his pillow. "Go away, Zaynab."

His sister's small body landed next to his, jolting the bed and sending a fresh throb of pain into his pounding skull. "You look awful," she said cheerfully, plucking away the hair plastered to his cheek. "Why are you all sweaty?" She let out a scandalized—and rather thrilled—gasp. "Were you *drinking*?"

Muntadhir pressed the silk pillow over his ears. "Ukhti, it's too early for this. Why are you in my room?"

"It's not that early," she said, ignoring the more important question—in his mind, at least. Zaynab's hands scrabbled around, tickling him, and she laughed as he tried to wriggle away. Abruptly, her fingers stilled, closing over something lying near his head.

"Is this an earring? Dhiru, why do you have a woman's earring in your bed?" Excitement lit her voice. "*Oh,* does it belong to that new singing girl from Babili?"

In a moment of sudden panic, Muntadhir shot out his hand to sweep the other side of the mattress. Relief coursed through him when he found it empty. The earring's owner must have already left, and thank God for it. That was *not* something he needed his gossipy thirteen-year-old sister to see.

He rolled over, squinting in the dark; Muntadhir's servants all knew to pull the shades before the emir woke from one of his "evenings," so Zaynab came to him in blurry pieces: her gray-gold eyes and small dark face, her mischievous smile . . . the intricate gold and emerald jhumka dangling from her fingers.

"Give me that." Muntadhir snatched the earring back as Zaynab giggled once more. "Could you at least make yourself useful and get me some water?"

Still grinning, Zaynab bounced off the bed and poured the contents of his blue glass pitcher into a white jade cup, making a face as she examined it. "Why does this smell funny?"

"It has medicine for my head."

She came back and offered the cup to him. "You shouldn't drink wine, akhi. It's forbidden."

"Lots of things are forbidden, little bird." Muntadhir drained the cup. He wasn't setting the greatest example for his sister, but at least last night's drinking had—technically—been in the service of his kingdom.

Zaynab rolled her eyes. "You know I hate when you call me that. I'm not a child anymore."

"Yes, but you still flit around everywhere, listening and seeing things that are not your business." Muntadhir tapped the top of her head. "A tall bird," he teased. "You and Ali are going to leave me behind with all this growing."

She fell back onto the bed. "I tried to see him," she complained, sounding glum. "Wajed brought the cadets over from the Royal Guard to spar. I went to the arena, but Abba made me leave. He said it was 'inappropriate,'" she added, flicking a hand dismissively.

Muntadhir was sympathetic. "You're getting older, Zaynab," he said gently. "You shouldn't be around all those men."

Zaynab glared at him. "You smell like wine and have some lady's earring in your bed. Why do you get to do whatever you want, and I can't even leave the harem anymore? If we were back in Am Gezira, I'd be able to go out. Our cousins do all the time!"

"But we're not in Am Gezira, and our cousins aren't princesses," Muntadhir said. He didn't entirely disagree with Zaynab, but he didn't feel up to debating Daevabad's archaic traditions with his sister right now. "Things are different here. People will talk."

"So let them talk!" Zaynab balled up her hands, her fists bunching the quilted blanket beneath her. "It's not fair! I'm *bored*. I can't even go to the market park in the Ayaanle Quarter anymore. That was my favorite place. Amma used to take me there every Friday to see the animals." Her lower lip trembled, making her look younger than her thirteen years. "Ali too."

Muntadhir sighed. "I know, Ukhti. I'm sorry . . ." Zaynab looked away, her face crumpling, and Muntadhir's chest tightened. "I'll take you, all right?" he suggested. "No one is going to stop me. We'll go by the Citadel on the way and drag Alizayd too."

Zaynab's face instantly brightened. "Really?"

He nodded. "I'll insist I need a particularly small zulfiqari to keep us safe. As long as *you* promise to deal with Ali's chattering. He'll probably subject us to an entire afternoon's ramble on the park's history or where they found the animals or God only knows what else."

"It's a deal." She smiled again, the grin lighting up her whole face. "You're a good brother, Dhiru."

"I try." He nodded toward the door. "Now will you let me go back to sleep?"

"You can't. Abba wants to see you."

Muntadhir's mood immediately darkened. "About what?"

"I didn't ask. He seemed annoyed." She inclined her head. "You should probably hurry."

"I see. Thanks for letting me know so quickly." His sister merely laughed at his sarcasm, and he shooed her away with a sigh. "Go on, you troublemaker. Let me get dressed."

Zaynab skipped off, and Muntadhir rolled out of bed, swearing under his breath. He hadn't expected to see his father until this evening: had he known he'd be summoned so early, he would never have had so much to drink last night.

He splashed some rosewater over his face, then rinsed his mouth and ran his hands through his hair and over his beard, attempting to smooth their disarray. He exchanged his rumpled waist cloth for a crisp dishdasha patterned with blue diamonds, then grabbed his cap and hurried out, wrapping his turban as he half jogged toward the arena. His limbs felt heavy; his abused body did not appreciate the speed at which it was being compelled to move.

When he finally reached the arena, Muntadhir took the stairs leading to the viewing platform with great care, easing one foot ahead of the other, and trying not to appear impaired. Ghassan would not be pleased to see him lurching around like a newborn karkadann.

The pavilion that overlooked the palace arena was well shaded, with drapes of brightly patterned gold and black silk and thickly planted potted ferns rising overhead to protect Daevabad's royals and their privileged retainers from the city's merciless midday heat. A half-dozen servants waved wetly gleaming palm fans, dipping the branches in a fountain of enchanted ice before churning the darkened space.

Muntadhir breathed deeply outside the curtained archway, inhaling the smoky scent of frankincense and trying to calm his pulse. His mouth tasted sour and thick, last night's wine not entirely gone. Not that it mattered. He could be impeccably turned out, and Ghassan would see through the facade—he always did. His father had a stare that opened a man up and dissected him out as he squirmed. A stare he was most accomplished at turning onto his eldest son.

At least today Muntadhir would be able to counter it with some useful information. Steeling himself, he stepped through the filmy curtain.

He winced. Light came in dappled rays through the drapes. The chatter of the men on the pavilion, the clash and sizzle of the zulfiqars below, and the delicate music coming from a pair of lutes all competed to make his head pound in a dizzying manner. Ahead, he caught sight of his father sitting on a brocaded cushion, his attention focused on the arena below.

Muntadhir began to move toward him, but he didn't get halfway there before a young Daeva man abruptly stepped in his path. Muntadhir jerked back in surprise, barely keeping his balance.

"Emir Muntadhir! Peace be upon you! I hope you are having a most excellent of mornings!"

The man was dressed in the garb of a priest . . . or maybe some sort of priest in training—Muntadhir was not up to deciphering the intricacies of the Daeva faith right now. A short crimson jacket went to the fellow's knees, underneath which he wore striped azure and fire-yellow trousers. A cap of the same color sat upon his wavy hair.

The effect was bright. Very bright. Far too bright for this particular morning, though there was something about the man's long-lashed black eyes, overly enthusiastic manner, and rural Divasti accent that tugged at Muntadhir's memory.

The pieces slowly came together in his foggy head. "Upon you peace," he answered warily. "Pramukh, yes? Kaveh's son?"

The other man nodded, grinning. He was actually rocking back and forth on his heels with excitement, and Muntadhir suddenly wondered if he wasn't the only one who'd had too much to drink.

"Jamshid! That is . . . I am meaning, that is my name," the other man replied, bumbling the Djinnistani words. He blushed, and even in his preoccupied state, Muntadhir could not help but note that it was rather fetching. "I cannot tell you how thrilled I am to join your service, Emir." He brought his fingers together in the Daeva blessing, then added a smart Geziri salute for good measure. "You will find none more loyal than me!"

Join my service? Muntadhir stared at Jamshid in complete confusion for a few heartbeats before his gaze slid to his father. Ghassan wasn't looking at him, confirmation in Muntadhir's mind that he'd just become the pawn in some new scheme.

He returned his attention to the bouncing, starry-eyed priest. His eyelashes really were suspiciously long, the effect captivating.

Muntadhir cleared his throat, shutting down the thought. There was no damn way this man was joining his service. He feigned a smile, inclining his head to motion Jamshid out of his way. "Would you mind . . ."

"But of course!" Jamshid sprang back. "Should I wait for you outside?"

"You do that." Muntadhir neatly stepped past him without a backward glance.

Ghassan didn't look up as Muntadhir approached. His admiring gaze was locked on the arena below.

"Look at him fight," his father said by way of greeting. Appreciation and proud awe—two sentiments he rarely directed toward Muntadhir—were clear in his voice. "I have never seen someone so young handle a zulfiqar with such skill."

There was only one person who'd earn that kind of praise from Ghassan al Qahtani, and as Muntadhir glanced down upon the sand, apprehension rising in his chest, he spotted Alizayd. His little brother was sparring against a soldier who looked twice his height and three times his bulk. Both fighters had their blades aflame, and a group of young cadets were ringed out in a wide circle around them, cheering their royal fellow.

Muntadhir frowned, stepping forward as he caught sight of the greenish haze at the heart of the whipping fire. "That's not a training blade."

Ghassan shrugged. "He's ready to move on."

Muntadhir whirled on his father. "He's *eleven*. Citadel cadets don't start using live blades until they're fifteen, if not older." He tensed, cringing as the weapons met with a clash. "He could be killed!"

Ghassan waved him off. "He would not have advanced if Wajed and his instructors did not think him prepared. I also spoke to Alizayd. He desires the challenge."

Muntadhir bit his lip. He knew his little brother well enough to know it wasn't the challenge Ali desired. It was the chance to prove himself. To prove to his fellow cadets—boys taken from hardscrabble villages in Am Gezira, the ones now shouting him on—that the half-Ayaanle prince was just as good as they were. Better. And child or not, Ali had a deadly focus in his eyes when he returned his opponent's strike, taking advantage of his small size to duck under the man's arm.

My future Qaid. The young man who, but for a quirk of timing and politics, could be in his older brother's thoroughly privileged position.

Troubled, Muntadhir forced himself to look away. "May I sit, Abba?" Ghassan nodded at a cushion, and Muntadhir sank into it. "Forgive my tardiness," he continued. "I didn't realize you wished to speak to me so early."

"It's noon, Muntadhir. If you didn't drink until dawn, this wouldn't seem early." Ghassan threw him an exasperated look. "You are too young to be so reliant on wine. If it doesn't put you in an early grave, it will make you a weak king."

Muntadhir had no doubt which of those possibilities bothered his father more. "I'll try to temper my intake," he said diplomatically. "Though last night was not without its uses."

He fell silent as a servant approached to pour him a cup of coffee from a steaming copper carafe. Muntadhir thanked him and took a long sip, willing the drink to dispel the pounding in his head.

"What uses?" Ghassan prodded.

"I think your suspicions about al-Danaf are correct," he replied, naming one of the northern Geziri governors. "I was out with his cousin last night, and he was making some rather interesting promises to one of my female companions. I'd say either they've learned to conjure gold from rocks or they're skimming from the caravan taxes due to the Treasury."

"Proof?"

Muntadhir shook his head. "But his wife is from a powerful clan. I suspect they would be none too pleased to learn the promises he was making to another woman." He took another sip of his coffee. "I thought I'd pass him over to you." It was their usual way: Muntadhir getting what he could with charm, and his father stepping in when it was time to turn to different—more violent—methods.

Ghassan shook his head, his mouth pressed in a grim line. "That bastard. To think I was considering him for your sister's hand."

Muntadhir went cold, even as he sputtered the hot drink. "What?"

"It would be smart to strengthen our relationship with the north. Alleviate some of the tension that has built over the past few decades."

"You'd give your daughter to a snake with a half century on her just to alleviate some tension?" Muntadhir's voice was sharp. "She doesn't even speak Geziriyya. Do you have any idea how lonely she'd be out there? How miserable?"

Ghassan waved him off the same way he'd waved off Muntadhir's concerns about Ali's safety. It was a profoundly irritating gesture. "It was only a thought. I would not do anything without talking to her. And clearly I'll do nothing of the sort now."

As though her opinion would matter. Muntadhir knew his father meant no true unkindness . . . but Zaynab was a princess, a powerful piece in the deadly game that was Daevabad's politics. Her future would be determined based on whatever course Ghassan deemed best for their reign.

"And the reason you had me summoned—does it have to do with Kaveh's rather loud son thinking that he's joining my service?"

"He *is* joining your service. He's offered himself for the Daeva Brigade. He'll train at the Citadel with the aim of becoming your personal guard, and in the meantime, he can join your circle. He's apparently quite the talented archer."

An *archer*? Muntadhir groaned. "No. Do not make me take some country noble with aspirations of being an Afshin under my wing. I beg you."

"Don't be such a snob." Ghassan's gaze returned to the arena as Ali landed another blow. "Jamshid is a Temple-educated Daeva noble. I'm sure he'll fit in with your little retinue of poets and singers well enough. Indeed, I want you to make sure of it."

Muntadhir frowned at the intent in his father's voice. "Is something going on?"

"No." Ghassan's mouth tightened. "But I think it would be good if Jamshid was in your orbit. If he was loyal—truly loyal. It cannot hurt us to have a reliable Daeva so highly placed." He shrugged. "And were that reliable Daeva to be in the grand wazir's household . . . all the better."

Even though they were speaking quietly in Geziriyya, Muntadhir darted a peek past his father's shoulder at the surrounding nobles to make sure no one was listening. "Do you suspect Kaveh of something?"

"You sound hopeful."

Muntadhir hesitated. He had been uneasy with his father's choice to name Kaveh e-Pramukh as grand wazir a few years back, but he'd been too young—and too fearful of disagreeing with the king—to protest. The decision had been made in the wake of Manizheh's and Rustam's murders at the hands of the ifrit when Daevabad itself was at the brink of civil chaos. No one had needed to hear the misgivings of an underaged Qahtani royal.

Ghassan must have sensed his thoughts. "Speak your mind, Emir."

"I don't trust him, Abba."

"Because he is Daeva?"

"No," Muntadhir replied, his voice firm. "You know I'm not like that. I trust many Daevas. But there are some we will never win over. I can feel it. You can *see* it. Behind the polite smiles, there's resentment in their eyes."

Ghassan's expression didn't waver. "And you think Kaveh is one of them? He has done very well as grand wazir."

"Of course he has. He's in no position to make any kind of move yet." Muntadhir twisted the silver ring on his thumb. "But I think a man as close as he reportedly was to Manizheh and Rustam is a man we should be careful of. Abba, there are times Kaveh looks at me . . . it's like he sees an insect. He never lets it color his actions, but I'd bet coin that behind his walls, he's calling us sand flies in need of swatting."

"All the more reason to put someone behind those walls."

"And his son is the best way? You could easily place a proper spy in his household."

Ghassan shook his head. "I don't want a spy. I want his son. I want someone I can use, someone Kaveh *knows* I can use, and a person he wouldn't dare risk."

Muntadhir knew what his father was truly saying. It was a dynamic he'd seen play out before: the sons of political opponents taken into the Citadel, ostensibly for honorable careers, but also so there would be a ready blade at their throat should their parents step out of line. Wives "invited" to serve as companions for the queen, then detained in the harem when suspicion fell upon their husbands.

His father wanted a hostage.

The memory of Jamshid's cheerful smile sent prickles of guilt across his skin. "Do you intend to harm him?" he finally asked.

"I hope not. You have a talent for dazzling people. There are courtiers who would spill blood to be one of your companions." Ghassan's eyes narrowed. "So take that bright-eyed, aspiring Afshin and make him your closest friend. Show Kaveh's son the charm, the riches, the women . . . the paradise his life could be. And make damn sure he knows his fortunes are tied to yours. To *ours*. It should not be difficult."

Muntadhir considered that. Knowing his father, he supposed he should be pleased Ghassan was asking him only to befriend Jamshid, not poison him or frame him in some sort of scandal. "That's it? Make him one of my companions?"

There was a flicker in his father's expression he couldn't decipher. "I would not be averse to you encouraging his tongue to spill about his life back in Zariaspa. About what he knows of his father's relationship with the Nahid siblings."

Muntadhir ran a finger around the edge of his coffee cup. Whether it was the wine still churning in his belly or his father's words, he'd lost his taste for it. "Understood. If that is all . . ."

Ali's cry drew his attention. Muntadhir turned just in time to see his brother's zulfiqar go spinning out of his hand.

Relief flooded through him. He doubted Ali wanted to lose, but the sooner his little brother was done playing with that fiery, poisoned death blade, the better.

Except Ali's opponent didn't stop. He charged after him, kicking his brother square in the chest. Ali fell hard, sprawling in the sand.

Muntadhir shot to his feet in outrage.

"Sit," Ghassan said flatly.

"But, Abba—"

"*Now.*"

Muntadhir sat, his skin burning as Ali's opponent stalked after him. The other cadets were frozen. His brother suddenly seemed horrifically young and small: a scared little kid scrambling backward, his terrified gray eyes darting between the looming bulk of his opponent and the spot where his zulfiqar had landed.

Men died trying to master the zulfiqar. The training was ruthless, meant to separate those who could properly wield and control such a destructive weapon from those who couldn't. But surely not here. Not the king's *son*, not before his own eyes.

"Abba," Muntadhir tried again, tensing as Ali barely ducked the next strike. Flames whipped around the warrior's copper sword as he lunged. "Abba, stop this. Tell him to stand down!" His voice broke in fear.

His father said nothing.

Ali's expression abruptly changed; determination sweeping over his features. He grabbed a handful of sand and hurled it in his opponent's face.

The man jerked back, his free hand going to his eyes. It was enough time for Ali to hook his foot around the other man's ankles, knocking him off balance and sending him tumbling to the ground. Ali drew his khanjar in the next moment, ramming it into the hand holding his opponent's zulfiqar. He did it again and again, and then *again*, the brutal movement drawing blood from the other warrior.

The warrior dropped the zulfiqar.

Muntadhir let out a shaky breath of relief. Despite his father's order, he'd risen back to his feet, drawing close to the platform's edge. He must have been visible, for Ali glanced up, meeting his eyes.

In the space of time it took for his little brother to give Muntadhir a trembling smile, his opponent had drawn his own khanjar.

He smashed the dagger's handle across Ali's face.

Ali yelped in pain, blood pouring from his nose. Muntadhir's angry shout was drowned by the whistle marking the end of the match.

Oh, someone is going to die. Muntadhir spun on his heel, reaching for his own blade. His khanjar was an emir's ornament, a jeweled symbol of authority before it was a weapon—but Muntadhir bet with enough force, he could still shove the dagger into the throat of the man who had just struck his brother.

Ghassan grabbed his wrist, jerking him close. "Stop."

"I'm not going to stop! Did you see what he just did?"

"Yes." His father's voice was firm, but Muntadhir didn't miss the dart of his eyes back to Ali before they returned to his eldest's face. "The match had yet to be called. Alizayd shouldn't have lost focus."

Muntadhir wrenched his arm free. *"Shouldn't have lost focus?* They were both disarmed! A man does that to your son, and you say nothing?"

Anger flashed in Ghassan's face, but it was a weary sort of anger. "I would rather see his nose broken before my eyes than hear of his death on a faraway battlefield. He is learning, Muntadhir. He's going to be Qaid. It is a violent, dangerous life, and neither you nor I do him any favors by softening his training."

Muntadhir looked at his little brother. His white sparring uniform was now filthy, stained by scorch marks, blood, and the arena's dirty sand. Ali pressed a grimy sleeve to his nose to stem the bleeding as he limped over to retrieve his zulfiqar.

The sight broke Muntadhir's heart. "Then I don't want him to be my Qaid," he burst out. "Dismiss him from the Citadel. Let him enjoy whatever is left of his childhood and have a normal life."

"He's never going to have a normal life," Ghassan said softly. "He is a prince from two powerful families. Such people do not have normal lives in our world. Especially not now. Not since . . ."

His father didn't finish the sentence. He didn't need to. Everyone knew the irreparable damage that had been done to their world with the death of the last Nahids. If Daevabad's politics had been deadly when Muntadhir was a child, the city's stability balancing on a knife's edge, it was nothing in comparison to the stakes now.

No. Ali was never going to have a normal life. None of them were. Muntadhir watched, feeling sick as Ali sheathed his zulfiqar. The blade looked far too big against his body.

"It is not for Alizayd alone that I do these things," his father chided, not ungently. "You have good political instincts, Muntadhir. You are charming, you are an excellent diplomat . . . But you are neither an ambassador nor a wazir. You are my successor. You need to harden your heart, or Daevabad will crush you. And you cannot risk that, my son. The city rises and falls with its king." His father met his gaze and for a moment, there was a hint of vulnerability in his eyes, an echo of the worry and fear and simple *affection* Ghassan had once shown his family so freely. It was gone the next moment. "Do you understand?"

Daevabad comes first. It was his father's mantra. The thing he said when brutally putting down those who dared to dissent. When ruining the lives of his young children.

Things Muntadhir would one day be expected to do.

Nausea welled inside him. "I . . . I should take Jamshid to the Citadel." It was the first excuse he could think of to leave.

Ghassan lifted his hand. "Go in peace."

"Upon you blessings." Muntadhir touched his heart and brow, backing away.

Jamshid was still there, and he was no less exuberant, leaping to his feet like someone had touched him with a hot coal. "Emir!"

"Please stop that." Muntadhir rubbed his head. He had no desire to go to the Citadel. Despite his promise to his father, the only thing he felt like doing was drinking away their conversation and the memories of Ali's pained cry and Zaynab's sad eyes. But his usual cup companions were likely still hungover in their beds, and Muntadhir knew his own weaknesses enough to know he was in no state to drink alone.

He cut his eyes at Jamshid. "Does your priesthood forbid wine?"

Jamshid looked baffled. "No?"

"Then you're coming with me."

JAMSHID STROLLED THE LENGTH OF THE CARVED WOODEN balcony. "This is an extraordinary view," he admired. "One can see all of Daevabad from up here."

Muntadhir made a grunt of assent from his cushion but didn't move. He didn't feel like looking down at the city he'd be expected to one day tyrannize, even if it was beautiful.

Jamshid turned around, leaning against the railing. "Is there something the matter, Emir?"

"Why would you ask that?"

"You look a bit sad. And I'd heard you were more talkative."

Muntadhir stared at the man in disbelief. People did not ask if the emir of Daevabad was *sad*. Not even his closest companions spoke so freely. Ah, they would have noticed his reticence surely, but they wouldn't dare question it. Instead, they'd compose poems to praise him or offer up diverting tales, all while discreetly beginning to water down his wine.

But Muntadhir couldn't find it in himself to be annoyed. After all, palace etiquette probably wasn't taught at the Daeva's Grand Temple. "Tell me of yourself," he asked, ignoring Jamshid's question. "Why did you wish to leave the priesthood? Are you no longer a believer?"

Jamshid shook his head. "I'm still a believer. But I didn't think shutting myself up with dusty texts was the best way to serve my people."

"And your father agreed? Kaveh seems so orthodox."

"My father is in Zariaspa on family business." Jamshid's knuckles paled as he tightened his grip on the wine cup. "He doesn't know yet."

"You left the Grand Temple and joined the Royal Guard without your father's permission?" Muntadhir was astonished . . . and rather intrigued. That was *not* the way things were typically done among Daevabad's powerful noble families, and the man before him didn't seem the rebellious type. At all.

Jamshid seemed amused by his reaction. "Does your father know everything about you?"

There was a twinkle in the other man's dark eyes that, combined with the question, sent a sharp buzz down Muntadhir's spine. He drew up, his gaze flickering over Jamshid. Under different circumstances, he might have wondered if there had been an undercurrent of intent lingering in those words. He might have been tempted to find out, with a flash of the smile he knew had broken a fair number of hearts in Daevabad and an invitation to sit.

But very few people in Daevabad looked at Muntadhir al Qahtani with such directness . . . and even fewer spoke to him with the kind of genuine warmth that emanated from Jamshid. Fewer still held such political delicacy as did this son of Kaveh. And so Muntadhir would have to play this with care.

He cleared his throat, trying to ignore the blood rushing under his skin. "My father knows everything," he found himself saying.

Jamshid laughed, a rich sound that sent Muntadhir's stomach fluttering. "I suppose that's true." He left the balcony, coming closer. "That must be difficult."

"It's terrible," Muntadhir agreed, suddenly having a hard time looking away from the other man. He wasn't a great beauty, but there was something pleasing about his winged brows and slightly old-fashioned mustache. To say nothing of the long-lashed black eyes that hadn't unlocked themselves from Muntadhir's. Still in his Temple attire, Jamshid looked as though he might have stepped out of one of the chipped paintings of the Nahid Council that clung to the palace's ancient walls.

Jamshid sat without invitation and then quickly stood back up, looking embarrassed. "Forgive me . . . am I allowed to sit? I know there's all sorts of protocol."

"Sit," Muntadhir urged. "Please. It's nice to get a break from protocol."

Jamshid smiled again. It seemed to be a thing he did easily—Muntadhir supposed people who grew up without having to worry about ridiculous court rules and its related political maneuvering did so. "My father would disagree. He's always worried we're showing our 'terrible' provincial ways." Jamshid made a face. "You'd think after a decade in Daevabad, I would have lost my accent."

"I like your accent," Muntadhir assured. He took a sip of his wine. "Why did you leave Zariaspa?"

"My father wanted me educated at the Grand Temple. Or so he says." Jamshid drank from his cup, his gaze fixing on the sky. "I suspect it was easier to start fresh here."

"What do you mean?" Muntadhir asked, his curiosity getting

the better of his urge not to follow his father's orders so immediately.

Jamshid glanced at him, looking surprised. "My mother . . . I assumed you knew."

Muntadhir winced. He did know, and his words had been clumsy. "Forgive me. Your mother died when you were young, correct? I didn't mean to bring it up."

"I don't mind. Truly. I don't get to speak about her with anyone. My father refuses." Jamshid's expression clouded. "She died when I was born, and they weren't married. I think she might have been a servant, but no one will tell me anything more about her. They're too ashamed."

Muntadhir frowned. "Why? You have your father's name. Is it that much of an issue?"

"For Daevas, yes. My people are obsessed with tracing their roots." He drank back the rest of his cup. "It determines what we do, who we marry . . . everything." He spoke lightly, but Muntadhir didn't miss the flash of pain in his face. "And half of my roots are missing."

"Maybe that just means you're free to write your own destiny. Maybe it's a gift," Muntadhir said softly, thinking of his Ali and Zaynab.

Jamshid stilled, his expression serious. When he finally spoke, his voice was solemn. "I *had* heard . . . that you tended to become overly poetic when drunk."

Muntadhir's eyes went wide as heat rushed to his face. Had Jamshid just . . . *insulted* him? He was shocked. Outside his family, no one dared speak to Daevabad's emir with such disrespect. They probably feared the king would execute them.

But as Jamshid's eyes danced with the jest and a laugh escaped his lips, it was not anger Muntadhir felt. He didn't know *what* he felt; there was a strange lightness twirling in his chest that was entirely unfamiliar.

He was pretty sure he *liked* it.

Even so, he tried to muster an indignant glare. "Your father is right to worry over your manners," Muntadhir shot back. "I was trying to be nice, you ass!"

"Then perhaps I am blessed to join your service." Jamshid smirked, and Muntadhir began to fear his father's assignment was going to be much more difficult than he had anticipated. "You'll have plenty of time to teach me."

Jamshid

This takes place less than a year after the preceding Muntadhir chapter. Spoilers for the first book.

The sounds beyond the closed door were really quite ridiculous. Jamshid e-Pramukh shifted on his feet, growing more apprehensive as he glanced at the wall of ceremonial weapons displayed along the long marble corridor in which he stood guard. It was a fearsome collection. A spear so large it could be hefted only by a giant and a mace studded with zahhak teeth. Dented shields, swords, and oh . . . a serrated axe with blood and gristle still encrusted in its teeth.

It was perhaps unsurprising decor considering the reputation of the formidable warlord from the Tukharistani frontier currently residing in these walls. The warlord rumored to be gathering soldiers and coin, intent on protecting his little fiefdom. The warlord who supposedly made a golden cup out of an enemy's skull and boiled a captured ifrit alive. The warlord who had greeted the emir of Daevabad boasting about how his ancestors had once drunk Geziri blood.

The warlord now ensconced in his bedroom with Muntadhir and what sounded like at least four other people, including the woman Jamshid was pretty sure was the warlord's wife and an extremely off-key singer.

Behind the closed door, Muntadhir laughed lightly, a teasing sound that caused Jamshid's stomach to flip. Jamshid couldn't make out his emir's words, but his jesting tone didn't sound afraid or intimidated. Then again, Muntadhir never sounded afraid or intimidated. Instead Daevabad's emir seemed to float through life wonderfully confident and amused, unbothered by concepts such as basic safety. Why would he? He had other people who worried about those things on his behalf.

People like Jamshid, who found himself gripping his dagger as the warlord let out a cackling bellow. The small dagger was the only weapon Jamshid had been allowed; Muntadhir mentioned that they wouldn't want to seem rude or distrustful. Heavens no. Far better for his emir to get murdered and then Jamshid and the rest of the Daevas persecuted for letting it happen.

Maybe you should have thought of that before quitting the Temple and joining the Royal Guard. Granted, when Jamshid presented himself to Ghassan, he'd thought he'd be joining the Daeva Brigade as an archer, proudly protecting his tribe's quarter. Not personally guarding Ghassan's eldest son and getting a crash course in Muntadhir's extremely specific kind of politics.

The door opened with a bang. Jamshid shot to attention as drunken laughter and warm candlelight spilled into the corridor. For a moment, he panicked, and then Muntadhir al Qahtani was standing there, framed in the doorway. No matter the noises and implied activity Jamshid had been listening to, Muntadhir looked untouched and remarkably sober. The silk of his pale silver-blue waist cloth was still pressed flat, the moonstone buttons running up the collar of his tunic, dyed and cut in the most modern style, still fastened. His silver turban, crowned with a sapphire and carnelian ornament, might have been slightly tilted, but this only gave him a more rakish air.

As if he needs to be more rakish, Jamshid thought, glad the blush he felt stealing into his cheeks would be difficult to notice in the dark hallway.

Muntadhir's gray gaze fell upon Jamshid and then he smiled. Muntadhir had a slow, drawling smile that brightened his entire face—a smile that did things to Jamshid's nerves he suspected were not professionally helpful. His eyes sparkled as he leaned closer to whisper in Jamshid's ear. He looked delighted and blissfully content, as though he'd opened the door simply to request more wine or perhaps another participant, and his breath was warm upon Jamshid's neck.

"We need to get out of here." Muntadhir spoke in Divasti, his tone still light and airy as though nothing were wrong. "Right away."

Jamshid jerked back, his eyes darting over Muntadhir's shoulder. A glimpse was enough to make him blush fully now. The party appeared to be in full swing, the warlord and his companions deeply unconcerned about Muntadhir's foray toward the door. Or perhaps simply more focused on the rather acrobatic moves being performed.

Acting on instinct, Jamshid quietly pulled Muntadhir out and eased the door closed. Keeping a hand on the small of his back, like they were completely normal men out for additional refreshments, Jamshid carefully led Muntadhir down the corridor.

"The door's down this way," he whispered.

Muntadhir stopped. "We can't go out the main door. Trust me."

"All right . . ." Jamshid swallowed. "We're a bit high up, but there was a window down the other way."

"Perfect." Muntadhir was already turning around. Jamshid raced to catch up, conscious of the sound of his boots clipping on the stone floor. Muntadhir had slipped his sandals back on, but his steps were silent. He clearly had more experience sneaking through darkened homes than the man who was ostensibly here to protect him.

The window was sandblasted glass, thick and hazy. Through the swirls of etched roses and climbing vines, the street was visible, but at least three stories down.

Muntadhir frowned. "Do you think we can break the glass?"

"No need." Jamshid placed his palms against the cool glass, calling heat into his hands. It began to simmer and melt, dripping down in glimmering molten waves until there was an opening big enough for them to slip through.

Muntadhir gave an impressed whistle. "When this is over, you need to teach me how to do that." He stepped through the window.

"Wait!" Jamshid grabbed his wrist. "We're three stories up, and you've been drinking. Are you sure you're going to be able to climb down?"

"It's better than staying here. And I'm perfectly steady, see?" Muntadhir held out his hand. "Not even I'm foolish enough to get drunk in front of massive, angry warriors with more weapons than wits."

Creator, help me. This was not what Jamshid had signed up for. But as he crawled after Muntadhir, he could not help the spike of thrill that raced through him. This *should* have been what he signed up for, because it was indeed more exciting than memorizing dusty texts in the Temple.

They went hand over foot down the tiled roof. Then it was a short drop to a garden balcony of lushly potted palms and hanging baskets of ferns. They crept through the flowers, Jamshid tapping Muntadhir's shoulder and nodding in the direction of a drainpipe.

"Do you think you can slide down that?" he asked.

The emir went a bit pale, but then there was an enraged bellow from above them. "Yes," Muntadhir agreed. He threw himself at the drainpipe with the zeal of a schoolboy and slid down. Jamshid waited until Muntadhir had stumbled away, cursing and limping, and then followed.

He landed far more gracefully than the emir, albeit in a puddle that sent a spray of dirty water across Muntadhir's fine clothes. Jamshid froze, certain he'd just broken some arcane rule of palace etiquette prescribing banishment for those who sullied their royals, but then he remembered that pretty much everything they were doing was a breach of etiquette. Besides, Muntadhir grabbed him by the wrist and pulled him forward.

"Come on!"

They hurried through the darkened alleys of what looked like a rather seedy section of the Tukharistani Quarter, far grittier than anything Jamshid was used to. Muntadhir seemed to know where he was going, however, taking the turns of the tight winding streets as if he had walked them all his life. As they neared one of the main avenues, Muntadhir loosened his turban to wrap one end over his nose and mouth.

"Do you do this often?" Jamshid could not help but ask.

"What? Sneak around my city?" Muntadhir winked, his steel eyes sparkling in the light of the painted glass lamps strung across the street. "I typically travel with far more companions and a great many more weapons, which makes the sneaking part difficult." He threaded his arm through Jamshid's and pulled him close. "But it might be fun to be anonymous for once. After all, who'd be expecting the Qahtani emir to be gallivanting around with only a Daeva for protection?"

Again the extremely unhelpful fluttering in Jamshid's belly. "I should remind you I've had less than a year of weapons training." *And I won't remind you that the only weapon on me right now is a tiny knife.*

Muntadhir patted his hand. "All the more challenge for us both."

Jamshid probably should have been unsettled by that, but as the two of them made their way into the bustling commercial heart of the Tukharistani district, arm in arm like normal citizens out for a night on the town, it was difficult to be upset. Jamshid had lived in Daevabad for more than a decade, but his life in the city had always been constricted. A mix of justified fear and prejudice kept most Daevas from venturing outside their quarter to mix with the djinn tribes, let alone any shafit. Jamshid's world instead revolved around the Temple and socializing with other nobles. Nights in the glittering Tukharistani district—in the company of the even more cosmopolitan prince—were a new and exhilarating experience.

"I can't believe I've never been here before," Jamshid remarked, inhaling the burnt caramel notes of the fiery skewered confections being sold by the stall ahead of them.

"You've never been to the Tukharistani district?" When Jamshid nodded, Muntadhir chuckled. "You weren't kidding when you said your father was overprotective."

"I'm surprised *your* father isn't more overprotective." But as soon as the words were out of his mouth, Jamshid regretted them. It felt impossible to check himself around Muntadhir, as though the emir couldn't have Jamshid killed and his family destroyed with a snap of his fingers. He rushed to apologize. "Forgive me. Not that—"

Muntadhir waved him off, the movement unsteady. "There's nothing to forgive. My father adheres to a different sort of protection."

"Meaning?"

"Meaning that it would be more dangerous for both Daevabad and me if I appeared weak." Muntadhir met his gaze. Behind his facecloth, it looked like he was attempting to smile. "If my father had his way, I would have spent my childhood in Am Gezira, living off the land with my cousins and battling zahhak."

Jamshid frowned. "So why didn't you?"

"My mother didn't want me to leave." A hint of old grief softened Muntadhir's voice. "We were very close."

You prying idiot. "I'm sorry," Jamshid blurted out. "I shouldn't be questioning you like this."

"And I probably shouldn't be answering. And yet I find myself continuously doing that with you, Pramukh. You would have made a good priest. Or an even better spy, were you so inclined."

Jamshid shuddered. "I don't think I'd make a very good spy."

"Ah, you never know." But then Muntadhir stumbled, nearly falling to his knees. "Oh, all right. So that's why they pulled out cushions when they started passing the mushrooms around."

"Passing the *what*?"

Muntadhir clutched his arm. "You should probably get me back to the palace."

JAMSHID TRIED NOT TO TRIP AS HE EASED MUNTADHIR INTO his bed. As intoxicated as Muntadhir was—and he was *out* of it: Muntadhir had spent their walk back to the palace reciting poetry to his hands and falling asleep—Jamshid didn't think collapsing onto the emir of Daevabad was wise. Finally Jamshid got him more or less onto the mattress, and Muntadhir let out a sigh of contentment that made Jamshid's thoughts go in a series of inappropriate directions.

Control yourself, he chided, a command that was easier chanted internally than obeyed as he leaned over Muntadhir's body to reach for a pillow. Jamshid was overly conscious of the silky feel of the sheets between his fingers. The plumpness of the pillow and the perfume of Muntadhir's breath. He slipped the pillow carefully under the emir's head, his heart going wild at the brief brush of Muntadhir's hair. He'd never seen the emir's head uncovered before. Muntadhir had beautiful hair, the black warmed by just a hint of russet. It was cut short, curling at the ends, and Jamshid found himself wondering what it would look like if it was grown out. If it would catch his fingers.

He swallowed loudly, aware that imagining how Muntadhir's hair would feel in his hands was not part of controlling himself. He let go of the pillow.

"Is there anything else I can do, Emir?" he asked, trying to steady his voice.

Muntadhir's eyes fluttered open. His gaze was still bleary, but lying down seemed to have helped, a little alertness returning to his expression. "Travel back in time and tell me not to eat anything tonight?"

"They haven't taught me that particular skill at the Citadel yet." A small, exhausted smile lit Muntadhir's face, and fresh worry knotted Jamshid up. "Are you sure I cannot call someone? Nisreen, perhaps? She could brew you a tonic or—"

"I'm fine. Truly. I mean . . . there are currently three of you and one of them is dancing with stars, but I'm at the point where I recognize only one is real. I just need to sleep." Muntadhir reached out, still looking a little dazed. His fingers brushed Jamshid's cheek, tracing down the line of his jaw. "You look very good in starlight."

Everything in Jamshid went still. Suddenly all he was conscious of was the press of Muntadhir's fingers and the heavy wonder in his gray eyes.

Kiss him.

Had it been any other man, under any other circumstances, Jamshid would have done just that. But Muntadhir was not a man—not really. He was a prince. The emir. And not only the emir, he was *very* obviously impaired, and so when Muntadhir's thumb moved over Jamshid's bottom lip, making everything in him tremble, Jamshid forced himself to stay still.

"We are not good for you," Muntadhir said softly.

Jamshid let out a choked breath. It was taking everything he had right now not to jump into this man's bed and crush his mouth to his, so the warning needed a moment to land. "Wh-what?"

Muntadhir's thumb went over his lips once more, and Jamshid would swear he actually did see stars.

"You would have been safer at your Temple. This place, this palace, it eats people up from the inside. It takes everything that is kind and gentle in your heart and turns it to stone." Muntadhir dropped his hand. "And you . . . you are good and perfect, and it is going to destroy you."

There was true fear in Muntadhir's glazed eyes. And though being warned in such a way by one of Daevabad's most cunning and powerful figures should have frightened Jamshid, it didn't.

Not until Jamshid sat back on his heels and caught a glimpse of the opposite wall. Muntadhir's chamber was opulent and almost absurdly lavish, with woven rugs so thick and soft that his feet sank deep into them, painted silk landscapes covering the walls and rosewood partitions carved so finely it looked like one was in a garden. It occupied a prime location in the ancient palace, its balcony offering an unparalleled view of both the city and the deep lake that surrounded it. This room had clearly always belonged to the highest of nobility.

And Jamshid knew that: because painted in pale fragments that still clung to the wall across from him was a circle of roaring shedus. The emblem of his blessed Nahids, long dead now. The winged lions that still symbolically guarded the Daeva Quarter, bordering the heavy gates his people made sure to keep clean and oiled should they ever need to be shut against the rest of the city.

You will always be a Daeva to them first. His father had shouted these words until he was blue in the face upon returning from Zariaspa to learn his son had traded in his Temple garb for a spot in the Qahtanis' army. *Do you understand that? Everything you do in their service reflects on us, every mistake risks us.*

Jamshid lowered his gaze. "Your concern is noted, my emir," he said, forcing a cool professionalism into his voice. "Is there anything else?"

He could hear Muntadhir swallow. Jamshid didn't want to look up. He didn't want to see the glimmer of regret in the other man's face that would soften him, that would make him seem real and genuine instead of the untouchable, deadly charisma of the emir who could—and would—ruin or elevate you with a single gesture.

"Would you stay?" Muntadhir's voice was faint. "Just poke me every once in a while, to make sure I haven't stopped breathing. And talk to me," he added, sounding like sleep was beginning to overtake him again. "It makes me feel less like I'm hallucinating."

"What would you like me to talk about?"

"Anything," Muntadhir answered. "I just want to hear your voice."

Dara

This scene is meant to take place during Nahri and Dara's journey to Daevabad, shortly after they flee Hierapolis. No spoilers.

This human-blooded scoundrel was going to be the death of him. Dara peeked again at the merchants arguing in the street, the cobbler angrily accusing the fruit seller of intentionally spilling his cart, and then darted a glance at Nahri.

"Will you please hurry up?" he implored. "He's going to come back any minute."

Surrounded by a pile of boots and leather slippers in various states of mending, Nahri languidly stretched out a foot, wiggling her toes in the shoe she was trying on.

"They're still fighting. Relax." She made a face and then removed the shoe, tossing it aside. "Too stiff."

Dara hissed under his breath. "For the love of the Creator, will you just pick something? It cannot make that much of a difference!"

"Maybe if *my* feet were made of fire, it wouldn't. But alas . . . oh." Her dark eyes sparkled as she plucked out a pair of leather boots. "These look comfortable. And how lovely," she remarked, admiring the swirling pattern of leaves stamped up the sides. "I bet I could trade them later."

Dara counted to ten in his head, reminding himself that this woman was the closest thing to a Nahid healer left in the world, he was an Afshin, and a pack of ifrit were after her. Losing his temper and causing the pile of shoes surrounding her to burst into flames was not an option.

Not a *good* option, at least.

"*Nahri*," he said, stressing her name. It felt strange to speak it, an intimacy Dara was not yet accustomed to, but she had pointedly stopped responding to *thief*, *girl*, and *human*. He raised his hands, half praying, half begging. "Our people have rules. If that human man comes in here and catches you, I cannot harm him."

"Why? Will you melt? Turn to ash?" She rolled her eyes. "What's the use in being some all-powerful djinn if you have to run and hide from humans?"

Blood might no longer pump through his veins, but Dara was certain some part of him was boiling. "I have told you a hundred times. I am *not* a djinn."

"I know." Nahri smiled sweetly. "It just gives me exquisite pleasure to make you angry."

Between her mocking grin and his roiling emotions, Dara was not quite prepared to hear the phrase *exquisite pleasure* in Nahri's teasing voice. "Please just steal something and be done with it," he said gruffly.

"Fine." She rose to her feet, still wearing the boots. "I suppose these will do." She picked up her bag, already filled with other pilfered items, and shoved it in his arms, taking back a pot she'd stolen and forced him to carry. "Let's go." She turned for the front door of the tiny shop.

Dara put an arm out to stop her. "You can't mean to go out that way. He'll see you!"

"He will," Nahri agreed, shoving past him. In horror, Dara watched as she stepped out of the shop, neatly winding between piles of leather soles and spilled fruit, heading directly for the arguing merchants.

I am not going to save her. I am not. Dara hurried after her.

As he expected, it was not a smooth exit. Nahri was fighting with the fruit seller, one hand on her hip. She was shouting in that human tongue Dara barely understood, but judging from the righteous fury in the fruit seller's face and the cobbler's stammering denial, she had taken sides. Within moments, the cobbler had thrown up his hands, seemingly cursed them both, and stormed off. Dara watched Nahri kneel to help the fruit seller. He appeared to be thanking her profusely, clearly unaware Nahri had been the one to stick one of the cobbler's tools in his cart's wheel. Upon spotting her pot, he began filling it with fruit, waving off her feigned protestations.

"You are . . . the most dishonest person I have ever met," Dara said when Nahri rejoined him. He was as awed as he was scandalized.

"Then you have lived a very boring number of centuries whose exact number you still refuse to disclose." As they walked, Nahri glanced up at him with another of her winks. "Surely you've broken at least one rule in your life. Stayed out past curfew, lied to your mother. Slept with the wrong woman."

I have slaughtered thousands of people like you.

"No," Dara lied. "Centuries of being dull and rule-abiding. Just as you say."

"Sounds like a waste of life to me."

She might have punched him. But Dara kept his mouth shut, masking his reaction and following Nahri as she continued through the market, discreetly filching vegetables and clothes like she was at harvest and the crop was coming from her personal garden. This was the third human town they'd visited after fleeing Hierapolis and the last he hoped to lay eyes on for a long time. They certainly had enough supplies to see them through the rest of the journey to Daevabad.

Daevabad. Its very name still filled Dara with grief. The prospect of actually being across the lake from his home seemed impossible. But then he spotted Nahri neatly cut a purse off a man twice Dara's size.

"You are done," Dara proclaimed, seizing her wrist and pulling Nahri through the crowd of shoppers. Humans shivered as he swept past, their vacant gazes trailing over him with unseeing eyes. He hated it. Dara already felt like a ghost with his own people, the Daevas he'd been avoiding since he'd been freed. Being surrounded by humans in their world of dirt and iron blood where he truly was an invisible wraith was too much.

They'd left their horses along a bed of lush grass bordering the river where Dara had summoned a smoky fog to shroud them. He dissipated it now and turned toward Nahri. "We should . . . wh-what are you doing?" he stammered. "Why are you *taking your clothes off*?"

Nahri continued unlacing the strips of torn cloth she'd used to make his spare tunic fit her much smaller frame. "Getting rid of this giant tent of a shirt and then bathing so I don't smell like a brooding fire warrior." She wrenched off the tunic, and Dara caught a glimpse of ebony curls spilling over bare shoulders before he swore under his breath and spun around.

"You are going to drown," he spat as he heard her splash into the river. "Then I will have been dragged across the world for nothing."

"Oh, did I pull you from some sort of engaging social life? What exactly were you doing before you met me? Prowling the plains and scowling at deer? Please. I bet saving a secret Nahid shafit is the most exciting thing that's ever happened to you, *Darayavahoush*." Nahri all but purred his name. Since prying it from him in the ruins of Hierapolis with her ridiculous stunt, she'd taken to using it as often as possible, probably to irritate him.

And it did irritate him. Because Creator, did Dara like hearing his name out of her mouth.

Get ahold of yourself. Dara sat with his back purposefully to the water, fighting the urge to check on her. It cut too close to his urge to *look* at her, and he was not letting this shafit thief beguile him any further. Despite his horrified shock when he first realized what Nahri was, Dara was beginning to have sympathy for whatever distant Nahid ancestor had crossed paths with one of her human ones. If they were anything like Nahri, they would have been all but impossible to resist. He scrubbed his hands through his hair, trying to think of anything that wasn't the sound of her swimming.

"Hurry up," he insisted. "We still have ground to cover before nightfall."

"And *you* still have a whole slew of questions to answer, like you promised back at Hierapolis. Maybe I'll stay in the river until you start talking about this supposed war Khayzur says you got yourself involved in."

Dread crawled over Dara. There were a vast number of things he did not wish to discuss with Nahri, and the war was chief among them.

But you are running out of time. Dara had already made up his mind to tell her: allowing Nahri to present herself before the Qahtani king without knowing the deadly history between their families would be abhorrent.

Especially since Dara had no intention of being at her side when she did. He had no intention of even going beyond Daevabad's gates. How could he? Not only had he lost the right to return home when he failed his people and his Nahids—if he was honest, he was afraid. Nahri might not know what he'd done during the war, but Dara was damn sure even fourteen centuries later, the djinn had not forgotten. He'd be locked up in one of the infamous cells beneath the palace and left to suffer for eternity. Which might be a fate he deserved, but not one he'd willingly rush into. He didn't hate himself *that* much.

The darkness of his closed eyes dimmed further, and Dara glanced up, blinking to see Nahri standing before him, outlined against the sun. She was dressed in her stolen clothes, beads of water still clinging to her cheeks and glistening in her hair.

Suleiman's eye, she is beautiful. The sight of her left him feeling breathless, which of course was not possible, as Dara did not breath, and the sentiment lasted only as long as it took Nahri to aim a hard kick at his foot.

"Are you done berating yourself over here for my thieving at the market? If it makes you feel better, you were a useless accomplice."

If only being a useless accomplice was the crime he was berating himself for. "You are the rudest person I have ever encountered," he said, trying to force some rancor into his voice.

Nahri snorted in derision, a mocking sound that had no business increasing Dara's extremely unhelpful desire to pull her into his lap. She picked her belt back up and unsheathed the dagger he'd given her. Sunlight played on the iron blade.

"Can you teach me how to throw this?"

"Why?"

"Because I'd like to be able to protect myself from the pack of ifrit hunting me?"

Dara winced. "Fair point. Let us travel a bit farther first. I do not like remaining this close to a human settlement."

They resaddled the horses, Dara silently noting that Nahri clearly remembered what he'd shown her. He arranged her new purchases, threading a cord through the handle of a pot.

He tapped the pot. "What exactly do you mean to do with this?"

"Teach myself to cook?" But Nahri didn't sound optimistic. "I stole some vegetables and figured if I boiled them with water . . . that's soup, isn't it?"

Dara frowned. "If you do not know how to cook and have always lived alone, what did you eat?"

"Whatever I got my hands on. When I had enough coin, I could buy some fried beans and occasionally a bit of grilled meat. Otherwise, it was mostly day-old bread and bruised fruit." Nahri flushed. "And when I was a child . . . a lot of garbage and other people's leftovers."

Garbage. A lifetime of hot home-cooked meals flashed before Dara's eyes. Despite the war that engulfed his world, Dara had grown up beloved and well cared for in a wealthy home full of bustling relatives, including the mother he adored and a dozen aunts who would have taken it as a personal affront if he'd left the house hungry. There was always a steaming bowl of stew, freshly fried dumplings, or butter pastry being pressed on him—a privilege he hadn't realized.

He gazed at Nahri, remembering anew the sharp lines of her face and the sallow color to her skin when they first met. He could not begin to imagine how lonely and difficult it must have been to grow up the way she did.

"I will cook something for you," Dara decided. "Conjure it anyway, I mean." He'd never actually *tried* to conjure food—he didn't need to eat often in whatever form this was—but conjuring food couldn't be much harder than conjuring wine, and he was exceedingly practiced at that.

A guarded expression slipped across her face. "And what's that going to cost me?"

A few more days of believing my worst crime is being a useless accomplice. A few more days for Dara to savor being an ordinary soldier with an irrational crush on an impossibility instead of the Scourge of Qui-zi.

"Merely your company and the promise not to stab me during knife-throwing lessons," Dara replied, trying to sound as sincere as possible. "I promise."

"Does that mean I *can* stab you if you don't successfully conjure up some food?"

Dara couldn't help but smile. "Whatever makes you happy, little thief."

Jamshid

This scene takes place toward the end of *The City of Brass*, picking up from the night Ali is attacked by an assassin and following through the next few days until the climactic battle on the lake. Spoilers for the first book.

It had been nearly a decade since Jamshid e-Pramukh joined Muntadhir al Qahtani's service; in that time, there had been a great many incidents that led him to question the decision to leave his safe, boring life at the Temple. But as he followed the emir through a cursed garden in the middle of the night, with an unconscious prince in his arms, Jamshid's regrets had never loomed larger.

Baba warned you not to get involved with them. He tried. You have no one to blame but yourself. Jamshid ducked to avoid a vine dangling across the muddy path. Scythe-like thorns jutted from the vine's pebbly bark, gleaming wetly in the moonlight. Just what was gleaming wetly Jamshid didn't want to know. The only sound beside the dripping leaves was Muntadhir's labored breathing. The emir was clearly struggling with his share of his brother's body, huffing and gasping as he held Alizayd's long legs tucked under his arms.

Good, a petty part of Jamshid thought. *I hope you struggle.* Since strolling onto the palace roof expecting his royal lover and instead interrupting an assassination attempt, he'd been struggling to keep a lid on his emotions. Jamshid liked to think he'd behaved in accordance with his training: he'd obeyed Alizayd's orders and gotten the prince to the Banu Nahida in time to save his life. He'd cleaned up the scene and then discreetly sought out Muntadhir, knowing he'd know what to do next. All in all, not bad for the captain of the emir's guard: the man who was expected to be Muntadhir's capable shadow, the man who protected Daevabad's next king and sorted out his messes. Jamshid had even had the presence of mind to interrupt Muntadhir back in Banu Nahri's bedroom when it seemed the emir was about to speak too freely about whatever the hell his brother had gotten himself involved in.

But there was no Banu Nahida here now. Jamshid was alone with Muntadhir in the eerie midnight garden, so the professional mask he clung to so desperately finally slipped.

"Why were you at Khanzada's?" he demanded.

Muntadhir swore as he accidentally knocked off one of Ali's sandals. "What?"

"Khanzada's," Jamshid pressed, hating the jealous edge in his voice. "Why were you there? We were supposed to meet after you were done stargazing with your siblings, remember? Why do you think I was on the roof?"

Muntadhir sighed. "You're really doing this? *Now?*" he asked, nodding to Alizayd's unconscious body hanging between them.

"*Yes.* It will give you less time to concoct a lie."

Muntadhir stopped walking, and the look he shot Jamshid over his shoulder was his royal one. This was the Muntadhir who could seduce a business rival as Jamshid quietly watched and order the imprisonment of a Daeva writer who'd spoken against Ghassan. "Lower your voice," he hissed. "You'll get us caught."

Jamshid had to bite his tongue, but he did as his emir commanded and stayed silent as they made their way to Alizayd's apartment. The canal was wilder in this part of the garden—crashing against the tall stone walls before rising in a reversed waterfall. It was an extraordinary sight, and had Jamshid the time, he might have stopped to admire it. Though Daevabad's palace frightened most people with its bloody past and unpredictable, vengeful magic, Jamshid found the place entrancing. It was like stepping into the pages of a storybook and seeing fables brought to life before his eyes.

But right now he did only as he was told. After a quick peek to make sure the apartment was empty and devoid of further assassins, he and Muntadhir carried Alizayd inside. The younger prince had yet to stir, and judging from the opium on his breath—Banu Nahri clearly took pain management seriously—he wouldn't be waking up anytime soon.

They laid him carefully on the bed. Muntadhir called a flame into one hand and then lifted his brother's shirt to check his bandages. Jamshid watched, saying nothing as his emir removed Alizayd's sandals and pulled a light sheet over his body. Alizayd muttered in his sleep, and Muntadhir pressed a kiss to his forehead. "You're going to be the death of me, idiot."

"Yes," Jamshid said evenly. "A number of your followers fear exactly that."

Muntadhir threw him another aggravated glare and then rose to his feet. "Come." They left Alizayd's bedroom, and Muntadhir pulled the door closed behind him before pointing to a cushion. "Sit."

Jamshid grated at the commands but sat. Muntadhir poured two cups of water from a pitcher, and Jamshid didn't miss that his hands were shaking. The emir might be acting like he had everything under control, but Jamshid was as experienced at reading the emotions of the man he'd been cursed to fall for as Muntadhir was at concealing them.

And Muntadhir was worried.

Jamshid was too. "Shouldn't we tell your father what happened? This is madness. An assassin guts your brother and you're not summoning the guard? What if there are other killers out there? They could come for you next!"

Muntadhir set one of the cups before him. "The assassin was shafit, right? You're sure?" he asked, ignoring Jamshid's question.

"Yes." Jamshid opened the coat he'd stolen to reveal the crimson blood staining his tunic underneath. "Trust me."

"And Ali told you to get rid of him? And make sure no one but Nahri knew he was hurt?"

"Yes."

"Fuck." Muntadhir sat back, looking more exhausted.

"Do you have any idea who it might have been? It looked . . . Muntadhir, it looked personal. A better assassin would have been quicker and gotten away. Whoever this was, he wanted to cause a lot of pain. Your brother is lucky to be alive."

Muntadhir paled. "But he's dead now? You're certain?"

Suleiman's eye, I hope so. Jamshid suppressed a shudder as he forced himself to recall the details. Alizayd's growled order and the sickening splash as the assassin's body hit the distant lake. *Had* the man been dead?

Or had Jamshid sent him to an even more brutal end?

The question made him ill. But he was a soldier, and this was what he had signed up for, wasn't it? Protecting the royal family and killing those who would threaten them?

And is that what you want to be? A killer?

"Jamshid?" Muntadhir prompted, sounding concerned. Whether that was concern for Jamshid or a loose end, Jamshid wasn't sure he wanted to know.

He cleared his throat. "Your brother bashed the assassin's head in, cut his throat with a telescope lens, and then ordered me to dump the body in the lake." Jamshid held his emir's gaze. "The assassin's dead. I'm certain. *Now* will you tell me what's going on?"

Muntadhir's face instantly closed off. "A family matter. Nothing I can't handle."

"Except *you* didn't handle it," Jamshid pointed out, growing angrier. "My Banu Nahida did. And if she gets in trouble—"

"She won't. I give you my word. Neither you nor Nahri will come to any harm over this. If my father gets wind of anything, I'll cover for you both."

That made Jamshid feel slightly better, but Nahri wasn't the only person he was worried about. "And you? I'm the captain of your guard. You're keeping something from me, I know it. You're tense and distracted and—"

"There's a Geziri-murdering, Qahtani-despising, millennia-old Afshin in my city. Of course I'm tense!"

"This started before Darayavahoush arrived," Jamshid persisted. "You've been acting strange ever since your brother moved back to the palace." Muntadhir exhaled, looking away, and Jamshid had to resist the urge to go shake him. "You can *trust* me. If there's something going on with Alizayd . . ."

"There's not."

"Muntadhir, you know what people say—"

"Then they're wrong," Muntadhir snapped. "I trust Ali with my life, and we are done with this conversation."

A few years ago, the heat in Muntadhir's command would have sent Jamshid to his knees in apology. Emir Muntadhir rarely spoke in genuine anger; he was a forgiving, good-humored man. If you betrayed him, you were likely to wake up without your spouse, your fortune, and your house—but you would wake up, which was more than one could expect if they displeased the king.

Jamshid wasn't going to his knees now though. Muntadhir didn't want to talk about the assassination attempt? *Fine.* Jamshid had other topics they could discuss. "Then if you are truly recovered from your worries about Alizayd, perhaps we can return to the conversation we started in the garden about you standing me up to visit Khanzada."

Muntadhir raised his eyes to the ceiling. "You really are spoiling for a fight."

Spoiling for a fight . . . oh, but this man made him see red. Jamshid set down his cup, fighting the desire to fling it at Muntadhir's head. "You lied to me. I haven't seen you in three months and then you abandon me on the roof to go get drunk with—"

"You were my first stop when I returned! God, I know I'm somewhat out of practice after trekking across the desert with Dara-I-would-like-to-shoot-you-full-of-arrows-yavahoush, but surely you remember me surprising you this afternoon?"

The knowing look Muntadhir gave Jamshid made part of him melt while also stoking his rage—an effect his royal lover excelled at. Jamshid very much remembered this afternoon. Feigning an errand, Muntadhir had quietly diverted from his royal procession to surprise Jamshid at the Pramukhs' home. Kaveh had been out, the servants easily dismissed, and the sudden shock of having his emir, looking incongruous and yet terribly fetching in dusty traveling clothes and overgrown beard . . . well, perhaps neither of them had been as discreet as they should have been.

And yet the memory, the precious slice of intimacy and domesticity they would never have—Muntadhir stretched out in Jamshid's plain bed, washing from the same basin, sneaking into the kitchen to scrounge for snacks—Muntadhir himself had just torn it to shreds.

"So is that it, then?" Jamshid asked. "I get you in the afternoon, Khanzada in the evening, some starry-eyed diplomat tomorrow morning . . . no wonder you stood me up. It must be hard to keep us all in track. You should hire an additional secretary."

"There would be no salary high enough." When Jamshid glared at him, Muntadhir raised his hands in a gesture of peace. "Listen, I'm sorry, okay? You're right and I apologize. I shouldn't have left you on the roof like that. I was distracted by a fight I had with my father, but that's no excuse."

The half-pleading jest in Muntadhir's gray eyes tore at Jamshid's heart, but Jamshid wasn't letting him slip away so easily. "And Khanzada? You told me it was over when you left with the Afshin. I wouldn't . . . I mean, this afternoon—" Jamshid stumbled for words. "I can't have that with you and then watch you go to her."

Muntadhir looked pained. "I can't end things with her yet. Jamshid, she's got half court at her salon every night, spilling secrets to her students. I can't look away from that kind of intelligence."

"Of course not," Jamshid said, his voice hollow. "Daevabad comes first."

Muntadhir flinched but said nothing. Neither of them did for a long moment, and the tense silence that sprawled between them ripped Jamshid apart. If this was love—choking back your own hurt out of fear of hurting another—it was as awful as it was precious. He wanted to rage at Muntadhir just as much as he wanted to make sure *no one* raged at Muntadhir.

Muntadhir rose to his feet. There was a stiffness in his posture that meant he was about to say something emir-like that would no doubt be frustrating.

"Daevabad will always come first," he said softly. "It must. I cannot offer you any more of my heart and my loyalty than I already have, Jamshid. I've always tried to be honest about that."

He had. If there was one thing Jamshid could not fault Muntadhir, it was that Muntadhir had always been honest, brutally honest, about where his Daeva lover ranked in comparison to his kingdom and family. For all that Muntadhir could be profligate and careless—with money, with wine, with hearts—he'd been cautious with Jamshid. It had been *Jamshid* who'd pursued Muntadhir. *Jamshid* who'd broken down the emir's well-constructed walls and initiated their first kisses, brazenly ignoring Muntadhir's warnings. For everything that Jamshid had learned about the cruelty of Daevabad's court, about what it was like to belong to a beaten, persecuted people in a city they should have ruled . . . part of him was still the country boy from Zariaspa raised on legends and romance.

"We could run away," he said, only half joking. "Explore the world and live off the humans like our ancestors."

Muntadhir gave him a broken smile. "I have a team of servants to dress me. How do you think I would take to the wild?"

I would teach you. I would do anything to be with you and see you free of your duties and safe from this city's awful, murderous politics. But Jamshid didn't say that. He already knew the answer.

Daevabad came first.

Muntadhir was still staring at him with a despair in his eyes that Jamshid didn't like. "Jamshid, about my duties. There's something I should tell you before you hear it from Kaveh. The fight with my father . . ." Muntadhir cleared his throat. "It was about your Banu Nahida."

"What about her?"

"He wants me to marry her."

Jamshid rocked back on his heels. "*Marry* her? But that's ridiculous," he sputtered, objecting before the words had even properly settled in his brain. "She's a Nahid. You're a—"

"A what?" Muntadhir had jerked up, surprised hurt in his expression. "A djinn? A sand fly?"

Jamshid backpedaled, ashamed how quickly he'd recoiled at the prospect of one of his sacred Nahids marrying a non-Daeva. Of course it should have been a possibility. It was the ideal alliance, and it made perfect sense that Ghassan—one of the few kings who made a concerted effort at improving things with the Daevas—would want to marry his heir to the Banu Nahida.

But she's not theirs. Banu Nahri was a miracle, a *Daeva* miracle. Her arrival in Daevabad at the Afshin's side had electrified their tribe. She was a blessing, the promise of a brighter future. And Jamshid *liked* her. She was witty and funny and, well, a little scary, but he liked her.

He didn't want to see her made into Ghassan's pawn.

"You can't marry her," Jamshid said again, more insistently. "It's not right. She just got to Daevabad. She doesn't deserve to be immediately ground up by your father."

Muntadhir's eyes flashed. "Thanks for assuming I'd be the sort of husband to allow my wife to be 'ground up.'" He was twisting one of his rings, the plain gold one he wore in memory of his mother. Muntadhir had elegant hands, his fingers untouched by calluses. Jamshid loved his hands; quietly lacing their fingers together had been their earliest form of intimacy: a sign from Muntadhir that he needed Jamshid to help extract him from whatever circumstance in which he'd gotten embroiled.

Then a far more personal cost of this marriage became clear. Nahri was Jamshid's Banu Nahida. If she married Muntadhir . . .

"We would be over," Jamshid said, realizing it aloud. "This . . . whatever this is between us. It would need to end. She's my Banu Nahida; I couldn't betray her like that."

There was no surprise in Muntadhir's face, only resignation. Of course his emir would have already worked this all out.

"Yes," he said quietly. "I imagined as much."

Jamshid felt like he was going to be sick. "Do you want to marry her?"

The uncertainty in Muntadhir's expression said it all. "No. But . . . it could be a new beginning for our tribes. I feel like I'm being selfish if I don't consider it."

So be selfish, Jamshid wanted to say. To shout. But he couldn't. Muntadhir didn't give up his mask easily, and right now he looked devastated. Jamshid had no doubt that if it hadn't been for him, Muntadhir would have already agreed and consigned himself to a political marriage for the good of his kingdom.

He was always going to have a political marriage. Muntadhir might have broken his heart more times than Jamshid could count, but Jamshid was the only one of them who had a choice. Muntadhir would never escape his fate. Jamshid could. If he wanted to give up his position or run back to Zariaspa, tongues would wag, his father would be furious, but there would be no real consequences.

Muntadhir spoke again. "I hope you know that if this ever got to be too much, I would still look out for you. It's not contingent on us being . . . well." He stumbled over his words, sounding uncharacteristically nervous. "I can find you another position. Anything you want, anywhere you want. You wouldn't have to worry about money or—"

Oh, my love. Jamshid's anger melted. "No." He closed the space between them and took Muntadhir's hand. "Someone just broke into the palace to try to assassinate *one* Qahtani prince, and the Afshin has the Daevas all riled up. I'm not leaving your side."

"My protector." Muntadhir gave him a small, haunted smile and brought Jamshid's hand to his mouth. He kissed his knuckles. "Maybe you could be my Afshin."

Jamshid pulled Muntadhir closer. He wrapped his arms around him, and Muntadhir finally let out a shaky breath, relaxing into his embrace. Jamshid gently removed his turban and ran his fingers through Muntadhir's hair. "You know when I was younger, I would have found that a terribly romantic comparison."

"Of course you would have." But Jamshid heard hesitation in the other man's voice. "May I ask you something?"

"Of course."

Muntadhir broke away to look Jamshid in the face. "What do you mean the Afshin has the Daevas all riled up?"

JAMSHID WATCHED AS DARA LEANED BACK AGAINST THE cushions that had been set up next to their feast and grinned at the rapt faces of the spellbound Daeva nobles surrounding him.

"It knocked me clean off my horse," the Afshin said, laughing as he continued the story he'd been sharing. "I barely even saw the damned thing. One moment I am examining my bow before the archery competition; the next, there is a blur of flying stone, and—" He smashed his hands together, then shook his head ruefully. "I awoke in the Nahid's hospital three days later. Years of looking forward to my first Navasatem and I spent the majority of it in a sickbed having my skull pieced back together."

Saman Pashanur, one of Kaveh's oldest acquaintances and a severe man Jamshid had never seen smile, leaned forward, looking as excited as a schoolboy. "Was it truly a shedu that struck you?"

Dara chuckled and picked up his date wine. A couple months ago no one Jamshid knew drank date wine. Now half his friends swore by it.

"Not quite," Dara answered. "Even in my day, it had been centuries since any of us had seen a real shedu. That which struck me was a statue, one of the ones that lined the palace walls. A Baga Nahid was experimenting in the hopes he could bewitch them to shoot flames over the arena." He smiled sadly. "I wish you could have seen the Daevabad of my youth, my friends. It was a jewel, a paradise of gardens and libraries with streets safe enough that a woman could walk upon them at night alone."

"We'll make it that way again," Saman said fervently. "One day. Now that the Creator has returned a Banu Nahida to us, anything is possible."

It could be a new beginning. But Jamshid was also realistic about such dreams, and he shifted uncomfortably as Muntadhir's words returned to him. He knew the kind of glory age the Daevas around him were dreaming of had no place for Geziri kings.

Even so he could not help but watch the Afshin. Jamshid wasn't immune to the way he entranced the rest of them. The very ease, the confidence with which Dara sat and grinned and laughed. His open nostalgia as he waxed poetic about the days of the Nahid Council and Daevabad before the invasion.

He's not afraid of them. It was a stance plenty of foolish young Daevas might boast of in the safety of their homes as they mocked the Geziris. But not like Dara did. The Afshin wasn't boasting. He wasn't trying to show off. He simply wasn't afraid of Ghassan's regime. He hadn't been beaten by the Royal Guard for the "crime" of looking a djinn soldier in the eye or had a politically outspoken parent disappear. Dara hadn't been crushed like the rest of them, raised to watch their words and bow their heads.

It was captivating. Jamshid couldn't fault the Daevas who'd been flocking to the Pramukhs' home since the Afshin had taken up residence there. It was easy to be lulled by Dara's words. By the dream of a world in which their people were legends.

"Not stuck in the palace with the Qahtanis circling her, Banu Nahri isn't—" The words pulled Jamshid back to attention. It was another of his father's acquaintances, a scholar in the Royal Library. "She spends every afternoon in the company of that crocodile prince. The djinn are already trying to convert her, to steal her away from our religion and culture."

"I wish them luck," Dara said drily. "Banu Nahri has a will that could break a zulfiqar. There is no convincing her of anything." But he looked briefly troubled. "Relations between the princes . . . surely this alliance people speak of between them is exaggerated. Muntadhir and Alizayd would seem obvious rivals."

"They are." It was the scholar again, his expression impassioned . . . or perhaps drunken. "People say Emir Muntadhir begged the king not to let his brother be raised as a warrior, but Queen Hatset interfered. They are setting us all up for catastrophe."

Jamshid wasn't sure what prospect was more ridiculous: Ghassan being cowed by anyone or the notoriously secretive Qahtani royals exposing family turmoil to outsiders. He did know, however, that he should probably quell such talk. If Kaveh had been here, he would have hushed them several treasonous comments ago. There were nearly a score of men dining with them tonight, and one did not speak freely of the regime when that many ears were listening.

But his father was at the palace and Jamshid was tired of feeling torn between his people and his emir. So when Saman started up again, railing about the djinn, Jamshid left. His spot was immediately claimed, the press of men all trying to get closer to the famed Afshin. No one seemed to notice him leave, but Jamshid was used to being overlooked.

He breathed more freely once he was outside in the courtyard that fronted the stables. With his father's elevation to grand wazir had come a large, well-appointed mansion close to the palace and set against the city's outer wall in a garden distract. It wasn't Zariaspa and never would be, but the fresh air blowing from the island's forest and the smell of flowers let Jamshid briefly imagine he'd escaped the city. He'd have done anything for a ride beneath the stars along the hill trails right now, but of course Daevas weren't permitted outside the city walls after sunset.

"May I join you?"

Jamshid jumped. It was the Afshin. The ground here was pebbled stone, but somehow Dara walked without a single sound, his steps undetectable.

"I'm not as good company as your audience back there," Jamshid warned.

Dara snorted. "I am glad to know I am not the only one for whom it feels like a performance."

Jamshid flushed. "I didn't mean it like that."

But the Afshin only smiled. "You need not apologize, Pramukh. Believe it or not, I find your honesty refreshing." He drew nearer to the stables and clicked his tongue, pulling a handful of sugar pieces from his pocket. Judging by the speed with which their horses—even his father's elderly half-lame mare—appeared, Jamshid was guessing Dara had made a habit of spoiling them. "You modern Daevas are all so fancy and glamorous that it makes me nervous. I talk too much when I am nervous. A whole group of you, and I cannot hold my tongue."

Jamshid couldn't believe what he was hearing. "*We're* glamorous? You have your own personal shrine in the Temple!"

Dara laughed. "A shrine built in a simpler time, trust me. All these feasts with foods from around the world, your silks and jewels and whatnot . . . let alone all the gossip and politics. I have never felt more like a dull, blundering traveler from another century than when I am at these parties."

Jamshid joined him at the fence. "I suppose a lot changes in fourteen hundred years."

"It is beyond change," Dara said softly. "It is an entirely new world."

The sadness in the other man's voice took him aback, but by the time Jamshid met his gaze, the Afshin was already shaking his head, blushing with embarrassment. "Forgive me. I tend toward brooding when I have had too much drink, and your date wine is *far* stronger than what I am used to."

"Was Daevabad really as you say?" Jamshid asked. "I can't imagine being able to walk alone in the shafit district nowadays, let alone celebrate our holidays so openly."

"It was all that and more. I do not quite know what I was expecting to find in Daevabad, but having to stop a mob of shafit from breaking into the Daeva Quarter on my first day back was not inspiring."

"It doesn't seem to have affected you much," Jamshid replied. "You seem so . . . unafraid."

"If I seem unafraid, it is because I am much practiced at hiding it. I spent the entire journey here worrying whether your djinn king would send me to rot in the dungeon or simply execute me. And I am afraid for my Banu Nahida," Dara confessed. "Very afraid. I fear for her every moment she is trapped in that palace, surrounded by sly-talking, glamorous djinn."

"She seems very capable. Smart and strong-willed like you said earlier."

Dara didn't look very reassured. Jamshid watched as he gave one of the horses a last pat. "You do not like when people speak poorly of the Qahtanis, I have noticed."

The change in subject threw him for a moment. "No, I don't," Jamshid admitted. "Beyond the fact that it's dangerous to speak poorly of them, I count Emir Muntadhir as a close personal friend."

"It seems a strange thing to be afraid of a close personal friend."

Jamshid cleared his throat. "It's complicated."

"No doubt." Dara turned to look at him. "Is he a good man?"

Yes. But Jamshid held his tongue, not missing how intently Dara was looking at him. He was a politician's son; he knew a shift in conversation when he heard it. "You just returned from traveling with him. Was that not enough time to form an opinion?"

"Yes. Of a clever diplomat trying to keep peace with an enemy returned from the dead. I want the opinion of someone who knows him better."

Why is he asking me this now? Could *Dara* have heard the rumors about Ghassan wanting to marry Nahri and Muntadhir? The prospect made Jamshid shudder; it was clear to anyone who spent time in his company that the Afshin's feelings for the Banu Nahida went beyond duty.

"Yes," he said finally. "Muntadhir is a good man and a very capable emir, which are not always complementary things. But he has a kind heart and tries to do right by his people and his kingdom."

"He has a weakness for drink."

Jamshid found himself bristling on Muntadhir's behalf. "Says the man who just admitted being overcome by date wine."

Dara's bright eyes danced. "Ah, you must be friend to him truly to be so defensive! Then let me ask you something else, Jamshid e-Pramukh, and I pray you answer just as truly. Do you think he will be a good king for *our* people?" When Jamshid opened his mouth, Dara held up a hand. "No, do not answer as a friend. Think on it. Tell me as a Daeva man."

Tell me as a Daeva man. There was weight behind those words coming from the Afshin who'd fought and died to free their people. *Did*

Jamshid think Muntadhir would be a good king? Strangely he'd never forced himself to objectively consider the question before. It didn't matter what Jamshid thought; Muntadhir was *going* to be king, and Jamshid had been sworn to him even before he fell in love. It was more a matter of Jamshid wanting to help him be the best king he could. And Muntadhir was a good person. He tried to do the right thing.

Unless the right thing isn't what Ghassan wants. Jamshid thought about Nahri. Would she have a say in this royal marriage? Would Muntadhir even care? How many times had he pleaded with Muntadhir to save some of the Daeva artists and poets he patronized when they slipped and said the wrong thing in public? How many times had he watched Muntadhir lower his head and hold his tongue when Kaveh was insulted at court? When his fellow djinn companions got drunk and asked Jamshid if he truly worshipped flames? Jamshid did know Muntadhir. Probably better than anyone. And each additional year he served him and loved him, he watched more of Muntadhir's spark—his goodness—dim beneath his father's fierce, unrelenting pressure.

"If he becomes king . . . sooner rather than later," Jamshid said hesitantly. "He means well, but his family . . . it's a lot of pressure. I think his father is determined to shape him in his own image. And with Alizayd, the sooner succession is confirmed, the better."

Dara tilted his head, seeming to regard all that. "It sounds like someone should kill Ghassan."

The blood left Jamshid's face. "What? *No.* That's not what—"

Dara burst into laughter. "Oh, but your face! It was a joke, my friend!" He clapped Jamshid on the back so hard that he nearly knocked him off his feet. "Be glad you are not a Nahid, else I would have flown to carry out your command."

"It wasn't a command," Jamshid said weakly, beginning to wonder just how much Dara had drunk and whether this extremely dangerous idea would stay with him. "I was just—"

"Afshin?" One of the Pramukh's servants stepped out from the entrance leading back to the compound. He bowed when he spotted

Jamshid. "Didn't mean to interrupt, my lords. There was an invitation for the Afshin, delivered personally, by, ah . . . a woman."

Jamshid stared at the man as he handed Dara the letter, baffled by his tone. "A woman?"

The servant met his gaze, knowing in his eyes. "A messenger from Khanzada's salon."

Oh, for the love of the Creator . . . "Khanzada sent the Afshin an invitation?"

With a look that all but said "leave me out of this," the other man nodded. "I figured it was best to pass along." He bowed again and was gone.

Dara toyed with the scroll. "Who is this Khanzada?"

If Dara was dazzled by a simple dinner with friends at the Pramukhs', Jamshid had no idea how he was supposed to describe Khanzada's glittering salon of obscenely wealthy patrons, world-renowned entertainers, magic, criminals, and sex.

"She's a famous singer and dancer from Agnivansha," Jamshid finally replied. "Recently arrived in Daevabad. She runs a salon that's quite popular with the city's noblemen."

Dara frowned, looking uncertain. It was a strange expression to see on the face of a man who'd just been joking about murdering Daevabad's king and could probably kill everyone in the house in under five minutes.

He handed the invitation to Jamshid. "Will you read it for me?"

Jamshid reluctantly opened the scroll and had to fight not to scowl as he scanned the overly flowery words. "She says she would be honored if you would grace her home with your presence tonight. They are putting on a special performance."

"A performance? Tonight?"

"Tonight." Jamshid handed it back. "You *are* famous, Afshin," he added when Dara blinked in surprise. "She's probably hoping some of your admirers will follow."

Dara looked thoughtful. "I have never been to the Agnivanshi Quarter."

"Really? But you grew up here."

"We were not permitted many things," Dara said, sounding embarrassed. He slipped the scroll into his coat. "Would you go with me?"

Jamshid didn't understand what he meant at first, and then the hopeful look in the Afshin's green eyes took a horrifying turn. "Wait, you *want* to go to Khanzada's?"

"I confess myself intrigued. I have not . . ." Dara seemed to be struggling for words. "There is so much I have not seen, have not experienced. I feel like an outsider in my own city, crashing about with blinders on."

"I'm not sure Khanzada's salon is the sort of experience you're after. All the gossip and deadly politics you're worried about? Those are things she excels at. She has an entire team of courtesans dedicated to extracting the kind of secrets that topple dynasties and ruin fortunes."

Dara didn't look intimidated in the slightest. "I assure you, I have very little interest in her courtesans. But I would like to see the Agnivanshi Quarter and hear some music. To learn how you Daevabadi men of today spend your nights. Please," he said again, looking at Jamshid with open beseeching. "I am sure to make a fool of myself without you."

Jamshid could think of few worse ways to spend his evening than playing babysitter to a very large—already tipsy—deadly warrior, with a list of grievances the length of his arm, and in the salon of a woman who hated him. And none of that even factored in Muntadhir's presence.

But Muntadhir probably won't be there. Since the attack on his brother, Muntadhir had been withdrawn and depressed. He'd been retiring to his apartments and the harem garden after court, places Jamshid couldn't follow without invitation.

And Dara just looked so eager. Jamshid was putting together a very different picture of the famed Afshin than the one people celebrated. Dara had lived a short, stifled life in a different world, returning to one in which he was lonely and bewildered. Jamshid could take him to hear some music, marvel at some novelty, and make absolutely sure no one lured him into one of the rooms below the dance floor.

"All right," Jamshid grumbled. "But only for a little while."

EVERYTHING HAD GONE SO TERRIBLY WRONG.

Jamshid raced down the corridor toward the infirmary, his mind spinning. He felt as though he'd been dashing back and forth across the city all night. To Khanzada's salon with Dara for their ill-fated evening out. Back home to warn his father of the Afshin's very nasty—and very public—spat with Muntadhir. And then to the palace, as swiftly as his horse would take him, when came the wild rumor that Darayavahoush had broken into the infirmary and kidnapped Nahri and Alizayd.

It's not possible. Yes, the fight with Muntadhir had been bad, and frankly reflected poorly on two men Jamshid typically held in high esteem. But surely that wouldn't be enough to convince Darayavahoush to do something so rash. Surely he *knew* how delicate the balance of power was in this city and that to abduct the Banu Nahida—to say nothing of Ghassan's youngest son—would invite the king's wrath upon every Daeva in a lethal show of retribution.

It had to be a rumor. Which Jamshid kept telling himself until he arrived at the infirmary.

The place was packed with soldiers. More soldiers than Jamshid would have thought could fit, so many soldiers that he could barely see beyond the wall of their bodies. And though serving Muntadhir had given Jamshid plenty of experience in being the only Daeva in the room, the hateful glares aimed at him as he pushed his way through made his blood run cold. There were no familiar faces here. These soldiers were proper Citadel men.

Alizayd's men. And the infirmary in which their prince had made a last stand was a wreck. Virtually all the furniture had been smashed, and the curtain ripped to shreds. Bits of wreckage were still smoldering, and blood—a lot of it—was splashed across one glistening stone column.

Jamshid froze; Ghassan himself stood before the bloodstained column. Muntadhir was at his side, his head lowered in shame, but it was Ghassan who held Jamshid's attention. The djinn king was dressed more plainly than Jamshid had ever seen him, his ebony robe swapped for a homespun shawl, which on another might have made him look like a harmless, worried old man.

It didn't age Ghassan. The rough garment made him somehow look even more terrifying, reminding Jamshid that Ghassan was not some softly bred city king. He'd been raised in a hard land and spent his first century on the battlefield as his infamous father's right-hand. He might think more fondly of Daevas than his predecessor, but he kept the city's peace by brute force. There was nothing Ghassan hated more than chaos. He burned to the ground any inkling of civil strife.

And what Dara had done tonight was so much worse than an inkling.

As if he could feel Jamshid's stare, Ghassan turned to regard him. The king's gray eyes—a mirror image of Muntadhir's—traced Jamshid from his head to his toes, and the rage in those eyes nearly sent Jamshid to the floor.

But then the visible anger was gone, replaced by the king's cool mask.

"Captain Pramukh." It sounded like Ghassan might have attempted to drawl Jamshid's name, but there was no playful court ruse here; there was deadly intent in every syllable of Ghassan's voice. "Your houseguest has made some very poor decisions tonight."

At those words, all Jamshid's years at Muntadhir's side, all Kaveh's careful tutelage, everything he had ever learned about surviving at court fled his mind. He probably should have dropped to his knees. Apologized profusely and begged for mercy.

But despite what had happened tonight, the memory of Dara's confidence and the defiance Jamshid had envied burned in him still. Jamshid would not grovel before Ghassan.

Instead he barely bowed his head. "How can I help, my king?"

At Ghassan's side, Muntadhir shot Jamshid a glance in warning.

But the king didn't react to Jamshid's bravado save a slight thinning of his lips. "You've been training with the Afshin since his arrival, yes?"

"I have."

"Then stay by the emir's side tonight. We go to meet them on the lake." Ghassan shoved what looked like a blood-soaked rag into Muntadhir's hands. "If your brother dies tonight because of you, I will see you punished in this life and the next."

The king swept past them both, and Muntadhir rocked back on his heels. He stared down at the bloody piece of fabric, and Jamshid's stomach flipped as he recognized it as the cap Alizayd had been wearing earlier.

Jamshid cleared his throat, his mouth dry. "Is he . . ."

"We don't know." Muntadhir looked like he was going to throw up. "Nahri's patients were hysterical. It sounds like the Afshin took them hostage, but . . . there's so much blood, Jamshid. If something happens to him—"

Jamshid gripped Muntadhir's wrist. "Nahri is a Nahid. She could have healed him with a single touch."

"This is all my fault," Muntadhir whispered. "I shouldn't have said those things at Khanzada's. I made him angry and now he has my little brother." He glanced up, his eyes bloodshot with drink and glimmering with tears. "Do you know how Darayavahoush's sister died, Jamshid?"

Jamshid did, and he had nothing to counter Muntadhir's fear. Because God forgive him, but Ghassan was right. Muntadhir had been a fool to speak so crudely of Nahri in front of Darayavahoush. He'd been cruel. His words had angered even Jamshid, but he at least would have settled for unbraiding Muntadhir later when they were alone.

Darayavahoush . . . the Afshin was not like them. He was from a different time, a different place. He was charming and funny and Jamshid genuinely liked him, but even as he smiled, Dara wore death like a cloak. Muntadhir in his royal arrogance had made an awful mistake.

Now they were all going to pay for it.

But Jamshid didn't say that. "Darayavahoush isn't a fool, Munta-dhir. And he knows me." For the Afshin's faults, he still struck Jam-shid as an honorable man. He'd be reluctant to harm another Daeva, particularly the son of the man who had hosted him. "I'll be at your side tonight, every moment of it, and I'll try to talk him down."

Muntadhir was trembling but nodded. "All right."

Jamshid resisted the urge to hug him. Muntadhir had to look strong tonight—especially in front of the Citadel men who would blame him if something happened to their favored prince.

So instead Jamshid bowed, deeper than he had with Ghassan. "Come, my emir. Let us be sure to get on the first boat that goes out."

AND JAMSHID HAD KEPT HIS PROMISE. HE HADN'T LEFT Muntadhir's side.

But he'd been very wrong about Dara's unwillingness to hurt him.

Ali

This was a scene I couldn't quite fit in *The Kingdom of Copper*, so I decided to pull it out and make it a slightly satirical look at some of the old folktales. It takes place about a year or two after *The City of Brass*. Spoilers for the first book.

It is said by the djinn in the deserts of Am Gezira that there is no sight lovelier than the glisten of water. Fire may burn in their blood, but it is water that gives life, water that is precious and rare in the ruins of the forgotten human kingdoms in which they make their homes. A man might find all his crimes forgiven should he discover a new well, a woman be made chief for inventing a new water catchment.

Therefore, one might imagine the sight of the mighty Sea of Reeds would bring a djinn to tears. Especially on a night such as this, when a thick cluster of stars stretched across the velvet sky like a jeweled garter, mirrored in shimmering movement in the expanse of ebony water below. There was not the barest breath of wind, and it was silent, a silence so deep it felt sacred, the air aromatic with salt rather than incense. A bright moon shone silver as a new coin, its light dappling the sea below. This far from the beach, there were no waves; instead, the sea slightly swelled, rising and falling like a breathing beast.

Such a comparison did not put Alizayd al Qahtani at rest.

He dipped his oar into the water, pressing his small boat farther. *A damn fool quest, Ali*, his friend Lubayd had declared. *You and your stupid heroics are going to get you snapped up by a shark.*

Ali frowned. Did sharks eat djinn? That suddenly seemed a question he should have asked before embarking alone upon such a dangerous mission. But the stolen girl's family had been desperate, her parents weeping, and when it came to helping people, well . . . Ali had never been one for thinking things through.

Just ahead, the water took on a strangely luminous appearance, as if it were shallower, revealing a golden sandbar far below. Ali rowed until he was over the patch and then put the oars aside, picking up the boat's anchor. He threw it in the water, letting the anchor's rope out as he gazed across the still sea. No land was visible, but Ali knew what lay beyond far to the northwest.

Egypt.

I wonder what it's like there. The foolish thought came to him that it might be nice to visit Nahri's old home, to wander after her in Cairo's streets, touring the grand mosques and trying the sticky fried sweets she'd laughingly described.

The rope jerked in his hands as the anchor hit the seabed and yanked Ali from his thoughts. What was the point of such fantasies when he'd never leave Am Gezira, and Nahri would never leave Daevabad, especially not now? Word had come last month that Emir Muntadhir and the Banu Nahida had married in a spectacular ceremony. It was supposed to be a new dawn for the djinn world, its warring royal families finally united in a political alliance Ali himself had subtly encouraged. An alliance he had betrayed a friend to support.

Enough. Pushing aside thoughts of Daevabad, Ali slipped out of his robe. Underneath he wore a sleeveless tunic and a waist-wrap. His zulfiqar tied to his back, he checked the bindings holding the khanjar at his waist and another small knife at his ankle. Weapons secure, he moved on to the small clay pot he'd been given with the boat. He unscrewed the top, scrunching his nose at the smell of bitumen and some acrid herb: a magical concoction the Sabaen djinn swore would make the sea path visible to him. Ali smeared it across his lids and under his eyes before stepping to the edge of the boat.

He dove. The water embraced him, warmer than he would

have expected, and welcoming, rushing to pull him deeper into its depths. Ali swam fast, much faster than any djinn—beings of smoke-less flame who typically fled water deeper than one's knees—should have been able to. A blessing and curse from the marid's possession on the lake.

The water abruptly vanished, and Ali tumbled onto perfectly dry sand. Before him stretched a narrow path, the water pulled back and suspended above the seabed as though contained by invis-ible glass. Beyond, he could see the black shadows of flitting fish against the moonlit water. An enormous stingray passed overhead, its blue-spotted body rustling like the hem of a woman's gown, and Ali gawked at the incredible sight.

It was beautiful. Magical. Which meant it was almost certainly deadly. The anchor rested beside him, tethering his boat. The sandy path extended until it hit a sheer rock wall covered in bright coral and undulating sea plants. At the base of the cliffs, and nearly hid-den by a burst of frilly red seaweed, a pair of doors gleamed white as bone.

Ali headed for them, sand crunching beneath his bare feet. Small wonder the doors gleamed in such a manner; they looked to have been carved from a single massive piece of mother-of-pearl. Adding to the effect, a jagged line separated the two like the mouth of a clam.

Taking a deep breath, Ali drew his zulfiqar and carefully nudged open the doors. They drew back with a whisper, revealing a tight corridor. He stepped inside.

They snapped shut behind him.

Ali jumped, his fingers tightening on his weapons, but nothing else happened. His heart was racing; the dark was so thick it was op-pressive.

Swallowing his dread, he urged his zulfiqar to brighten. The blade obeyed, bursting into flames. Fiery tendrils danced down its copper length, throwing light upon the corridor's sandstone walls and grimy cobbled floor.

And upon the gleaming steel swords of several dozen warriors.

Ali instantly dropped into a fighting stance. But he needn't have—the warriors didn't move a muscle. They were *statues*, he realized, gazing in shock at their placid faces. Some appeared to be crafted from stone, others from bits of shell and coral. The eerie thing was that no matter what material they were made of, they all held identical steel swords. They were otherwise a remarkably diverse lot: their clothes a mix of Rumi togas, Nabatean wraps, Sabaen tunics, Egyptian pleated skirts, and garments Ali couldn't recognize. Statues that might have been taken from a dozen different civilizations during the thousands of years humans had called this land home.

He stepped closer, examining a statue wearing a carved thobe. A tooth-cleaning stick was tucked into its fraying belt, the minuscule stone details a perfect replica.

Almost too perfect. Ali shivered, studying the lines in the statue's face and what might have been a pox scar. Trepidation gripped him, his imagination racing.

Get the girl, he told himself. *And get out.*

He kept walking, his zulfiqar in one hand and his khanjar in the other, the only sounds the snapping of flames and his quickened breath. The zulfiqar's firelight flickered on the close walls, illuminating an intricately carved facade of mysterious figures and bizarre animals. What appeared to be an alphabet was entirely indecipherable, a scrawl of lines and perfectly round circles.

These look human-made. Ali pressed his zulfiqar closer. A lot of the cliffs and sandstone tombs back in Bir Nabat were covered in similar carvings: long-dead kings and hunters caught in action, forgotten deities and prayers in lost tongues. But these drawings went in a grislier direction: giant sea snakes devouring fleeing humans and lion-headed bulls roaring among a pile of severed limbs.

The end of the corridor beckoned, shining in the distance: another set of pearly gates. Unable to fight the feeling this was all a trap, Ali stepped through.

The moment he crossed the threshold, the chamber lit up, dozens of suspended glass lanterns swirling to life and illuminating an enormous cavern—easily twice the size of his father's throne room.

And *entirely* filled with treasure.

Mountains of gold coins, glass beads, and cowrie shells surrounded chests overflowing with jewels in every hue—emeralds and rubies and sapphires larger than his fist. Strands of pearls long enough to bind a man, animals of carved ebon wood and ivory, brass bowls of frankincense, ambergris, and musk. Folded brocades of silk and precious damask cloth. Even the walls were plated in gold, inlaid with jade and coral in sweeping floral designs. None of it was organized—on the contrary, shattered vases littered the ground and necklaces worth a kingdom were strewn across broken furniture. Several marble columns had collapsed, and the sheared stone face of a bearded man lay covered in dust. It looked as though some wrathful spirit had wreaked vengeance upon whatever human civilization had once called this place home, dragged it into the sea, and filled it with the plundered treasure of its murdered people.

Which frankly . . . seemed a possibility considering the magical world. Ali couldn't take his eyes off the fortune surrounding him. A single handful would change the lives of the villagers who had bravely sheltered him; several handfuls might buy more. Safety. Security. Soldiers. A way to challenge the grim future his father had handed him.

A way to make it easier for him to decide to simply execute you. Ali continued on without touching any of the precious items.

Ahead an orchard of jeweled trees burst from the marble floor, trunks of brown topaz braided with brass that stretched to the ceiling. Their branches were heavy with fruit and flowers in glass and precious stone. Golden birds perched between emerald leaves, frozen in the act of tending to quartz eggs, coral worms in their sculpted beaks. At the base of each tree was a silver plinth. Ali stepped closer and then stilled. Upon each plinth—of which there were dozens—was a shrouded form.

A body. Some of the shrouds had started to rot, revealing rusted bangles hanging from skeletal wrists and tarnished ornaments twisted around decaying black braids. And there on a plinth toward the back was a single shroud-less girl, the smoky shimmer of her brown skin a dead giveaway she was djinn.

Ali dashed to her side, sighing in relief when he saw her chest still rising and falling. She certainly looked like she could be the daughter of the wealthy Geziri governor who begged his assistance. A heavy gold collar ringed her neck, floral medallions of blue lapis, amber rock crystal, and bright rubies laying against the hollow of her throat. She wore an embroidered purple robe patterned in ikat, but it was unfastened and had fallen back to reveal the rose silk gown clinging to her body. Her lips were colored with ocher and a stylized bird—its wings outstretched—was painted over her delicate brows. Her long black hair was uncovered, the top portions arranged in elaborate braids around gold discs that hung from her ears.

"Abla?" Ali called softly. "Is that you?"

There was no response. But Ali would swear her mouth moved slightly, her lips seeming to purse.

"Abla?" He reached out to shake her shoulder. "Are you—"

A pair of lovely gray eyes fluttered open, her long lashes batting. She stretched her arms languidly above her head, the robe falling farther back, and smiled. "You're supposed to kiss me."

Ali could not have been more baffled if the girl had jumped from the plinth and turned into one of the stone soldiers from the corridor. "I'm supposed to do what?"

She pushed up into a sitting position, her tresses falling in midnight waves. "Kiss me," she teased. "Haven't you ever heard a story?"

Heat filled his cheeks. "I don't . . . I mean, there are rules forbidding that sort of thing."

She tilted her head, seeming to study him. "Where are you *from*? If I didn't know better, I'd say your accent sounds Daevabadi, but that's . . ." Her eyes went wide. "Oh my God, you're *him*, aren't you? You're the—!"

"Shhh." He held a finger to his mouth. "Let's get acquainted when we're not surrounded by decaying bodies. Where is the creature that took you?"

Abla shivered. "I don't know. It grabbed me when I was collecting shells and returns once a day—in the morning, I think. Makes me drink some awful tea that keeps me asleep."

"In the morning?" Ali repeated, his heart sinking as he remembered the line of burning dawn he'd seen in the sky just before diving. When she nodded, he took her hand. "Let's go. We don't have much time."

She glanced behind him. "Where are the rest of your men?"

"It's just me."

"Just you?" A trace of uncertainty crossed her face. "Forgive me . . . how soon did you say dawn is?"

The chamber gave a violent tremor. "Soon," a voice boomed, a sound like the grating of rocks. "Quite soon."

Ali spun around as a wash of foul heat swept over him. They had been caught.

The creature that had sneaked up on them looked far too large to have done so. Twice the height of an elephant, it had the body and horns of a bull, the tortured, purpling face of a woman, the wings of a bat, and a striped serpent's tail that vanished into the depths of the jeweled orchard. Instead of hooves, its front feet ended in taloned hands, and as it reared on its powerful hind legs, it raised an enormous trident.

Ali gaped. "*That's* the thing that took you?" The smell of iron blood, of decay and dust and utter foreignness gagged him again. Whatever the beast was, it seemed as alien to the sea as the pair of fire-blooded djinn standing before it. An earth demon, he realized, stunned. Such creatures were said to be exceedingly rare, beings that belonged to the age of legends.

The creature grinned; stained ivory tusks jutted from its crimson mouth.

"The heroes always come," it sneered. "Chasing their beauties to their deaths." It regarded him with glittering eyes. "A fine addition to my stone warriors, a slave of Bilqis I will make."

Abla rolled her eyes. "I keep trying to tell it that we don't belong to Bilqis." She turned to the creature. "The djinn are free! Suleiman has been dead for thousands of years!"

The creature snarled. "Lies. The djinn always lie. Who has set the marid, the children of the accursed Tiamat, to flight if not Suleiman?"

Ali blinked, thoroughly confused, but Abla waved him off. "It's been rambling about marid and Tiamat for days. Not that it matters." She put a hand on her hip, raising her chin defiantly. "You've not challenged just any warrior, beast . . . this is the Afshin-slayer, Alizayd al Qahtani."

The creature tossed the trident from hand to hand. "I know of no Afshin, and I do not fear its slayer. I am Shardunazatu, He Who Humbles." It lurched closer, looming over them. "Ten thousand years I ruled this land, shaking human cities into dust and bringing up mountains with a clap of my hands until the wicked Tiamat imprisoned me! But she shall despair when she meets my army of stone warriors, yes!" Its giant eyes pinned him, looking like churning pits of mud. "And you shall lead them!"

From the corridor came the distinct sound of marching, stone sliding against stone. The earth demon's army . . . surely it didn't mean—

Shardunazatu charged forward.

Shoving Abla out of the way, Ali met the first thrust of the demon's trident with his zulfiqar, the metals clashing in a spray of sparks. The creature reared back, and Ali lunged forward, intending to plunge the zulfiqar into a patch of exposed belly.

It was like he'd attacked a block of iron. His zulfiqar stuck hard, the shock reverberating through his arms. He kept his wits—and grip—and let loose his magic, the flames racing across the demon's chest.

Shardunazatu laughed and then it opened its horrible mouth wide. A torrent of mud gushed out, extinguishing the zulfiqar's flames as easily as Ali might have stomped out a candle. The smell of rot filled the air, foul and thick.

It grinned, towering over him. "Not all earthen creatures are as weak as humans, little djinn. And there's not much magic for a fire-blood to pull from under the sea."

Its tail moved in the blink of an eye. No longer a serpent's tail, rather something like living unbaked clay. It smashed into Ali's ankles, sweeping him off his feet as a taloned hand ripped the zulfiqar from his grip.

Ali tried to scramble back, but its tail had wrapped his legs, bubbling mud rippling across his body, heavy and smothering. It pinned him completely, encasing his arms and creeping up his neck. His fingers went numb and then horribly still, the sensation slithering down his wrists.

Shardunazatu was turning him into stone.

He could hear Abla screaming his name. Gagging on the awful smell and desperate to wrestle free, Ali tried to call upon his magic, but he'd no sooner sparked a flame than another gush of mud extinguished it. A wave of tar-like bile rolled over his face, and he choked, the foul substance pushing through his clamped lips.

He called for his fire again, but it did nothing more than bake the mud covering his limbs.

There's not much magic for a fire-blood to pull from under the sea.

Acting on instinct, Ali reached once again for magic. But he didn't try to conjure a flame or a smothering cloud of smoke. Instead he pulled on the distantly cold presence that had been swimming silently in his mind since the marid took him. The part of Ali that delighted when he dove into the sea, that sent his senses tingling when he walked past a hidden spring.

Everything went very quiet. And then a violent shiver swept Ali's body, icy water pouring from his skin. In seconds, the stone had dissolved, gray mud dripping from his limbs. His eyes snapped open, an almost predatory focus narrowing his gaze.

Shardunazatu appeared before him, an offensive thing of living dirt and molten rock that had no place in Ali's sea. And yet that wasn't all the earth demon contained. There was moisture in Shardunazatu: iron blood in its veins, liquid lubricating its joints, the delicate gurgle of humors and fluid in its spine and brain. The wet muscles that moved its mouth into a befuddled frown.

Ali seized its tail, yanking at the liquid with his mind's eye. Silver blood burst from the demon's skin, flooding past his fingers. Shardunazatu screeched and whipped his tail, throwing Ali across the room.

He landed hard, cracking the wall behind him and causing a mountain of coins to collapse. But Ali barely felt the impact. He rose lightly to his feet with an unnatural grace, the world still gray. Magic, more powerful than anything he'd known, pulsed in his veins, an ancient anger stealing over him. How dare this earthen abomination challenge him in his own waters? His zulfiqar flew to his hand on a wave, and Ali rushed forward.

Shardunazatu struck with the trident. But Ali was stronger now, the sea outside the cave beating in his head, in his blood. Catching the trident between the forks of his zulfiqar, he twisted hard, wrenching the weapon from the demon's hands and sending it skittering across the floor. He ducked a swipe of Shardunazatu's talons that would have left him in gory ribbons and then dashed his zulfiqar across its giant muddy eyes. The creature shrieked, grabbing its face.

"Alizayd!"

At the sound of his name, the marid presence vanished from his mind. Ali stumbled. Abla darted forward, grabbing his wrist and pulling him back.

Shardunazatu was screeching, a bellow like an earthquake. "A trick!" it wailed, clutching its ruined eyes. "Marid liar, I'll send you back to Tiamat in bloody waves!"

Ali was barely aware of the nonsensical charge, too busy dodging the creature's tail as it lashed the floor. He and Abla were almost at the pearly doors. But as they ran, he could not help but give the chamber one last admiring look. Whatever humans had designed this place had done an incredible job. It really did look like a thing from a story, a tale to be told in crowded coffeehouses and women's courtyards. A long-vanished world. A palace of gold, a temple of jewels.

A city of brass.

The doors burst open. Shardunazatu's stone army had arrived.

Had they not been the enslaved and transfigured bodies of long-dead warriors eager to murder him, Ali might have marveled at the sight of the statues rushing to surround them, moving as smoothly as living men, their massive broadswords glinting in the candlelight. But right now even Ali's curiosity had limits.

"Run!" he shouted.

A warrior dressed in the garb of a Rumi soldier lurched at him, and Ali shoved the trident in its chest. The statue shivered and burst apart, shattering into shell fragments. But in the time it took Ali to strike, three more had encircled him. Ali ducked, letting two of the statues smash into each other. He buried the trident in the knees of the third, diving out of the way and rolling to his feet.

Shardunazatu was still howling, searching blindly for the djinn. More stone warriors were emerging from the orchard. Then with a single motion, the slain girls abruptly sat up, the shrouds falling away from their exposed skulls. The statues he'd destroyed were already piecing themselves back together, mud wrapping the stone fragments like living mortar.

Ali's regret vanished. The sea could have this place. He caught up with Abla, grabbing her hand as they entered the corridor, the statues hot on their heels.

But the pearl doors that had clamped shut behind him were still closed. Ali tried to smash through, but neither his shoulder nor his zulfiqar nor the trident had any success. Beyond the doors, he could sense the weight of the sea over the enchanted path, aching to burst free.

The warriors were but moments away. Ali stepped back, edging himself and Abla into a small niche in the wall.

He met her frightened eyes. "When I tell you, take a deep breath and hold it for as long as you can." He secured the trident to his back, feeling oddly fond of it, and then pulled Abla close, clutching her tight enough to provoke a gasp.

Ali closed his eyes, the weight of the ocean dragging on his shoulders, part of his heart longing for its embrace. And then a word—in a language he did not speak—slipped his mouth.

"*Come.*"

The seabed shook.

Water crashed through the pearly doors, smashing them aside as though they were paper. As if the ocean were a thing alive, a creature long annoyed by this dry human refuge, eager to stamp out the alien upstart and take back its home.

In seconds, the water was at his neck. "Abla, hold your breath!" Ali took his own deep breath as the water closed over his head, but he'd learned long ago when an assassin threw him down a desolate desert well that he needn't be concerned with such things.

Ali couldn't drown.

Still holding Abla, he waited until the force of the water had lessened and then slipped out, swimming hard.

They broke through the surface a minute later. Abla thrashed in his arms, spluttering and gasping for air. She was a wreck: Shardunazatu's foul-smelling blood sticking to her messy braids, her makeup running down her face in streaks and one earring missing. Gashes covered her arms, her fine robe long gone.

"Are you all right?" he breathed.

Abla let out a wail. "No! We were almost killed by a mob of statues!"

Ali swam for his boat and helped her inside. "The ruins were fascinating, though, no? I've never seen a place like that. I didn't even think creatures like Shardunazatu still existed. Imagine the kinds of things he has seen."

Abla gave him a horrified look. "You sound ready to go back and have a conversation with the damned thing."

Ali pulled himself into the boat. He could not help but feel strangely giddy, a side effect from his latest brush with death that he suspected was not a healthy reaction.

He dipped his oars into the water. "I don't know . . . might be interesting to know what else lives below the surface."

ABLA'S PEOPLE FEASTED ALI AND HIS COMPANIONS FROM Bir Nabat through the day and into the night, with a riot of enchanted fireworks and wild drumming that Ali suspected would keep at least three generations of the local humans from ever visiting the area again. The djinn town of Saba was one of the largest in Am Gezira, built upon the ruins of an even more ancient human one. The first port of call for traders coming from Ta Ntry, Saba was also wealthy, a thing on full display in the sumptuous garments and jeweled ornaments of its people, as well as the fine food they'd laid out.

Ali had dug into the food without reservation—he hadn't seen a feast like this in years and neither he nor his companions had shown much prudence in gorging, especially since not a moment seemed to pass that one of the Sabaens wasn't pressing some new delicacy upon him. He sat heavily on plump cushions. An unreasonably expensive robe lay lightly upon his shoulders, one of several robes of honor he'd been given. This one was linen and silk, painted in bright blue and orange diamonds.

He spotted Abla's father—the town's governor—approaching. His face was wet with tears; the man had yet to stop weeping since Ali had brought back his daughter. Ali attempted to rise, fighting the anchor of honey cakes, fenugreek-flavored stew, roasted lamb, and grilled fish sitting in his stomach.

Abla's father waved him down. "Sit, my son, sit!" the governor cried. Fresh tears glimmered in his eyes. "I should be your chair for the prize that you have returned me, oh Prince of Daevabad!"

Passed out in the cushion next to Ali, Lubayd let out a smoky snore. His closest friend in Am Gezira, Lubayd had seemed determined to eat himself to death while they were in the south. On Ali's right sat Aqisa, Bir Nabat's fiercest fighter, very much awake and alert. She'd spent most of their trip shooting suspicious glares at everyone, her hand curling around her khanjar whenever someone looked too long upon them.

The governor touched his heart and knelt before him. "As you have returned my treasure to me, Prince Alizayd, I wish to grant you a similar one."

Ali swayed, nearly dropping his cup. "Mmm," he managed, trying to keep from toppling over. He squinted in an effort to keep his eyes open. The governor had tripled . . . no, of course, he hadn't. That was ridiculous. He'd been joined instead by Abla in a bright crimson and gold gown and a dour-looking man wearing an unbound ghutra in the manner of a cleric.

The governor continued. "My Abla has told me of your bravery.

She confesses her love for you, a thing I bless." He took Ali's hands. "I wish for you to marry her. I give you my daughter and my lands, Alizayd al Qahtani. Take this port, take its wealth and its prestige and its power, as only the smallest recompense for your deeds."

Ali blinked, brought rather violently back to the present. The governor's eyes were bright with happy tears, Abla was giving him a hungry smile, and the cleric looked rather weary of the whole experience.

"W-wait," Ali stammered. "What's happening?"

"Marry my daughter, Alizayd al Qahtani," the older man urged, still clutching his hands. "Saba is a far better place for you. You can build support here. We have forts dating back to the days of Bilqis, and it is an ideal location to defend. If need be, one can be across the Sea of Reeds and safely in Ta Ntry in a matter of days."

Ali straightened up, implications of treason banishing his exhaustion. "I can't do that, Governor. It's a lovely offer," he quickly added, seeing Abla's expression crumple. "But I can't accept it."

The other man drew up, offense in his face. "Is there something wrong with my Abla? With my home?"

"No, of course not!" Ali's mind spun. "I—"

"—have a woman waiting back in Bir Nabat." It was Lubayd, his friend awake and calm in the face of Ali's mounting panic. He patted Ali on the back. "The sheikh here wants to wait until his first quarter century, make sure everything is proper."

"Oh . . . but that is fairly soon, no?" the governor persisted. "Send for her. A man in your position should have more than one wife anyway."

Lubayd saved him again. "Aye, you know how women can be . . ." He grinned, cutting his eyes at Aqisa as she threw him an annoyed look. "His bride is the jealous type. Won't agree to share him with anyone."

The governor met Ali's gaze. "Is this true?"

God forgive me. "Yes," Ali lied, hating himself for doing so but not wishing to insult the man further. He glanced at Abla. "I'm sorry, my lady. I am deeply honored to be asked. But I know you'll find someone even more worthy of you than I."

The governor appeared despondent. "I must give you *something*. You saved my daughter's life."

Ali paused. "Now that you mention it . . . could I take a look at your gardens?"

ALI STEPPED OVER THE NARROW CANAL, THEN KNELT TO examine the way its stone corners joined together. Water rushed past, clean and cool, heading for Saba's apricot orchard. He straightened up, making a notation on the scroll he was carrying, and took a deep breath of the night air, savoring the tang of rich earth and vegetation. His feet sank into the mud as he headed toward the muskmelon fields, the ragged hem of his waist cloth trailing in the dirt.

"What happened to your fancy robe?" Lubayd asked, pulling an apricot from one of the trees.

"I packed it away," Ali replied absentmindedly. "We will get more for it up north if it's clean."

"You're going to *sell* it?"

"I have no need for such a garment, and Bir Nabat could use the money. Our crops are doing better, but there won't be enough excess to sell for at least another year." Ali knelt again, admiring the muskmelons. The vines were thick and strong, the fruit heavy. How did they grow them like this?

Lubayd exhaled. "Ali, we've known each other some time now. We are friends, yes?"

"Of course. I owe you my life."

"Then as your friend . . . can I ask you something?"

Ali nodded, pressing his palms against the soil. "Certainly."

"What the fuck is wrong with you?"

He glanced back in surprise. "*What?*"

Lubayd threw up his hands. "Why are you crawling around in the dirt when you could be having that lovely girl take that fancy robe off you?"

Ali flushed. Abla had been rather beautiful, and the image Lubayd conjured was not helpful in forgetting that fact. "Don't be disrespectful," he rebuked. "Besides, she's not my type."

"What? Not Daeva?"

Ali glared at him. "Don't start."

Lubayd rolled his eyes. "Oh, everyone else is allowed to say it, but not me?"

"You should know better."

"Yes, I know you were more unbearable than usual when news came of your brother's wedding, and you write her love letters every week."

The interest in my country, in improving your Arabic . . . I take it that was all a pretense? Nahri's words in the flooded tunnels beneath the palace returned to him. Ali could still remember how stiff her voice had been, a forced aloofness that did nothing to hide the hurt in her dark eyes.

No, it hadn't been a pretense. Rather, Ali hadn't realized his time with Nahri had been a light—and one he hadn't deserved—until it was too late. Her memory haunted him still.

"They're not . . . *love* letters," he stammered out. "I mean—I see things here that I think are interesting. That Nahri would think were interesting. Useful. It's more academic than anything."

"Sure it is," Lubayd said, clearly not believing a word. "Marry this Abla, my friend. Please. You need to move on."

Caught out, Ali flustered for a different response. "Did you not hear what else the governor offered, Lubayd? A place to build support? The marriage alone would look like I was attempting to build political alliances in Am Gezira."

Lubayd gave him a knowing look. "Maybe you *should* be building political alliances here. Better than waiting to get assassinated."

Ali rose to his feet. "I can't do that to my family." He wiped his hands on his waist cloth. "I'm going to ask the governor if we can have some of these seeds."

"I'm not sure that was the seed he was interested in."

"I will stab you with Shardunazatu's trident."

Lubayd snorted. "You would never. And you better not bring that cursed thing back to Bir Nabat. Only you'd be foolish enough to carry off a stolen weapon from a sea demon."

"Earth demon," Ali corrected. But talking about his fight with Shardunazatu brought back another part of it. "Lubayd, have you ever heard of Tiamat?"

"Like Bet il Tiamat? Yes, believe it or not, I know the name of the giant ocean to our south."

Ali shook his head. "Not the ocean. Just Tiamat. Shardunazatu spoke of them as old foes." He paused, trying to scrounge through his memories. "I'd swear I heard the name before, some primeval divinity of the humans or something . . . but the earth demon was saying other things. Talking about war, about someone having sent the marid fleeing . . ."

"Doesn't sound like a fight to get caught up in." Lubayd shrugged. "Who knows? Maybe being locked up in some underwater chamber for millennia with a bunch of statues drove it mad."

A surge of cool water rushed beneath Ali's feet, swiftly rising to his ankles. Someone must have shifted one of the stone cairns in the canal farther upstream. The water glistened in the moonlight, sweeping away a handful of dead leaves with a rustling noise that sounded too close to the marid whispers Ali still heard in his nightmares.

He stepped back onto the dry path. "You're probably right. Come on, let's go back to the feast and get out of here before one of us ends up married."

The Scout

This scene was originally an alternative prologue for *The Kingdom of Copper*. Spoilers for the first two books.

S o, what did you do?"

Cao Pran bristled at the question, and his horse danced nervously on the snowy path in response. He shot a look at the Geziri soldier riding alongside him. "Who says I did anything?"

Jahal snorted. "Because soldiers don't get tossed out of the Citadel and sent to scout the northern border of Daevastana unless they did something wrong." His gray eyes twinkled with amusement . . . and not a little of his characteristic smugness. Because Jahal was entirely swathed in furs, his eyes were all that could be seen of him. Ice crusted on the spiky black fur of his cloak, made from some former beast, some animal of earth and crimson blood.

The sight turned Pran's stomach. Though Jahal looked warm, Pran could not yet bear to cover himself in furs like the humans in this region did. It seemed wrong, unclean.

In the meantime, he was quite cold.

Jahal pressed again. "I'm your superior officer, you know," he reminded Pran for what felt like the hundredth time. "I could order you to tell me." He let the threat linger, his eyes still sparkling as if they were joking, as if Pran also found it amusing, the constant intimidations that his companion could gut him without charge or simply abandon him in this wild land. "So tell me. Did you try to catch a bribe from some minister's cousin? Sleep with the wrong woman? The wrong man?"

Just tell him. It's easier. Pran exhaled, his breath coming out in a smoky burst that clouded in the frigid air. "I've got a bit of a problem when it comes to wine and punctuality," he confessed. "Missed my watch a time too many."

"You missed your watch?" Jahal repeated in disbelief. "That hardly seems worth freezing to death on the edge of the world." He chuckled. "Too bad you're Tukharistani. If you were Geziri, you would have gotten by with a warning."

You think I don't know that? But Pran bit back the retort, knowing Jahal would not appreciate it. They'd been traveling together for over month. It was a miserable mission, one assigned every century or so to check upon a part of the world rarely given thought back in distant Daevabad. Really, the only reason they were out here at all was to collect as much tribute as possible from the savage Daeva fire worshippers who called this place home.

He pulled his cloak closer, shooting a pained grimace at his desolate surroundings. Snow swirled through the dark forest, falling silently upon the icy blanket already smothering the valley floor. Past the bare trees, a river ran fierce under a delicate crust of ice, and in the distance, rocky, snow-covered peaks tore at the sky. It was a world devoid of color—just black, gray, and white.

And a touch of orange as he conjured a pair of flames to warm his hands. *Our people were not meant for such a place.* Pran felt that in every drop of his fiery blood, an instinctual urge to retreat. Not to the brass city of the Nahids—no, he was done with Daevabad—but to something older, to the scalding sands his ancestors before Suleiman would have called home.

A wolf howled, pulling Pran from his reverie. He shuddered as a cold gust blew through the scarf covering his face. "Why in the Creator's name would anyone choose to live out here?"

"Who knows? The Daevas are all crazy." Jahal pulled a clay pipe from his bag and began packing it with hashish.

Pran nodded at the pipe. "I take it that's what got you sent here?" His "superior" had spent more than half their nights in a hashish-induced fog.

"This?" Jahal gestured to the pipe. "No. I slept with the wrong woman. Several, actually." The pipe smoldered in his hand, the hashish catching light. "I suspect one of them must have finally complained."

Pran went a little still. There was something unnerving about the way Jahal had phrased that last part, an implication he didn't like but didn't feel comfortable questioning.

So he changed the subject. "How long have you been out here?"

"Couple decades." Jahal puffed out, sparks fluttering upon the snowy ground. "Though never this far north. Don't think anyone's been this far north in a hundred years. The palace must be getting desperate for new people to tax."

"I guess." Politics had never been Pran's thing. He was from a military family, meant for the Royal Guard like his father and grandfather before him, but he'd been content to serve as a foot soldier, except when he'd been more content to sleep off a hard night. "I mean . . . I suppose things *have* been bad in Daevabad. We got our rations reduced just before I left, and our salaries cut before that." He fingered the worn hem on his sleeve. "Can't remember the last time we got new uniforms."

"The fire worshippers are probably stealing from the Treasury. They've been extra-mutinous since their Scourge got turned into a pile of ash. Though I bet that was a battle to witness." Jahal whistled. "Could you imagine? The Scourge of Qui-zi against the crocodile prince?"

Pran stared at his reins. "Not many of those witnesses survived," he said softly. "I had a friend on that boat, and the Afshin put a sword through his throat."

"Sorry to hear that." There was little sympathy behind the words, more a phrase thrown out so that Jahal could continue. "You would have trained with him, though, right? With Alizayd al Qahtani?"

Pran actually laughed. "No. Royal zulfiqaris and wine-swilling

Tukharistani infantrymen don't typically train together at the Citadel." He paused, recalling his memories of the intense young prince. "Used to watch him spar, though. Everyone did; he was terrifying with that blade. He's in Am Gezira now, right? Leading a garrison?"

Jahal's voice sounded a little tight. "Something like that."

Pran shifted in his saddle, trying to relieve his cramping muscles. "Shouldn't we be in Sugdam by now?" Sugdam was their next stop, a small Daeva village at the other end of the valley.

"Knowing our luck, the fire worshippers heard we were coming and sabotaged the marker stones."

"We could stop," Pran suggested. "Make camp for the night."

"Our tent's not going to offer much protection against this weather, and the snow's only getting worse. Let's keep going." Jahal nodded forward. "That might be smoke up ahead."

Pran saw nothing of the sort, but prayed Jahal was correct. He hated spending the night with Daevas—their demon-black eyes filled with resentment toward the foreign soldiers who claimed lodging and food in the evening and a hefty tax payment the next morning—but right now he'd take a fuming fire worshipper over the snow.

They stayed silent as they spurred their horses faster. Darkness fell swiftly around them. A wolf howled again, and from deep in the black forest, Pran heard the crash of deadwood, perhaps an old tree finally collapsing under the weight of the snow. A shadow swooped through the woods ahead, and he jumped. *An owl*, he decided, his heart beating faster.

Thankfully they hadn't been riding long when he caught glimpses of the smoke Jahal mentioned and then something far more promising: a stone cottage nestled in a snowy glen.

The cottage was small but well built, with firelight flickering from behind the thick curtains covering its narrow windows. A felt tent had been constructed to its rear—Pran could smell the musk of grain and horses. The remnants of a garden—nothing but blackened roots and empty trellises in this bitter winter—clung to one stone wall.

Pran slid off his horse, immediately colder once he parted from the animal's warmth. He retrieved one of his bags, checking to make sure his sword hadn't frozen in its sheath before leading his horse to the tent. Jahal followed, freeing his zulfiqar.

Pran frowned. "Are you expecting trouble?"

"You never know with Daevas."

But the tent was empty. A soft orange gloom filled the air, a reflection of the snow-bright night sky outside. On the opposite side, a rough wooden trough waited, filled with grain—enough for at least a half-dozen horses. Some sort of storage rack, a metal Pran couldn't identify, sprouted from the frozen ground like the skeleton of a tree. A single pair of reins hung from one limb, the others empty.

Pran's unease grew. "Riders are due back," he realized, glancing again at the grain. He spotted a similar trough in the opposite corner. "Could be quite a few."

Jahal pulled free his saddle and dumped it unceremoniously on the ground. "Well, should they show up, they'll find themselves with company." He nodded at Pran's horse. "Hurry up. That cottage looks warm, and I'm starving."

Pran quickly unsaddled his horse. They stomped back to the cottage, the snow gathering in knee-high drifts.

Jahal pounded on the thick pine door. "Royal Guard!" he shouted in broken Divasti. "Open up!"

They waited a long moment, but there was no response. Jahal cursed and banged on the door again, this time with the hilt of his zulfiqar.

"I'm not going to be pleasant company if you make me break down this door!"

It opened a moment later. Pran tensed, but it was a young woman who greeted them, hastily veiled in a faded floral chador the color of ash. Her black eyes—God, he never got used to that total absence of color—swept their faces, darting to Jahal's zulfiqar and widening with alarm.

Even so, she stepped boldly into their path, blocking the doorway with her body as she held one edge of the chador across her face. "Can I help you?"

"We need a place to spend the night."

Pran didn't miss the way her dark eyes flickered to the snow-swirled forest before she responded. She was definitely expecting someone. "We've no room."

"There's that famous Daeva hospitality." Jahal raised his zulfiqar, letting a glitter of fire dance upon its copper surface. "I suggest you make room."

The woman instantly backed away. Pran averted his eyes, embarrassed by Jahal's behavior.

His mouth fell open as he crossed the threshold. Expecting the home of some magic-poor trader or fire-cult ascetic—for who else would live in this frozen wasteland?—Pran anticipated little more than a stone hearth and shabby rugs.

What greeted his eyes was anything but. The inside of the cottage was warm and well lit, filled with dozens of oil lamps in brass and gold, glass and sculpted stone. Candles burned in ornate chandeliers and cedar smoldered in silver braziers. An enormous fireplace tiled in the colors of a setting sun dominated the western wall, while another was given over to shelves packed with books crammed into every available nook. Opposite the books was a large worktable covered in twisted glassware and bizarre copper instruments. A wooden ladder led to a lofted bed, with more bed folds—at least a dozen—tucked neatly away beneath the structure. A fire altar smoldered in the eastern corner, filling the room with the aroma of incense.

In all, it looked like the lair of some sort of crazed scholar and her minions, or perhaps that of an alchemist who'd inhaled the fumes of one too many experiments. Neither possibility helped with his growing disquiet.

Jahal didn't seem as bothered. "No room?" he crowed. "You could host a score of men in comfort here." Not bothering to remove his muddy boots, he explored the cottage, running his hands over the instruments. "When are your people expected back?"

The girl dropped her gaze, her fingers trembling on the chador. "Soon," she insisted, pointing to a sheet spread on the floor. "I was just preparing dinner."

Pran glanced at the sheet. Upon its brocaded surface rested several covered silver tureens. Small bowls were scattered between them, filled with chopped greens and yogurt, browned onions and speckled radishes. A feast.

Jahal made a face. "I guess I'm hungry enough for Daeva food." He kicked off his boots, splattering the rug with mud. "You can serve us."

The girl opened her mouth to protest. "It is not meant for—"

Jahal laid a hand on the hilt of his zulfiqar, and she went pale, stepping back to let him pass.

Pran removed his boots more neatly, though he doubted one polite gesture would excuse Jahal's rudeness.

"Wine," Jahal demanded as he sat down. "Surely with a place like this, you have wine. Warm it first."

Pran shrugged out of his icy cloak, hanging it on a chair near the fire before joining his fellow scout. "Captain . . . ," he started. "She seems pretty scared. Maybe we should . . ."

Jahal cut him off with a wave. "Don't. I've lived amongst these people for decades now. You've got to keep them scared, make sure they know who's in control." He picked up a fine-worked silver chalice and held it up to the dancing firelight. "I mean, look at this thing. You'd have to be crazy to be able to afford something like this and still choose to live in this desolate, snowy hell."

"Maybe they're illusionists."

Jahal rapped his knuckles on the chalice. "Feels real to me." He dropped the chalice and then lifted the top off one of the silver tureens. A thick stew simmered inside: some sort of leafy green with lentils, smelling of cream and spices. "Doesn't look too bad for a bunch of vegetarians."

His stomach grumbling, Pran unwrapped a warm cloth bundle beside him to reveal discs of fresh-baked bread. Starving, he dug into the food without reservation.

The girl returned. She'd wrapped her chador across her face so she could hold a large platter, upon which a teapot and samovar of wine rested, with both hands. She set it down and went to step back.

Jahal grabbed her wrist. "Join us."

She tried to wrench free, but Jahal was stronger, pulling her down to sit beside him. "What? Worried your baba won't like you dining with strange men?" Still holding her wrist, he reached for her chador with the other hand and then yanked it off her head, laughing as she tried to snatch it back. "A pretty thing you are living out here in the wilderness."

The knot in Pran's stomach tightened. "Captain . . ."

"Oh, calm yourself. We're just having fun." Jahal let go of the girl but only after tossing her chador in the fireplace. He laughed as the flames licked at the cloth. "Consider it an act of worship." He nodded at his chalice. "Come now, Daeva, the wine won't fill itself."

Looking close to tears, the girl obeyed, filling their chalices with shaky hands. Pran didn't know what to say. Jahal had always been obnoxious to the Daevas they called upon, leering at their women and insulting their faith. But not like this.

Because we've never come upon a Daeva woman alone before, he realized, suddenly remembering what Jahal had implied got him kicked out of the Citadel. Unsettled, he reached for the wine, a familiar companion. He took a small sip, and then a longer one. God, it was good. Date wine . . . a little sweeter than he typically liked but warm, swirling in his belly like some sort of nectar.

Strange to find date wine this far north, he mused, wine being one of the things he did know well. Even back in Daevabad, it wasn't particularly popular, considered a bit old-fashioned. Although he was pretty sure he recalled a Daeva soldier once telling him they drank it in honor of the Afshins, for whom it had been a ceremonial drink. But Pran didn't remember for certain. That soldier had been thrown out of the Royal Guard shortly after the Scourge's death, along with the rest of the Daevas, the fire worshippers now banned from enlisting.

Jahal must have shared his opinion about the wine, finishing his cup even before Pran did. He held it out for more as the wind howled outside. "I don't think your people are coming back tonight, dear one."

The girl lifted her gaze. Though she was trembling, there was a bit of defiance in her expression. "You should hope not."

Jahal's eyes lit in outrage. "What did you say?"

Pran raised his hands, trying to defuse the tension between them. "The food was really quite delicious," he said quickly. "Thank you. But it's been a long journey, and I know we're both tired." He gestured to the bedrolls stacked neatly beneath the loft. "Captain, why don't you and I borrow a pair of those and get some sleep?"

"You can go ahead," Jahal said coldly. "The Daeva and I need to have a conversation about hospitality."

Pran bit his lip. "Captain, you heard her . . . her people are coming back. Maybe it's best we—"

"It's best you mind your own affairs and go to bed. Unless you've suddenly learned the way to Sugdam." He shot Pran a hard look. "It's a very inhospitable land, Pran. You wouldn't want to get lost."

The threat stopped him cold. The girl was staring at him, her eyes imploring. But he had no doubt Jahal meant his words.

She's just a fire worshipper, Pran told himself. By the Most High, people said the Daevas out here were so feral they slept with their own fathers.

He cleared his throat. "I understand."

"Then good night."

Pran stood up, his legs shaking as he turned around. He kept his back purposefully to them as he retrieved one of the bedrolls. He unfurled it as far away from the feast as he could, in a dark corner under the loft, crowded with supplies. He lay down, still facing away.

There was a clatter, the dish or the chalice being shoved aside. A muffled scream. "You think you're so much better than us," he heard Jahal hiss. "All of you do."

Pran curled into a ball, catching sight of a glimmer of metal as he covered his ears. He didn't want to hear this.

And then he drew up like a shot, the gleam of metal coming into better focus.

It was a massive silver bow.

He blinked rapidly, convinced he was seeing things. Half concealed in a quilted pad, the enormous bow was probably half Pran's height and with a heft both imposing and impossibly delicate; its silver surface was covered in fine brass filigree. It looked like a weapon from some fable, not a thing meant to be wielded by any modern man. An artifact, priceless and deadly.

That's what he told himself . . . before he noticed the quill of arrows beside it, their ends fletched with fresh feathers.

The door slammed open.

Pran scrambled up, his heart in his throat. Expecting to see some gigantic warrior, the vengeful archer he assumed matched the fearsome bow, he whirled around, reaching for his sword.

He dropped his hand. It was another Daeva woman at the door, and well . . . not a particularly scary one. She was even shorter than the girl. Older too, at least a century and a half if the silver in her roughly shorn curls was anything to judge by. Dressed in the thick coat and baggy pants Daeva men typically wore, the woman had a hunting knife tucked in her belt and a felt chador resting on her shoulders.

Her eyes, though, those were sharp: somehow even blacker than the rest of the Daevas, hooded and owlish. They ignored him, her gaze settling upon Jahal like the raptor she resembled. Bloodless lips pressed in a thin line.

Jahal sneered. He had ahold of the girl by her braids. "This auntie is who I was supposed to be so afraid of?"

The girl was staring at the woman with open veneration. "Yes."

The Daeva woman snapped her fingers, and Pran heard Jahal's hand shatter from across the room.

The Geziri soldier screamed, dropping the girl. Pran watched as he clutched his ruined hand, the fingers pointing in a constellation of directions.

The older woman hadn't moved. She glanced at the girl. "Are you all right?" she asked.

The girl nodded, still shaking. "They-they said they were from the Royal Guard."

The older woman nodded and then moved, approaching Jahal

like a leopard might an injured hare: her movements achingly graceful, her face a mix of mild curiosity and cool hunger. "A Geziri man
trying to take what's not his," she said curtly. "How very like his
king."

Jahal clutched his injured hand, his eyes wild with pain. "You
fucking witch!" he shrieked. "What did you do to me?"

Pran didn't move, rooted to his spot and frozen in shock. Jahal
couldn't really think the woman had done that to him. That was impossible. Too much wine, maybe . . .

Still gasping, Jahal reached for his zulfiqar as the woman drew
nearer, but he was slowed by pain. She kicked it away easily and seized
his wrist. There was the sudden scent of acrid smoke on the air.

The next noise that came from Jahal's mouth made his shrieks
seem like whispers.

He *howled*, a sound that grew wet and choked as black blood
streamed from his mouth, joining the blood dripping from his eyes,
his ears, and his nose. His body convulsed, seizing with enough violence to shatter bones, as ash beaded off his skin like human sweat.
And yet he didn't collapse, didn't stop screaming, held in thrall by
one of the woman's delicate hands. The younger girl stood watching,
her face a mask of bitter vengeance.

"An interesting sensation, is it not?" the Daeva woman mused.
"To have one's blood abruptly reverse direction? It should kill you,
of course, obliterate your heart. There's a trick to keep it beating
throughout: one that took me quite a bit of practice to master."

Pran's mouth fell open, his mind and eyes unable to reconcile
what was before him. Appearances be damned, the woman could be
no djinn. His race didn't have that kind of power.

Except . . . there were ones who once did.

"What arrogance you have . . . ," the woman marveled. "To go
raiding across a land that is not yours, to look upon, to *touch* a woman
who does not want you."

Her crisp voice was clipped, the accent almost familiar. No, it
was familiar, Pran realized. It was Daevabadi, high-class.

Really high-class.

The books on the shelves, the twisted glasswork and metal instruments covering the table. The *scalpel*.

A Daeva woman who could break a man's bones from across the room, who could make his blood flow in the opposite direction. In dawning horror, Pran's eyes again fell on the terrible bow, a thing fallen from myth.

He shot to his feet. He should have helped Jahal, but the grisly scene before him, his mind shouting ridiculous conclusions and half-remembered tales of his family's ancestral home in ruined Qui-zi, banished any sense of duty he might have had—along with most of his other senses. He fled, tearing out the door with neither his coat nor his boots.

He raced headlong into the snowy dark, thinking of nothing but putting distance between himself and Jahal's screams, now fading to gurgled shrieks. Besides Jahal's cries, the breaking of sticks beneath Pran's feet and the pant of his breath were the only sounds, the falling snow dampening the rest of the world. The frozen trees were black, stark skeletons against the gray sky, dead things suddenly welcoming: for with each one he passed, he was farther away from the impossible event he'd just witnessed. He'd run all the way to Sugdam, all the way back to Daevabad, if it would save him from the woman with the cold voice and the deadly touch. He scrambled up a snowy bank, his heart racing.

There was no sound as he gathered himself. And then there was a whistle on the icy air.

Something sharp punched through his back, sending him tumbling down the incline. He landed twisted on his side and gasped for air, pain and pressure ripping through him.

A bloody arrow protruded from the left side of his chest.

God have mercy. Black spots blossomed before his eyes as Pran sucked uselessly for breath. The arrow must have gone through one of his lungs. Foamy hot blood gushed from the wound, melting the snow beneath him. He swooned, vaguely aware of the glen growing brighter with the flicker of approaching firelight. Some Daeva mob, no doubt, coming to finish him off.

But it was no mob that emerged from the black trees with their torches held high. It was a single man, and he carried no fire.

He *was* fire.

Skin of pressed light, so vivid it nearly hurt to look upon. Hands and bare feet the color of coal. Golden eyes and fire-blackened fangs. The man moved forward with deadly grace, with a darting speed like a snake. The enormous bow Pran had seen back in the cottage was held half drawn in his clawed hands.

Pran would have screamed could he have drawn a single breath. It was an ifrit. The worst nightmare of his people, their mortal enemy. A choked whimper escaped his lips. The glen was darkening again, shadows growing at the corners of his vision as his life's blood spread across the snow. He was dying, he knew, the things he was seeing making no sense.

They couldn't make sense, couldn't be possible. For as the ifrit drew nearer, raising his bow once again, Pran spotted a black tattoo on his golden temple that had no business being there. An arrow crossed over a stylized wing.

An Afshin mark.

Pran didn't have much time to contemplate it. There was a glimmer of silver, and then the next arrow ripped through his throat. He was aware of falling backward, of blood filling his mouth, of the icy pricks still swirling down from the sky and the gaunt trees looming over him. His death was quick.

Indeed, it was so quick that Pran died before he could fathom the implications of what he and Jahal had just run into out here in the wilds of Daevastana. What it would mean for the elderly parents he'd left behind in Daevabad, rising now to make an early cup of tea, their home in the shadow of the Qui-zi memorial. For the soldiers he'd trained alongside in the Citadel, grumbling as they strapped on weapons long overdue for replacement. For an already stressed kingdom and a crumbling magical city.

For a certain young woman from Cairo.

Nahri

I took these Nahri scenes from an old (and very different!) version of *The Kingdom of Copper*. I've reworked them so they feel like something that could have happened before that book, looking at aspects of Nahri's marriage to Muntadhir and her role as the Banu Nahida. Spoilers for the first book.

Banu Nahida, *stop!*"

Nahri didn't stop. Instead, she sprinted down the corridor to her infirmary. Her heart racing, she didn't waste time glancing back to see how many guards from the Treasury were pursuing her, but judging from the pounding of feet, it was at least half a dozen.

You fool, she chided herself as she ran. *You never should have let your skills get that rusty.*

Two chattering scribes ambled out from the direction of the library, their arms heavy with scrolls. Nahri nearly crashed into the first and then intentionally tripped the second, sending him and his scrolls sprawling across the floor. The documents bounced and rolled down the corridor. She could only hope they tripped up a couple of her pursuers.

"Nahri, damn it, stop!" It was her husband this time. He sounded out of breath, and she wasn't surprised; Emir Muntadhir wasn't the type to physically exert himself—at least not in this way. That she'd roused him from his circle of drunk poets to play unintentional partner to her heist had been miracle enough.

The guards sounded closer. Nahri could see the half-open doors to her infirmary just ahead. She put on a burst of extra speed.

"Nisreen!" she shouted. "Help me!"

Nisreen must have been close. In seconds, she was at the doorway, a wickedly sharp scalpel in one hand and her eyes bright with alarm as she noticed the running guards.

"Banu Nahida!" she gasped. "What in the Creator's name—?"

Nahri grabbed the edge of the door and shoved Nisreen out as she flew over the threshold. "Forgive me," she rushed before slamming the door in the older woman's bewildered face. She whirled around, pressed her palms against the intricate metalwork on the closed door, and then dragged them down, hissing in pain as the studs tore into her skin, her blood slippery on the decorative panels.

"Protect me," she commanded confidently in Divasti—she'd already practiced the enchantment in preparation.

She'd practiced . . . and now nothing happened.

Nahri panicked, holding the door closed against Nisreen's shoving on the other side. She kicked it hard and cursed loudly in Arabic. "Damn it, I said 'protect me'!"

The blood smoked—her blood, the blood and magic of the people who'd built this place so many centuries ago. Nahri backed away as the metal grating twisted together, firmly locking the doors just as something heavy smashed into them.

She heard several muffled voices arguing on the other side of the door, including Muntadhir's distinctly irritated tone. She'd never heard him so angry, and considering the number of fights they'd gotten into during the three years they'd been married, that was saying a lot.

There was more pounding on the door.

"Banu Nahri!" she heard Nisreen yell. Judging from the alarm in her voice, she'd learned what Nahri *might* have stolen. "Please let me in. We can discuss this!"

"Sorry!" Nahri sang out. "The door . . . you know how unpredictable palace magic can be!"

Behind her, a tray clattered to the floor. Nahri turned around to meet the astonished eyes of her patients and aides. The infirmary was on the quiet side this afternoon—and by quiet, she meant not so full that people were literally pushed into the garden. The hundred beds were all occupied—they always were nowadays—but only a few of her patients had visitors.

Nahri gave them all a severe look and then jerked her head at the door. "Any of you go near that and you'll have plague sores in some very uncomfortable places, understand?"

No one spoke, but enough people went pale and drew back to convince her that they understood. Nahri dashed across the infirmary to her private workspace and yanked the curtain closed behind her, trying to ignore the battering on her door and the enraged—and unusually detailed—threats from Muntadhir. Only then did she dig out the shard of white stone she'd shoved in her bodice back in the Treasury. It was barely the size of her thumb, and though it shone prettily in the light, the rock otherwise wasn't much to look at.

There was a nervous shuffling, and then a short Daeva woman with silver hair stood up from where she'd been hiding behind a pile of texts.

"Is that it?" she asked hopefully.

Nahri gazed at the shard. "If you believe the stories." For if the stories were to be believed, this tiny white rock was one of the only pieces left of Iram—the legendary city of the pillars. Nahri knew conflicting tales of Iram. Back home in Cairo, she'd heard it mentioned as a city destroyed for its wickedness thousands of years ago. Some of the djinn took issue with that, muttering that the humans really shouldn't have been there and how were their ancestors to know how destructive celestial fire winds could be.

But Nahri wasn't interested in the Iram fragment for its stories.

She was interested in it because it was apparently the only cure for one of the trickiest curses in their world: the loss of one's magic. And by apparently, Nahri had read of this effect only in a single Nahid text, a reference that made clear how tricky and unpredictable the enchantment was to get right. She would also have to *destroy* the Iram fragment—the rare rock so prized that the few remaining shards were kept in the Treasury—in order to have any chance of success. To get access to the Treasury alone, she'd had to bait Muntadhir into a fight regarding her dowry, a ruse she doubted she could pull off a second time.

The Daeva woman—Delaram—approached, wringing her hands. "Are you sure about this, Banu Nahida? I do not wish to bring you further trouble. I'm not worth that risk."

"You are my patient and thus worth any risk," Nahri insisted as she strode over to her desk and plucked free the Nahid notes nestled between two Arabic books—she kept her workspace as messy as possible to discourage would-be snoopers. She ran her fingers along the ancient paper, tracing the inkblots and whirled script her ancestors had long ago laid down. She'd read the notes so often, she had them memorized, but the feel of something tangible her legendary relatives had read and used and touched themselves reassured her.

And Delaram *was* worth it, having lost her magic after being cursed by a cruel husband. By chance, her affliction was also the reason Nahri might have found the cure in the first place. Without her magic, Delaram had spent the last few decades of her life dusting, sweeping, and reorganizing the library in the Grand Temple after overeager students swirled through it like destructive academic cyclones. She was so diligent in her work—and in taking the reins of this domain of knowledge—that she had uncovered at least a dozen new Nahid texts hidden beneath the floorboards and tucked into cracks.

But that work didn't make her a noble. It didn't make her a djinn. Daeva cleaning women weren't worth the "destruction of such a valuable item," and so Nahri had been turned down when she requested the Iram fragment, even as she pleaded that the curse was shortening Delaram's life.

Really, I had no choice but *to steal it.* Nahri tossed and caught the shard in one hand and then got to work.

In her absence, the fire pit had died down to smoldering ash. "Naar," she commanded, and the flames answered back, crackling and snapping as they raced to reach her fingers. The heat scorched her face but did not hurt. Nahri knelt, pulling a prepared basket from underneath the nearest couch.

"Earth from your homeland," she murmured, taking a handful of soil gathered from Daevabad's hills and tossing it into the fire. "Water purified in the name of the Creator." She poured in a vial of water taken earlier from her fire altar. There was a hiss of steam as it hit the flames, the drops too few to affect the blaze.

"Nahri, don't you *dare* destroy that shard! Open the damned door!"

Oh, go jump in the lake, Muntadhir. She could only imagine how embarrassed he was to have been locked out by his wife, and it gave her an almost distracting amount of pleasure.

But she could exult later—she needed to focus now. Nahri exhaled, adding the air from her lungs to the fire's smoke. Holding the Iram shard in one hand, she reached for a scalpel with the other and then drew a sharp line across her palm, blood immediately swelling to drown the small white rock. Nahid blood: deadly to the ifrit, capable of undoing all manner of magic, and one of the most powerful substances in the world.

The Iram fragment exploded.

Nahri yelped in pain and swore, but her hand was already healing. She tossed the burning remains of the shard into the fire and then cradled her hand to her chest.

"Are you hurt?" Delaram gasped.

"I'm fine," Nahri said through gritted teeth. Maybe Nisreen had had a point—a small one—about not messing with magic she didn't understand. With her good hand, she urged Delaram closer to the blaze. "Breathe in the smoke, as much as you can."

Something smashed into the doors so hard the entire infirmary shook. Bits of plaster rained down from the ceiling.

"BANU NAHIDA!" Ghassan thundered, and the sound of the king's rage was enough to send a shiver of fear down her back. A few of her patients let out startled cries. "Stop what you're doing right now!"

Without waiting for her response, whatever hit the door did so again. The metalwork keeping it closed began to groan and snap.

But it held, and that meant there was still a chance.

"Keep breathing in the smoke, Delaram. Keep breathing . . ."

Delaram cast a nervous glance back at her, but kept sucking in the pungent smoke until, overwhelmed, Nahri's patient started to choke.

"Delaram!"

Delaram fell to her knees and Nahri dropped to her side.

"I'm fine," the other woman wheezed through the smoke whirling around her face. Delicate white fragments sparkled in the air. She massaged her throat. "I just . . ." She trailed off and then lifted her hand.

Flames danced between her patient's fingers. "Is this . . . is this *me*?" Delaram whispered.

"It's you." Nahri smiled—and then the doors finally smashed open.

Ah, but alas, the infirmary was so crowded. And Ghassan was so intimidating that her patients fled hastily to avoid him and his soldiers, causing more of a delay and commotion than they might have if they had simply stayed put.

Which meant by the time he had wrenched back the curtain with a very undignified curse, Delaram was gone and Nahri was sitting at her desk, going over notes about her patients with a professional healer's diligence.

"Where is it?" Ghassan demanded. "I swear to God, girl, if you've damaged that shard . . ."

She gave the king the most innocent face she could. "What shard?"

NAHRI FELL TO HER KNEES BEFORE THE ANCIENT ALTAR and pressed her fingertips together, closing her eyes. She bowed her head and then carefully plucked a long stick of cedar incense from the silver tray of consecrated tools at her side. She stood up on her toes, holding the incense to the flames burning merrily in the altar's cupola until it started to smolder. Once it was burning, she began relighting the glass oil lamps floating in the giant silver fountain below.

She paused as she lit the last, taking a moment to appreciate the beauty of the fire altar before her. Central to the Daeva faith, the striking design of the altars had persisted through the centuries. A basin—usually silver—of purified water with a brazier-like structure rising in its middle in which burned a fire of cedarwood, a fire extinguished only upon a devotee's death. The brazier was to be carefully swept of ash at dawn each day, marking the sun's return. The flaming glass oil lamps in the basin below kept the water at a constant simmer.

Nahri stayed silent a few moments longer. Although not often one for prayer, she was conscious of her weighty role in the Daeva faith and had learned to play her part accordingly. When she turned around, the lower part of her face was veiled in Nahid white silk, but her eyes were free to take in the people massed below her. She raised her right hand, her palm outward in blessing.

Four thousand men, women, and children—worshippers packed to the walls—pressed their hands together and bowed their heads in respect.

A few years of leading ceremonies at the Grand Temple had yet to reduce the awe Nahri felt upon such a demonstration. The Temple itself still routinely took her breath away. Constructed nearly three millennia ago, the massive stone ziggurat was a work on par with the Great Pyramids outside Cairo. The main prayer hall mimicked the design of the palace's throne room, though styled in a far more austere fashion. Two rows of columns, studded with sandstone discs in a variety of colors, held up the distant ceiling, and shrines lined the walls, dedicated to the most lionized figures in their tribe's long history.

Nahri stepped away from the altar. On the platform below, a line of scarlet-robed priests kept her separated from the rest of the worshippers. They'd already given at least a half-dozen sermons praising her and her extended family and calling upon the Creator to favor her work. Thankfully Nahri had never been asked to give a sermon; she would have had no idea what to say. Moreover, traditionally Nahids weren't expected to interact with worshippers in the

Grand Temple or even deign to notice them. They were supposed to float above all, lofty and cool, figures worthy of distant veneration.

But Nahri had never been one for lofty veneration. She stepped onto the lower platform, heading for the crowd.

The priests parted to let her through. A young acolyte, his shaven head covered in ash, dashed out from the shadows, wooden stool in hand, while a few of his fellows urged the crowd into the semblance of a queue. None resisted, the worshippers eager to comply in hopes of addressing her.

She studied the crowd. It was entirely Daeva save a scattering of Tukharistanis—Nahri had been surprised to learn there were a number of families among the trading cities of Tukharistan who'd quietly kept their original faith despite the djinn war. Beyond that, it was a diverse group. Ascetics in fraying robes shared space next to bejeweled nobles while wide-eyed northern pilgrims jostled weary Daevabadi sophisticates. Near the front, Nahri spotted a little girl fidgeting beside her father. She wore a plain dress of yellow felt, her black hair styled in four braids intertwined with sweet basil.

Nahri caught her eye and winked, beckoning her forward.

Clearly too young to worry about protocol, the little girl gave Nahri a gap-toothed grin and darted from her father's grip to rush forward. She threw her small arms around Nahri's knees in a tight embrace.

Nahri noticed a few of the priests wince. When her ancestors ruled, anyone who dared lay a hand on a Nahid outside of the act of being healed would have had such a limb lopped off, a tradition—one of many—that Nahri had decided needed revisiting.

"Banu Nahida!" The little girl beamed as she stepped back, her eyes crinkling in awe.

Her father hurried to join them, bowing in respect. He nudged his daughter's shoulder. "May the fires . . ."

"Oh!" The girl pressed her hands together. "May the fires burn brightly for you!"

"And for you, child," Nahri replied with a smile as she blessed them, marking the girl's forehead with ash. Their accent was unfamiliar. Pilgrims, Nahri assumed. A lot of her tribesmen came from outer Daevastana to pray at the Grand Temple. "Where are you from?"

"Panchekanth, my lady," the girl's father answered. At Nahri's visible confusion, he explained, "A ruined human city on the edge of Daevastana. I would not expect you to know it."

Nahri touched her heart. "I'm honored you made the journey. I pray the Creator rewards your devotion."

He bowed deeply, looking close to tears. "Thank you, my lady." The little girl gave Nahri another hug, waving as they wove their way through the crowd.

Nahri smiled beneath her veil. She'd come to live for moments like this, encounters that gave her the confidence to stand before the Daevas and the courage to ignore Ghassan's ominous insinuations about her "holding court." She told herself it was pragmatism. And if these moments also left a warm glow in her heart?

Well, Nahri was not going to deny herself even the rare bit of happiness she could steal in Daevabad.

The little girl and her father finally disappeared, swallowed by the crowd, and Nahri beckoned to another. About half the people who came to her did so with various ailments. She healed the easiest cases immediately, sending the more complicated ones on to the infirmary. She tried to see as many petitioners as she could, but as the sun climbed high behind the marble screens looking out at the landscaped courtyard, she began itching to return to the infirmary. Things had a tendency to go catastrophically wrong when she wasn't there.

Nahri blessed the pilgrims in front of her and then stood, motioning for the priests. The crowds had grown far too large for her to personally bless them all. Nahri knew many would return tomorrow. Some came day after day. She kept an eye out for familiar faces, never failing to be warmed by their obvious delight when they finally came before her.

Kartir appeared at her shoulder. Though the Grand Priest was nearly in his third century, he often proved surprisingly spry—especially when he was going to embark on a lecture. Which judging from his crossed arms and weary expression, Nahri was about to receive.

"Banu Nahida, are you *actively* looking for new ways to provoke the Qahtanis?"

"Why, whatever do you mean, Grand Priest?"

Ghassan could stare the skin off someone who displeased him, but the piercing gaze Kartir gave Nahri right now actually took her aback for a second.

Then she flashed him a conspiratorial smile. "No one actually *caught* me with anything."

Kartir gave her another severe look as they started walking down the steps. "You and I both know that doesn't matter. The more powerful and popular you become here, the more danger you're in." The priest softened his voice. "I know you want to be a good Banu Nahida, but I would rather see you alive and treating nothing but bruises than being executed because you reached too far."

"I'm careful, Kartir," she said, trying to assure him. And Creator knew Nahri was; she rather enjoyed not being murdered by the king. "But I've given Ghassan what *he* wanted," she added, a note of bitterness slipping into her voice. "I won't let him stop me from taking care of my patients."

It was a poor moment for them to pass by Dara's shrine. The curtain was drawn back to reveal the brass statue inside, that of a Daeva warrior on horseback, standing proudly upright in his stirrups to aim an arrow at his pursuers. Fat wax candles and oil lamps threw jagged light on the dozens of offerings scattered about the base of the statue. No blades were allowed in the temple, so small ceramic tokens depicting a variety of ceremonial weapons—mostly arrows—had been brought instead.

Though Dara's shrine was one of the most popular, there were no devotees there now. Nahri stopped before she could think better of it and gazed at the enormous silver bow suspended behind the statue. She wondered if it was a replica or if it had been his during his mortal life. If his fingers had clutched the grip and drawn back the bowstring.

Yes, maybe he used it to shoot down shafit like you at Qui-zi. Nahri closed her eyes. It had been nearly four years and Nahri had yet to come to terms with the man who had entered her life on a sandstorm and ripped out of it just as violently. The man she was fairly certain had loved her, who she might have one day loved in return, and then who had betrayed her trust in a way Nahri didn't think she'd ever completely recover from.

Kartir cleared his throat. "I can make sure no one will bother you if you'd like to pray."

"No." Nahri had tried to pray here, and it usually wasn't long before she was either crying and throwing accusations at a statue or—in a humiliating moment of weakness the morning before her wedding—begging Dara a final time to return and save her. She'd learned the hard way that bottling up her emotions and moving on was the only path to survival, whether in Cairo or in Daevabad.

She turned away from the shrine. "I should get back to the palace."

NAHRI FLOATED IN THE NILE, THE COOL WATER A BALM against the hot sun. The river was still, too still, but she paid it little mind. With the wind rustling through the reeds and insects buzzing in the trees, it was far too peaceful to be bothered over something like motionless water.

That smell, though. That was bothersome, like seared metal and burnt hair. She wrinkled her nose, but the stench had been getting worse as the water grew warmer. Disgusted, she finally straightened up, meaning to wade back to land.

Her feet didn't so much as touch the muddy bottom—Nahri must have drifted farther out. She floundered and briefly went under, getting a mouthful of water. She spat it out, recoiling. It wasn't water.

It was blood.

"Gulbahar!"

She turned toward the voice—only to see a dark reptilian form slip into the river.

A crocodile.

"Mama!" Nahri tried to escape, splashing and kicking in desperation as the creature swam toward her. The bloodred water rippled over its scales, implying a massive *body. It was as if she had been pinned in place, the riverbank growing only more distant.*

"MAMA!"

Teeth clamped around Nahri's ankles, and then before she could scream, she was dragged under the water.

"NAHRI? NAHRI, *WAKE UP*!"

Nahri woke with a start. She gasped, a cold sweat breaking across her skin.

Muntadhir was hovering over her. "Are you okay?" he asked, his hand on her shoulder. "You were crying in your sleep and screaming that human language of yours."

I was? Nahri blinked, the details of the nightmare already receding. Sharp teeth and a river of blood. Terror. Raw and wrenching and unlike anything she'd ever felt before.

And a *name*. There had been a name, hadn't there?

She was suddenly conscious of Muntadhir staring at her. "I'm fine," she insisted. Nahri shook off his hand, peeling away the sheets to slip from her bed. She crossed the room, the marble floor past the rug a cold shock on her bare feet, and poured herself a glass of water from a pitcher resting on a small table. A breeze played with the linen curtains, smelling of wet earth and jasmine. Beyond the door leading to the balcony, the gardens were entirely black. She doubted it was even close to dawn.

Muntadhir spoke again, his voice soft. "I get them too. Nightmares, I mean. Of that night on the boat. I often think that if I had just moved faster—"

"Why are you here?" It came out ruder than she meant, but Nahri was not discussing that night with him.

Muntadhir visibly started at her tone and then raised an eyebrow. "Now that's just insulting."

Nahri cleared her throat, a little heat creeping into her cheeks. "I mean, why are you *still* here?"

"I fell asleep." Muntadhir shrugged. He lay back on her rumpled sheets, the picture of royal indolence as he crossed his wrists behind his head. "I didn't know I was to hurry from my wife's bed like a wide-eyed concubine."

"An image you must have a degree of familiarity with."

He gave her an even look, nodding at her messy hair and disheveled shift. "I speak Divasti, Nahri. You were definitely *not* objecting to my presence earlier."

There was no fighting the blush now, but Nahri held her ground. "Do you want some sort of praise? You've slept with half of Daevabad. I'd hope you'd have some skill."

"Only you could make that sound like an insult." But Muntadhir finally rolled out of her bed, reaching for his clothes. "You're right, though—maybe it would be better not to fall asleep beside you. I'm sure your mother's notes are full of suggestions for Qahtani blood."

"So stop coming," she snapped. "Surely you have beds aplenty to occupy you."

He looked taken aback. "God, Nahri, it was a *joke*. Why must you always be so prickly about everything?" He lazily tied the bindings on his waist-wrap. "And I do believe you were there when my father pointed out that if I wasn't using certain parts to give him a grandchild, I must not need them at all." He shuddered. "So I think I'll keep visiting."

Nahri said nothing. The nightmare was still on her mind, a memory, a meaning trying to connect. There had been a *name*. A voice. An inexplicably vast absence yawning through her chest.

Muntadhir pulled on his robe and then hesitated. "Actually, on that note . . . there was something else." He picked up the black bag he'd brought with him, one that Nahri had ignored, assuming it to be wine or God only knew what intended for the evening amusements he had planned after visiting her. "I brought you something." He motioned toward the cold embers in her fireplace; Daevabad's nights were warm enough for Nahri, and the soft light of her flickering fire altar was all she needed to sleep. "Do you mind?"

Nahri shrugged. "I'll let you stay if a gift is involved."

Muntadhir squatted at the hearth and relit the fire with a snap of his fingers. "You know if you were a courtier, you'd be investigated for corruption talking like that."

"How fortunate that my position is hereditary."

He sat in one of the cushioned chairs in front of the fire. Nahri took the opposite one, propping her feet on a plump ottoman and watching as he pulled what appeared to be a large book from the bag.

She frowned. "I didn't think you could read."

"Yes, I'm aware how I measure up against your royal pen pal."

Nahri instantly stiffened. "I don't know what you're talking about."

Muntadhir gave her a measured gaze. "I'm the Emir of Daevabad. Do you really think I wouldn't find out another man has been writing to my wife?"

Everything about his response made Nahri's temper rise. "What a lovely way to remind me that you keep spies in my quarters. Surely they are talented enough to have informed you that those letters get immediately burned in my fire altar?"

"Not immediately they don't," Muntadhir countered.

Nahri dropped her gaze. Ali and his stupid letters. He'd taken to writing her after he was dispatched to his garrison in Am Gezira. Not often, and perhaps suspecting they'd be intercepted, he didn't dare touch on that night on the boat. Instead his notes had been almost impersonal ramblings that, just like their reluctant friendship, had drawn her in with equal amounts endearing naivete and wit. Sketches of ancient ruins, descriptions of local healing plants, any bits of news he'd learned of neighboring Egypt, stories about the nearby humans.

They were mundane, and yet they always ended the same way. Written in a rough transcription of the Egyptian dialect she'd taught him: "I'm so sorry. I pray God grants you some happiness."

Even if she hadn't been worried about getting caught, Nahri wouldn't have written back. She didn't trust the tug on her heart that Ali—her enemy in every way—still had. If it had not been for that affection, she might have noticed the quiet way he was waiting for soldiers that horrible night instead of begging him to escape alongside Dara and her.

Nahri crossed her arms over her chest. "You mentioned a gift, not an interrogation. Can we move on to that part?"

Muntadhir rolled his eyes, but held out the cloth-covered book. Nahri carefully unwrapped it. A stylized painting of a winged lion—the shedu that was the emblem of her family—roaring at a rising sun was centered on the book's cover. The next page was a garden scene rendered in painstakingly miniature details, and the following one a handsome soldier on horseback.

"They're your uncle's," Muntadhir explained. "He used to paint and sketch on the side. Not many have an appreciation for Daeva art in the palace, but I always thought Rustam was talented."

He was. Nahri was among those with little understanding of art, but even she could see the spark her uncle had managed to catch in his subjects: the gleam of ornaments in a dancer's vibrant costume, the wearied slump of an old scholar surrounded by simmering glass vials. "Where did you find these?"

"Various collectors."

Nahri turned the page to a painting of the infirmary's garden and a shafit servant with a slightly mischievous smile gathering what she was surprised to recognize as molokhia plants. She traced the bumpy edge of a brushstroke. Nahri had nothing so personal, so precious of the uncle she'd never met. Beyond the pavilion outside, there was a small grove where Rustam had tended oranges and rare herbs, and she was tempted to take the book there now. To sit and linger with it in a place he had spent so much time. To feel *some* connection with her vanished family.

Instead, she closed the book, unwilling to let her husband see such a weakness. Muntadhir was not a thoughtful man: it wasn't that he was unkind; instead she suspected that a lifetime in the palace, wined and dined as the heir to the powerful Qahtani throne, had simply shaped him to be a man who didn't think of others. She couldn't imagine him coming up with such a gift, let alone taking the time to track down a bunch of scattered artwork.

She could, however, think of someone else who would have done such a thing . . . someone who would have been all too happy to let

Muntadhir take the credit. "I'll be sure to thank Jamshid the next time I see him."

Muntadhir sighed. He glanced at the low table between them, and his fingers twitched, as if wishing for a cup of wine to ease his discomfort. "You don't always have to make this so hard, Nahri."

"What?"

"*This.*" He beckoned between them. "Us. The stunt at the Treasury. You completely humiliated me. And for what? I might have helped you of my own accord."

"Please. As though you don't snap to your father's commands as quickly as the rest of us. You certainly had no qualms about ordering the guards to chase me down."

Muntadhir flinched, taking a controlled breath. "I'm just trying to say our marriage doesn't have to be as miserable as you seem determined to make it. We're not getting out of this and you know it."

"So you've brought me what? A peace offering?"

"Does that seem so unreasonable?" When Nahri gave him a skeptical look, Muntadhir pressed on. "I don't expect some great love story, but we could attempt not to hate each other. We could attempt . . . to fulfill the actual reason we were married in the first place."

She shifted, the meaning of his deliberate words clearer, and gestured to the crumpled sheets on her bed. "We just did."

"Our people don't conceive as easily as your humans," Muntadhir said gently. "Once every few months is not going to produce the heir everyone is expecting."

The heir everyone is expecting. Even for Nahri—who prided herself on being pragmatic, who knew this was all transactional—the blunt reminder of her worth was too much. "I'm the Banu Nahida of Daevabad, not some broodmare," she snapped. "Believe it or not, I occasionally have other duties to attend to."

"I *know*, Nahri. Believe it or not, I feel similarly." Muntadhir scrubbed a hand through his hair. "Can I speak frankly?"

"I cannot imagine there's a way to get more candid."

That brought a half-smile to his face. "Fair. All right . . . I cannot help but feel like every time we . . . *fulfill* the actual reason we were married, you pull away more. And I don't understand. When we were first married, we used to talk. We used to *try.* Now I can't get a word out of you that isn't barbed."

His comment took her aback, as did the fact that he was right. When they were first married, Muntadhir had determinedly courted her. They might not have slept *together,* but he insisted they share a bed more nights than not, as well as conversation, even if it was just him passing on court gossip over a cup of wine. And oddly enough, Nahri had started to somewhat enjoy the bizarre ending to her day. Their nights together got her out of the infirmary, and his gossip was often useful, filling in the gaps of her political knowledge. Muntadhir was nothing if not a storyteller, and Nahri could not help but laugh at the ridiculous scandals he shared of poets who hexed their competitors and merchant nobles who were tricked into buying invisibility cloaks that inevitably failed when they got caught in bed with djinn who weren't their spouses.

It was a courtship with an obvious goal, and Muntadhir never hid his intentions. He proceeded slowly: massaging her hands after a long surgery and then eventually her neck and her calves. Meanwhile, the whispers and not-so-veiled comments had gotten unbearable; the king replacing the domestic staff in both their apartments with servants who obviously reported every intimate detail—or lack thereof—directly to him. And so a year into their marriage, after her own generous cup of wine, a mix of curiosity, weariness, and pressure had finally gotten the better of her. Nahri had doused the lights, closed her eyes, and gruffly told Muntadhir to get on with it.

He had complied . . . and she had enjoyed it. It would be pointless to pretend otherwise; it was, as she admitted, one of his only skills. But finally consummating their marriage had—in a way she still didn't understand—poisoned any budding affection she had for him. For it had been an intimacy whose depth Nahri didn't realize until it was too late, one she didn't want to share with him.

"See?" he prodded, pulling Nahri from her thoughts. "You're

doing it right now. Retreating into your head instead of talking to me."

Nahri scowled. She didn't like being read so easily.

Muntadhir reached for her hand. "What I said back there about my father and refusing to visit your bed: I was joking. If you need a break . . ."

"We can't take a break," Nahri murmured. "People would talk."

And Ghassan would find out. The king was a determined man and there was little more he desired than a grandchild with Nahid blood. He probably had a servant keep a book with the dates and lengths of time Muntadhir spent in her bedroom, a maid to check her sheets. They were invasions of her privacy that Nahri could not even dwell upon without wanting to burn the palace down. Knowing that something so personal was reported to the man she hated most in the world, the man who held her life and the lives of everyone she cared about in his hand . . .

That was why Nahri could not warm to Muntadhir.

Because despite everything she told herself—that she had consented to this marriage and taken the Qahtanis for every coin she could, that to be married off for political gain was the fate of every woman of noble blood, that her husband at least was decent and handsome and cared for her satisfaction—it all faded before one undeniable truth: neither she nor Muntadhir wanted this. Nahri was a prize to the Qahtanis; she had given herself, her very body, in marriage to save her life and stop Ghassan's bloodletting of her people. Were she to deny him now, there would be a cost.

"Then what *do* you want?" Muntadhir implored, sounding frustrated. "Talk to me. What will make this easier for you?"

Nothing will make this easier for me. Nahri pulled her hand out of his to trace her fingers over the shedu her uncle had painted. Had art been an escape for Rustam, a way to make his life as Ghassan's prisoner easier?

Art that Ghassan's son now gave to Rustam's only surviving relative in the hopes of visiting her bed more often.

"What number would satisfy you?" Nahri finally asked.

"What do you mean?"

She met Muntadhir's gaze, her voice toneless. "You said you weren't satisfied with how often I let you try for an heir. So how many nights a month would you prefer?"

"Nahri, for God's sake, you know that's not what I—"

"Isn't it?" She tapped her fingers on the painting again. "Don't be shy, Emir. You've already paid."

Muntadhir recoiled. But before Nahri could feel a moment's regret—for the words had been cruel—anger washed across his face. Good. Nahri preferred anger to vulnerability.

He glared at her. "You're not the only one who doesn't want this. Who lost a chance at happiness with someone else."

"Our situations are not *remotely* the same," Nahri snapped, unable to keep the feigned detachment in her voice at such an insinuation. She had no idea who he was referring to and didn't care. Muntadhir was not the one expected to carry an enemy's child. "And I'm finished with this conversation."

He pressed his lips into a thin, bloodless line, but he didn't argue. Instead he dressed in silence and then picked up his bag.

"You can take back the book if you like," Nahri said stiffly, though it killed her to do so. "I know it didn't buy you what you wanted."

Muntadhir gave her a weary look. "The book is yours. I told you the night I burned our marriage mask, Nahri: I'm not that kind of man." He sighed. "You know, there are times that I think you and I could actually be good at ruling together. Even if we never loved each other. But you clearly need a bit of a break from me."

"We can't—"

"I'll handle the whispers, all right? Believe it or not, I know how to handle *some* things around here, and I promise I won't put you at risk. Just let me know when you're ready for me to visit again."

Nahri's eyes pricked with tears at his unexpected kindness and the weight of their conversation. At the weight of the entire *day*. A day that had started with her believing she might have outmaneuvered the Qahtanis for once. A day in which she'd stood proudly in the Temple before her people.

A day that had ended with a rude reminder of just how powerless she truly was.

"Thank you, Emir Muntadhir," she said uncomfortably, with as much politeness as possible. It would not do to entirely reject her reluctant yet powerful ally. "Good night."

"Good night, Banu Nahida."

Ali

This scene takes place during *The Kingdom of Copper*, a few days after Nahri, Ali, and Zaynab visit the Daeva temple. There are spoilers for the first two books.

Ali glanced between the sketch in his lap and the hospital garden, then tapped his pencil against his chin.

"Perhaps another shade tree." He said the words to himself, for there was no one else in the ruins of the garden's half-collapsed gazebo. There never was. The gazebo's once finely carved wooden columns were so peppered through with termite holes that most had snapped, and what was left of the roof was held up only by a sprawling fig tree. Add in the tangled flowering vines that hid the interior and the winged snakes that liked to nest in the canopy, and it made for an excellent spot to get paperwork done without being bothered—provided one did not stand up too quickly. The winged snakes came out only at night, but that didn't mean they appreciated their sleep being disturbed during the day.

The gazebo was *usually* a good spot to be alone anyway.

"That arrogant, condescending mule . . ." A purple-swathed figure stomped through the vines, yanking back a tree bough and releasing it in the direction of the completed contracts Ali had neatly stacked on the remains of an old stone bench.

Ali had a split second to decide between saving his paperwork and protecting himself from a sudden intruder—a decision that several years of being hunted by assassins should have made intuitive—so of course he dove for his papers, skidding across the rocky ground on his shins and lunging for the scrolls before they flew in the rain-soaked shrubs.

"Alizayd, *by the Most High*." It was Nahri. "Are you trying to give me a heart attack, jumping out of a bush like that?"

Ali climbed back to his feet, keeping his head low to avoid the gazebo's leafy canopy. "Says the woman running in here as though a magical beast were after her." He frowned, taking in Nahri's flushed cheeks and disheveled headscarf. "Wait . . . *is* a magical beast after you?"

Nahri's expression darkened. "Worse. Kaveh."

Ali shuddered. "Is he still here?"

"No, I think it was meant to be a surprise visit. He was probably hoping to catch me doing something scandalous with the shafit, like treating them as equals or exchanging a kind word. Do you mind if I sit?" She sighed, gesturing to the bench. "I need to just breathe and not see people for a few minutes."

Ali quickly started gathering his things. "Of course. It's your hospital."

Nahri waved him off. "You can stay. You don't count."

Ali wasn't sure whether that was a compliment or an insult. "Are you sure?"

"Yes. Just don't . . . God, how hard did you throw yourself at the ground? You're bleeding all over the place!"

Ali glanced down at his legs to see blood blossoming through his clothes. Ah, so that was why his shins burned so badly. "It's fine. Just a scrape."

But Nahri was already rising to her feet again. She pulled the paperwork out of his hands and pushed him onto the opposite bench. "Just a scrape . . . save me from the pride of idiot men. Roll up your pants."

A little embarrassed, Ali nonetheless obeyed. Then he realized he no longer *had* skin between his ankles and knees, and blood was filling his sandals. "Oh."

"Oh, indeed." Nahri rolled her eyes and then, with the ease of a professional who did this every day, firmly clasped the back of his calves. Ali jumped at her touch.

She glanced up. "Did that hurt? It doesn't feel like anything's broken."

"No," Ali managed as the rain began striking the gazebo roof faster in pace with his racing heart. Her hands were just so soft. "I'm fine."

"Good." Nahri closed her eyes and a wave of coolness swept through Ali like he'd submerged his legs into an icy pond. He shivered, watching in fascination as his wounds stopped bleeding and scabbed over. In seconds, there was nothing but healthy skin covering his shins, as though he'd never been injured.

"God be praised," he breathed. "You must never tire of seeing that."

"The ancestral duty has its occasional advantages. Better?"

"Yes," he admitted. "Thank you."

"Add it to the debt you already owe me." Nahri let go of his calves. "I hope the papers were worth it."

Ali kicked his sandals out of the gazebo, hoping by the time he had to walk back, the rain would have rinsed the blood away. "Not having to read and annotate all these contracts again is very much worth it. Did you know people sneak in literal curses against competitors in construction contracts here?"

"No. No, I did not."

"Neither did I. Now everything is getting read twice."

"Sounds monotonous."

Ali shrugged. "I don't mind a bit of monotony now and then. It balances out the brushes with death."

Nahri snorted before reclining against the trunk of the fig tree. A brief smile crossed her face as she closed her eyes again. "I suppose it does."

She said nothing else, seeming content to rest. Despite her assurances that he could stay in the gazebo, Ali hesitated. It was probably best he leave. Five years ago, he would have insisted on doing so. The optics were even worse now, for Ali could only imagine how tongues would wag if Emir Muntadhir's ambitious younger brother was spotted secluded with his wife in a remote garden. Daevabad lived for such gossip.

And some died for such gossip.

But Nahri had asked him to stay. And this was the warmest— well, least barbed—conversation they'd had since that awful night on the lake. It felt fleeting and precious, and he realized how much he wanted it.

So Ali stayed. He returned to his spot on the opposite bench and retrieved his sketch. Thankfully it hadn't gotten wet when he dropped it, and he fell back into his work, trying to envision which plants and trees would best fit the space. The rain had picked up, the water droplets drumming against the leaves like music, and the humid air was thick with moisture and rich with the aroma of wet earth and flowers. It was intensely, almost hypnotizingly peaceful. And oddly enough, it was rather nice to have Nahri with him, the silence between them comfortable.

Comfortable enough that he wasn't sure how much time had passed when Nahri spoke again. "What is that you're drawing?"

Ali didn't look up from his sketch. "Just planning what to plant in the garden."

"Did they teach you much about gardening in the Citadel?"

"The most I learned about plants in the Citadel was to avoid thorned bushes if you needed to jump out of a window. Gardening, farming . . . those things I learned in Bir Nabat."

Nahri frowned. "I thought you were sent there to lead a garrison."

Ah, yes, his father's old lie. "Not quite," Ali replied, not wanting to delve into violent family secrets right now. "Bir Nabat is built in the ruins of a human oasis town, and I've been trying to restore their irrigation systems. Trust me . . . I've spent *way* more time thinking about plants and crop yields than I have about Citadel techniques in the past few years."

"Alizayd al Qahtani the farmer." Nahri smiled again. "I have a hard time picturing it."

"More like Alizayd al Qahtani the canal-digger. The glamorous life every prince dreams of."

She was still studying him. "But you liked it there."

Ali felt his smile fade. "Yes."

"Do you want to go back?"

I don't know. Ali looked away. Her dark gaze was too assessing. Nahri might think him a good liar, but Ali knew he wasn't, especially not with her.

But the question stayed with him. Truth be told . . . Ali didn't know. The idea of even having a choice was an alien concept. People like Ali didn't get to decide things like that for themselves.

"Whatever is best for my family," he finally said.

There was a long moment of silence, the only sound the dripping leaves. Ali would swear he could feel the weight of Nahri's gaze, but she didn't call him out on his evasive answer or reply with a sarcastic response.

"I suppose this can be a dangerous place to want things," she murmured.

"Yes," he agreed simply.

Nahri stood up. "Let me see." She snatched the sketch from Ali's hands and elbowed him aside to make room for her to sit beside him.

"I'm not a very good artist," he warned.

"No, you're not. But I can figure it out." She tilted the drawing. "Healing herbs?" she asked, reading the Arabic note aloud.

"I know the garden is mainly meant for recreation—well, for your patients to relax in, anyway." Ali pointed to the sketch he'd done of a weeping cypress. "So we'll put in plenty of shade trees and flowers, swings and recliners . . . a new fountain. But if we have the room, we might as well grow some plants you can use. There's a good spot right here for a bed of herbs."

"There's that Geziri practicality." Nahri bent over the piece of parchment between them. She was so close now that Ali could see the sheen of moisture on her face. A few locks of hair had slipped out of her scarf and were plastered to her damp skin. He inhaled sharply, catching the scent of the cedar ash that marked her brow and the jasmine blossoms braided into her hair.

She glanced up at the sound. Their gazes caught, and then she seemed to blush, an expression of embarrassment of which he hadn't thought the ever-confident Banu Nahida capable.

She quickly cleared her throat. "Is this an orange tree?"

"An orange what . . . uh, yes," Ali stammered, still taken aback by her nearness. "I figured we could transplant a sapling from your uncle's grove back at the palace. Or a different kind of tree," he offered. It was difficult to think when Nahri was watching him so intensely. "Lemon or lime—whatever you want, really."

"No . . . the orange is perfect." Nahri hesitated. "It's very thoughtful of you."

Ali rubbed the back of his neck, feeling sheepish. "You seemed fond of it."

"Of course I'm fond of it. Its roots knock intruders onto their asses." She gave him a warmer smile this time, her eyes dancing with a mischievous edge that sent nerves fluttering in his chest. "I wouldn't have thought you had equally fond memories."

The allusion to their ill-fated reunion didn't miss him. "I shouldn't have been where I wasn't invited," Ali said with as much diplomacy as he could.

"Well, listen to you learning." Nahri handed back the sketch. "Maybe I can trick Kaveh into coming by my orange grove and getting swallowed by the ground."

"Was his visit that bad?"

Nahri scowled. "I hate the way he talks to me . . . the way so many of them do. Like I'm this half-feral child they need to clean up and protect. Men like Kaveh would rather me be a silent icon they can worship instead of a leader who actually challenges them. It's infuriating."

"I don't think it's just about protecting you," Ali said, remembering their visit to the Temple and the horrified shock of the priests and Kaveh when Nahri announced her plan. "I think they're afraid. I think you do more than challenge them."

"What do you mean?"

"You shame them."

"How do I *shame* them? I've behaved diplomatically at every damn turn!"

"Yes, you and your famous diplomacy. You oh so *diplomatically* went to the Daeva temple and *diplomatically* turned over centuries worth of ignorant beliefs about the shafit. The kinds of things people make themselves believe so they can look upon others as inferiors and still think of themselves as righteous. That's hard for people to hear," Ali said, thinking back to the bones they'd found of the slaughtered Nahid healers in the remains of the apothecary. He and his people had their own history to reckon with.

His words hung heavy for a moment. And then Nahri, in the most deadpan sarcastic tone he'd ever heard, said, "You really did go full hearing-voices-and-wandering-the-desert religious back in Am Gezira, didn't you?"

"I'm trying to help. You know that, right?"

"I know." She sighed and no matter what fleeting embarrassment had passed between them earlier, she moved closer again, bringing her knees to her chest. She shook out the end of her chador, scattering water droplets over the mossy ground. "Is this rain your doing by the way?"

The unexpected question sent a shot of fear through him. "Of course not."

"A shame." Nahri glanced at him, and in the darkness of her eyes, there was no accusation or jest. She just looked very, very tired. "I was hoping you might keep it up a few days more."

At that moment, Ali desperately wished he was better with his words. He wished he could say something, anything to ease the sorrow in her expression. "Any more rain and this roof is going to collapse," he said, trying for a joke. "You'd be trapped with me."

She gave him another small smile and nudged his shoulder. "You're not always so bad. Even when you're talking like an over-wrought Friday preacher."

"May I speak like that again?" When Nahri nodded, Ali continued. "You should be proud. This hospital, bringing in Subha and facing down your priests . . . it's incredibly brave. You're doing wonderful things here. Don't let others make you feel small because they're struggling to measure up."

Nahri stared at him. He couldn't read the emotion churning in her eyes, but then she exhaled, like part of a weight had been lifted. "Thank you. It's nice to hear *someone* doesn't think I'm being a naive fool for wanting to bring the shafit and the Daevas together."

"We overwrought Friday preachers are known for our wisdom. Occasionally."

They sat together in silence again. She'd settled against the bench with her shoulder brushing his, and when she glanced up at the vine-choked canopy, Ali followed her gaze.

"Do you think this will bear fruit?"

Ali didn't know if that was a metaphor or an attempt to change the subject. "I'm not sure."

"I thought you were a farmer now."

"Canal-digger. Different specialty."

"Ah, of course. Forgive the grave error in misdiagnosing your heart's desire."

"And what about yours?" Ali asked, glancing down at her. "I've confessed my preference for a life of crop rotation rather than royal duties. What would you do if you weren't the Banu Nahida? And don't say doctor or pharmacist. That's cheating."

"I like cheating." Nahri shrugged. "I don't know . . . I've never really thought about it."

"You've never fantasized about a different life?"

"I don't believe in dreaming. It sets you up for disappointment."

"That is *the* most depressing thing I've ever heard, and I had a sheikh when I was six who spent an entire year detailing every punishment in the afterlife. Come on," he encouraged. "Besides, it's not dreaming. It's a fantasy that you know won't come true. A distraction. Wine poet," Ali teased, thinking of the furthest thing from Nahri he could. "Simurgh trainer. My father's most patient scribe."

Nahri swatted his arm. "I would rather be poisoned. Hmm, if I couldn't be a doctor . . . bookseller, perhaps."

"Bookseller?"

"Yes," she replied, sounding surer. "I think I'd like having my own business. I like talking to people, I like books, and most of all, I like convincing customers to part with their money. And could you imagine having all those books? Being able to read anything you want and fill your brain with new information every day?"

Ali grinned. "Yes, I remember how eager you were to get your hands on everything in the library."

"Excuse me, I'm not the one who got blown off a shelf and smashed against the wall for their curiosity."

He flushed, remembering their trip to the library catacombs. "It hurt so much," he admitted. "I was trying to act fine and unfazed, but I was seeing stars the entire time."

Nahri laughed. It was a genuine, deep laugh, not one of her mocking snickers. Ali couldn't remember the last time he'd heard it. He wanted to grab it, to memorize the way her grin lit her face and keep it there for as long as he could—both in real life and in his memory.

But her smile was already fading. "I really enjoyed those afternoons," she confessed, a hint of vulnerability slipping into her voice. "I was so overwhelmed when I first got to Daevabad. Everyone's expectations, the politics I couldn't understand—it was crushing. It was nice to slip away for a few hours a day. To speak Arabic and get my questions answered without you making me feel ignorant." She stared at her hands. "It was nice to feel like I had a friend."

Any teasing jest Ali might have offered died on his lips. "Could we be friends again? Or not friends!" he amended when Nahri's expression fell further. "Just two people who occasionally meet in an extremely dangerous gazebo to fantasize about the different lives they'd rather be living."

She was already shaking her head. "I don't think that's a good idea, Ali."

Ali. It was the first time Nahri had called him that since he'd returned to Daevabad.

"Is it because of that night on the boat?" he asked. "I'm sorry. I didn't—"

Nahri took his hand. Her fingers slipped between his and Ali instantly shut up. His eyes darted to her face, but she was staring at her lap, as though to avoid looking at him directly. Even so, there was no missing the flash of grief in her expression, an echo of the loneliness that seemed to cling to Nahri like a shadow.

"It's not because of that night on the boat," she said finally. "It's because this . . . this feels too easy. Like I could make a mistake. And I can't. Not again."

Ali opened and closed his mouth. "I-I don't understand."

She sighed. "It's like you said before: you'll do what's best for your family. I'll do what's best for the Daevas. If there ever came a time when either of us had to make a choice . . ." Nahri met his gaze, and the sadness in her dark eyes sliced Ali to the core. "I think it would be easier if we weren't friends."

Nahri let go of his hand. Ali said nothing as she rose to her feet and carefully placed her chador upon her head, reassuming her mantle of duty. He almost wished he could argue with her, but as usual, Nahri had cut straight to the truth.

"Is there nothing I can do to help you?" Ali asked, aching for her. "It breaks my heart to see you so unhappy."

"Smuggle me out if your father lets you leave?" It sounded like she was trying to make a joke, but there was no denying the undercurrent of misery in her voice. "Surely Bir Nabat could use a good bookseller."

Ali forced a smile, even as despair stole over him. "I'll keep an eye out for Banu Nahida–size traveling trunks."

"That would be appreciated." Nahri moved to leave, slipping through the tangled branches. "Though actually . . . there is something you could do. I mean, only if it's easy. Since you're already planning the garden."

"What?" he asked. She hadn't fully turned around, and the profile of her face was only partially visible behind the chador draping her cheek.

Her voice was hesitant, embarrassed. "There are these little purple flowers that grow in the hills. I've never seen them up close—

your father doesn't let me leave the city walls. But do you know what I'm talking about?"

Ali was surprised to realize he did. "I think they're called irises."

"Could we grow them here?" Nahri asked. "They're one of the first flowers to bloom in spring, and the sight of them has always made me hopeful."

"Then I will grow them everywhere," Ali said automatically. Realizing it came out like some sort of solemn vow, he quickly added, "I'll try anyway."

The ghost of what might have been a smile curved her lips. "Thanks."

Ali watched Nahri make her way back through the vines. He held his silence even as a dozen half-formed sentences rose to his tongue, sentiments and emotions he couldn't untangle.

So instead he quietly called upon the marid magic he'd denied having and very carefully stilled the rain before it could fall on her head.

Zaynab

This scene takes place directly after the events in *The Kingdom of Copper*. Spoilers for the first two books.

*L*ike this?" Ali asked, bending low to let her examine his turban.

"No, not like that. Let me . . ." Zaynab quickly rewrapped the turban, the fabric feather-light in her hands. "You want the folds crisper. And you'll need jewelry." She turned away, humming as she selected a few pieces from the pile on her bed.

Ali made a face as she draped pearls around his neck. "If I didn't know better, I'd think you were enjoying this."

"I'm loving this. It's like playing with dolls again and you'll owe me a favor." Zaynab picked up the tray of incense, swinging it over Ali's head to let the smoke scent his clothes.

"I have mentioned the whole 'in a hurry' part, yes?"

"Royals don't worry about punctuality." She slipped a silver ring over his thumb. "A pink diamond for Ta Ntry. Were you wise, little brother, you'd make sure at least one element of your daily dress is Ntaran. Remind people you come from **two** powerful families."

"Zaynab, there has not been a day in my life someone hasn't reminded me of the fact that I'm Ayaanle. Usually rudely." Ali stepped back and straightened up. "How do I look?"

Zaynab blinked. She might have been the architect behind their plan to steal Muntadhir's ceremonial clothes in a last-minute effort to save Nahri's meeting with the priests at the Temple, but the sight of her brother in royal garb still took her aback. There was little of the chattering young boy who used to follow her around the harem garden in the tall, *imposing man standing before her now. With the help of one her maids, they'd used some spellwork to lengthen the ebony robe so that it smoked around Ali's ankles, black as night. He looked striking in the Qahtani colors, the purple and gold pattern twisted together. He still wore his zulfiqar and khanjar, the deadly blades with their well-worn handles a contrast to his finery that set them off even more.*

"You look like a king," Zaynab said softly, her heart wrenching in the way it always did when she was torn between her brothers. It was just so hard. She loved Muntadhir and wanted only the best for him. But after a lifetime of being treated as slightly "other" by both Geziri and Ayaanle noblewomen, Zaynab could not deny the fierce pride that burned in her to see an Ayaanle man dressed like a king. "Make sure Amma never sees you in this," she warned. "It would give her far too many dangerous ideas."

Ali shuddered. "Don't even joke like that. She hears everything." He ran a hand over his beard. "Do you think this is going to work?"

"Do you have any other ideas?"

"I could promise Dhiru that I'll jump in the lake again if he goes to the Temple."

Zaynab smacked his shoulder. "Don't you joke like that." She gestured at the pile of scrolls he'd been carting around. Ali and paperwork were constant companions lately. "Do you need any of that?"

Ali sorted through the pile. "Maybe some of the basic plans . . . though the priests already know most of this. It's the shafit part we need to convince them of." He stuck a scroll under his arm. "God, I hope this works. I can't let her down again."

Can't let *her* down again. *Not the hospital. Nahri. Zaynab wondered if Ali even heard it. If her clueless brother had any idea the dangerous path he seemed determined to race down.*

She took his other arm. "We'll figure it out," she promised. "Now come on. We still need to steal Muntadhir's horse."

A JOLT OF FRESH PAIN BROUGHT ZAYNAB BACK TO THE PRESent, her memories of Ali fading. She flinched and rasped out, "Are you almost done?"

"No," the shafit physician—Subha, Zaynab remembered—answered. "Hold still."

"Do you know how much longer—"

"You should stop talking." Zaynab was shocked to be so rudely interrupted, but the doctor didn't even glance up from her work. "Your throat is injured and needs rest. Next time you plan to spend the night screaming at half the city, take some warm olive oil first."

Zaynab thought "screaming at half the city" a trite way to describe warning Daevabad's Geziris that their relics were about to kill them, but she was too exhausted and grief-stricken to argue. Instead she just grimaced and tried to keep still as Subha splinted her wrist. Her entire body ached. Zaynab used to consider herself an experienced rider; Muntadhir had been putting her in saddles since she could walk. But last night she'd learned the hard way that there was cantering the private trails in the palace gardens and then there was galloping madly through Daevabad, dodging fleeing djinn and moaning ghouls to shout warnings to any Geziris within earshot.

The lesson had been worth it, however. By the time the deadly copper vapor engulfed the Geziri Quarter, moving like a hungry malevolent fog, her people were ready: their relics removed and buried. Zaynab might have destroyed her voice, and she wouldn't be getting near a horse for days, but she and Aqisa had saved thousands of lives. They were heroes.

Zaynab didn't feel like a hero, though. Heroes didn't get their little brothers killed by dragging them back to a city they might finally have escaped. Again, the memory of Ali in royal clothes played in Zaynab's mind. He'd made a life for himself in Am Gezira. He had been happy.

Now he was very likely dead. For Zaynab and Aqisa had completed only the first part of their mission. They were to warn the Geziri Quarter of the plague coming for them, yes. But then they were supposed to go to the Citadel. To alert Ali and the officers who'd joined his rebellion that a worse coup had already arrived, and the army—Daevabad's feared Royal Guard, its thousands of well-armed, well-trained warriors—was needed to save the day.

But by the time they'd arrived, there had been no Citadel.

Zaynab and Aqisa had instead come upon a scene from hell: Zaydi al Qahtani's mighty fortress—the first place her family had built in Daevabad and the last place Ali was seen—was no more. Its massive tower had been ripped from its moorings, smashed, and dropped in the lake. The rest had fared little better. Every structure had been reduced to rubble and its courtyard left a muddy pit, scarred by water-and-blood-filled trenches as though a gargantuan beast had raked its claws over the ground.

And the bodies. More bodies than Zaynab could count. Crushed and drowned and ripped apart—their bloody scraps of uniform often the only thing that identified them as once living men. They were half buried by wreckage and littered across the wet sand, floating in the lake and pinned beneath the fallen tower. Scores had been clearly eaten alive, the remains of ghouls entangled with their ruined limbs.

Zaynab had snapped. She'd galloped for the pit, screaming Ali's name. But as if giving action to her grief, an earthquake had torn through the island. Her horse had shied and thrown her, and Zaynab had landed badly, breaking her wrist in the process. Surrounded by shaking buildings, panicked crowds, and falling debris, she'd scrambled for shelter. But not in time to miss the sight of the sky itself fracturing, the veil that separated their kingdom from the human world peeling away. As it vanished, it took with it the conjured fires of the djinn digging for survivors. The enchanted flying rugs they'd been using to whisk the injured to help. And as every bit of magic in Daevabad was stripped away, the real screaming had started.

By then Aqisa had caught up and dragged her to her feet, throwing Zaynab on her horse and racing for the hospital. "I will chain you to a post if you try to leave," the warrior woman had warned as she left Zaynab under Subha's care. "I will look for your brother. You don't need to see that."

Zaynab had been too dazed by pain and shock to argue, and it was only after Aqisa left that Zaynab realized the meaning of her words.

Aqisa didn't expect to find Ali alive.

That had been hours ago. The square of sky Zaynab could see through the window now was a pale early morning blue, the crimson of dawn gone. But if dawn was already gone . . .

No one called the adhan for fajr. The realization made her sick; Zaynab could never in her life recall that happening. Not that she herself felt capable of praying right now. If she tried to call upon God, she was going to start sobbing and not be able to stop.

Amma, I need you. I need Abba. I need my brothers.

There was no one in her mind to answer, though, so Zaynab inhaled, trying to steady herself. "Has there been any news from the palace?"

The doctor shook her head. "Everything I've heard is madness. People are shouting that another Suleiman has come to take our magic away and bring the wrath of the Creator down upon us."

"Do you believe that?"

"No." Subha gave her a dark look. "I think the gods washed their hands of this place a long time ago."

Movement from the doorway caught her eye, and then Aqisa stepped in. Any relief Zaynab might have felt upon seeing her companion was fleeting. Aqisa was covered in blood and her face ashen.

"Aqisa!" Zaynab moved to go to her before a jolt of pain reminded her Subha was still finishing her splint. "Help her! She's hurt."

"I'm not. It isn't my blood," Aqisa said hoarsely. She might not be hurt, but she was in bad shape all the same, staggering inside with her deadly grace gone to lean heavily against the wall. She looked haunted, more shaken than Zaynab imagined her proudly rude, seemingly fearless friend could ever be.

Her heart crashed to the floor. "You found him."

Aqisa managed a bare shake of her head. "Not Ali. I found Lubayd. An ifrit killed him." Tears glistened in her gray eyes. "Put an axe through his back. The stupid fool. He had no business getting killed by an ifrit."

Lubayd. Ali's cackling great bear of a friend and another man who wouldn't have been in Daevabad if not for Zaynab's machinations. "Aqisa, I'm sorry. I'm so sorry."

Aqisa waved her off. "This wasn't you, Zaynab. This . . . this isn't any of us."

Subha had finished with Zaynab's wrist splint, the smell of lime and plaster ripe in the air.

"Lubayd was a kind man," Subha said softly. "I kept having to kick him out for smoking in the hospital, but he was always so sweet with the workers' children."

"I will kill the creature who did it. I swear before God." Aqisa wiped her eyes and then took a shaky breath. "Zaynab, your brother . . . I spoke to the survivors I could find. They all said the same thing. The ifrit that killed Lubayd . . . it took Alizayd."

"What-what do you mean, it *took* him?" Zaynab demanded. "Where?"

"I don't know. They said it vanished. There was a bolt of lightning and they were both gone."

Gone. The word rang through her head. Zaynab opened her mouth, but she had no words. She would have rather found Ali's body herself, no matter the state. She could have burned him and prayed in the way of their people. He would have at least died a martyr and opened his eyes to Paradise.

Now he would awaken to a human master. To centuries of suffering at the hands of the people whose world he'd so admired.

"This is my fault," she choked. "This is all my fault. I should have never brought him—"

"Zaynab." Aqisa was suddenly there, gripping her shoulders. "Listen to me. None of this is your fault. You could not have known the city was about to be attacked. And Alizayd could still be alive. We don't know what the ifrit wanted with him."

Tears burned in Zaynab's eyes. "They only ever want one thing."

"You don't know that," Aqisa maintained. "The ifrit might be working with the Daevas behind this. Why else would it be here now?"

Subha gasped. "*Daevas* are behind this?"

"It was that spineless grand wazir who killed the king and released the poison targeting my people." Aqisa spat. "I will kill him too."

Aqisa's murderous declarations brought Zaynab briefly out of the numbing cloud of grief threatening to consume her. She didn't have time to mourn.

"I don't think it's all the Daevas," she said. "Nahri is the one who alerted us, after all. She and Muntadhir stayed behind at the palace so we could warn the Geziri Quarter and then bring Ali and the Royal Guard back to fight."

Subha was pacing. "This isn't good. I have dozens of Daeva patients here: victims of the attack on the Navasatem parade. If word gets around that Daevas were behind what happened to the Citadel . . ." She looked at Zaynab. "Do you have allies outside the palace who could help us? Any relatives?"

"My father and grandfather were only children. I have a few distant cousins and uncles serving in Daevabad, but . . ." Zaynab swallowed the lump in her throat. "They would have been in the palace or the Citadel."

"And your mother's side?" the doctor pressed. "The queen funded half this place. She must have connections, kin—"

"Most went back to Ta Ntry with her." Saying it aloud made Zaynab feel violently alone. Her father was dead, her mother a world away. Muntadhir and Nahri were across the city and Ali . . .

She took a sharp breath against the pain in her chest. No, Zaynab wouldn't think of Ali right now.

"So you have no allies," Subha said bluntly. "A princess with no power is just a person taking up a bed in the hospital. How are we to prevent what's left of the Royal Guard from coming here and taking vengeance on my Daeva patients?"

"Because she *is* the princess." Aqisa's eyes flashed. "The Royal Guard will listen to her. Zaynab is as much Zaydi al Qahtani's descendant as are her brothers. Our people are loyal. They'll rally behind her."

"Your people are conservative," Subha argued. "They're more likely to lock her up in a mansion for her own protection while they fight over the remains of her father's regime and the city falls apart." When Aqisa let out a hiss, Subha scoffed. "Don't glare at me. I've seen my own people abandoned too many times to be frightened by a scowling bandit."

"I will show you a scowling—"

"That's enough." Zaynab turned to Aqisa. "Who have you been speaking to out there?"

With one last glare at the doctor, Aqisa answered, "Soldiers mostly. There's a few dozen who survived, but no one very senior. I've found a couple of nobles that look ready to wet themselves, the chief gardener, and the minister of honored provisions."

"Honored provisions?" Subha asked. "Does that mean weapons?"

"It means robes," Zaynab said weakly. "Robes of honor for guests."

"Ah." The doctor pinched the bridge of her nose. "We're all going to die."

"We're not going to die." Clutching Aqisa, Zaynab climbed shakily to her feet. Her legs felt like they'd been turned to rubber where they didn't hurt, and a foul odor scented the air. Zaynab wrinkled her nose only to realize that *she* was the source of the odor. Her dress was filthy and mud, blood, and God only knew what else stained the dark cloak she'd hastily wrapped around her body.

Fortunately her turban was still intact, and she was able to pull enough of the tail free to veil her face. "Let me go talk to these people."

Aqisa stared at her. "You look like a ghoul."

"A royal one?"

The warrior woman slanted her head. "Maybe?"

"A great source of comfort you are. It will have to do." Cradling her splinted arm, Zaynab followed Aqisa out of the small room and into the hospital's main corridor.

Raised voices came from the courtyard, the Geziri cadence familiar but damnably incomprehensible. Despite several discreet tutors, Zaynab had never mastered her father's language, and it was a rejection that had never stopped stinging.

Now she hoped it wasn't a weakness that prevented her from taking what reins of power she could.

"Idiots!" Aqisa barked in Djinnistani as they entered the courtyard of arguing djinn. Zaynab silently blessed her for switching languages. "Stop weeping and gnashing your teeth. Your princess is here to speak with you."

Zaynab had not known men could shut up so fast. She stepped out from behind Aqisa. About a dozen Geziri men stared back at her, dressed in a motley assortment of bloody uniforms and torn clothing. Not a single face was familiar, and Zaynab fought the instinct to recoil.

"Your-Your Highness," a man with a *very* broken nose stammered. His eyes went wide over the swollen bruise that was his face and then he abruptly lowered his gaze, dropping to one knee so fast it had to hurt. He smacked the man next to him and then they were all kneeling and no one looking at her at all.

Which succeeded only in making Zaynab feel more out of place. She likely knew some of their women; the wives and daughters she'd have confidently ruled in the harem. That was the kind of power Zaynab was familiar with: the strings of command that ran through the world of women and could bring down a throne. Money, marriage and trade alliances, a whisper of gossip . . . those were the tools Zaynab had mastered, and she wielded them with the lovely smile her courtiers tried so hard to earn. She *liked* that power. She'd used it to save Ali's life and bring him home; she'd been trying to use it to settle the brewing war between her brothers. Zaynab often hated the physical constrictions of her role—which she knew stemmed more from her father's worries about her safety than from propriety—and ached to see more of the city, more of the *world*. But the role was at least familiar.

None of this was familiar. Zaynab had no business addressing soldiers. It should have been Muntadhir; it should have been Ali.

It should be, but it can't *be—it can only be you. And every moment you waste endangers them further.*

Zaynab squared her shoulders and tried to remember everything she'd ever seen her mother do. Hatset dealt with men all the time, not bothering to feign obedience to the royal custom of secluding noble women. "You forget I ruled my own court in Ta Ntry, dear daughter," she'd said more than once. "I do not care for the peculiar customs of this Daeva rock."

Oh, Amma, I could really use you right now. Summoning some courage,

Zaynab spoke, letting command color her voice. "I'd like to hear what's going on. Starting with what we know about the attack on the palace."

An elderly man in a wrinkled steward's coat stepped forward. "Not much, Princess, I apologize. You and the Lady Aqisa appear to be the only djinn who escaped. Prince Alizayd barricaded the shafit district and the Geziri Quarter earlier this evening; we would know if someone had tried to get in."

A chill went down Zaynab's spine. "Barricaded? What do you mean?"

A few of the men exchanged glances. "He closed off the gates to the midan," the steward explained gently, in a tone that made Zaynab feel like a fool. "He had the walls fortified and guard posts set up. It means our neighborhoods—the Geziri and shafit ones—are fairly well protected and separated from the rest of the city. Which puts a strong wall and soldiers between us and whoever attacked the palace, but—"

"But means anyone on the other side is trapped," Zaynab finished.

"This is all the fault of the fire worshippers," a soldier hissed. "It was Daeva fighters on the beach. We should get rid of the ones here before they turn on us."

"If anyone lays a hand on the Daevas in this hospital, they're going to lose it," Zaynab snapped. She must have had a bit of her father in her voice because half the men immediately shrank back. "It was Banu Nahri herself who came to me so I could warn the rest of you about the poison. I won't hear abuse against her tribe." She regarded the group of men again, remembering what Aqisa had said about how few soldiers had survived the attack on the Citadel. "We need help. Wajed left Daevabad before the attack, but he couldn't have gone far. Are any of you scouts? We may not have magic, but surely we could get a few messengers out by boat and horse."

An immediate disquiet seemed to come over the group. A few of the men shifted, but no one spoke.

Great, so now she'd gone full Ghassan and scared them into

silence. "What?" she prompted, trying to sound less intimidating. "What is it?"

"There . . . there are no boats, Princess," one of the soldiers replied. "Two ifrit came last night and set fire to the docks. They spared nothing, not even small craft, and killed several men trying to put out the flames. We have no way to get off the island."

Aqisa swore. "Can we not build rafts?"

The soldier shook his head. "Sure. Build a raft. We shall take bets on whether it's an ifrit or the marid in the lake that kills you first."

Zaynab laid a hand on Aqisa's wrist before the other woman responded with something violent. She could feel the awful weight of the men's stares. They were frightened and unsure, and she was a Qahtani. She was supposed to be in charge.

But Zaynab had no idea how to take charge of a situation like this.

"Has there been any word on my brothers?" She hated asking. Zaynab could only imagine how weak it made her sound, but she couldn't help it. She had an almost physical need to see her family, to clutch Muntadhir and Ali close and figure out what to do next together.

The steward's expression fell. "No, Your Highness."

"Princess Zaynab?"

Zaynab glanced back. An enormous shafit man was standing in the archway, a bloodstained apron full of medical instruments tied around his waist and a nervous expression on his face.

"F-forgive me," he stammered. "My wife—Dr. Sen said I should get you."

Aqisa had edged closer to Zaynab, her sword half drawn. "Why?" she asked, sounding suspicious.

"We found a survivor from the palace."

THE CHILD WAS SMALL, AND WITH HIS KNEES PULLED tight against his chest and rocking under a blanket, he appeared even smaller. Zaynab could make out little else about him—his age, his dress, his background—for he was entirely covered in blood and ash, his black eyes standing out wide and haunted in his dirty face.

The darkness of his eyes threw her. "Daeva?" she whispered to Subha as her husband, Parimal, returned to the boy's side and began gently wiping his face.

The doctor shook her head. "Shafit, but he owes his life to a Daeva. Apparently, they're rounding up all the djinn and shafit who survived the attack on the palace and herding them into the library. A Daeva scholar grabbed him and smuggled him out by claiming he was the boy's uncle. Our soldiers found him in the midan trying to climb the wall."

"Why did you bring him all the way up here?" They were in a well-appointed room on the top floor of the hospital that Parimal had said was Nahri's office. With a fountain full of lotus flowers and an elegant window seat of plush embroidered cushions and intricate wooden screens, it was a lovely place—but not the most natural one to treat a traumatized child.

"Because of what else he's saying." Subha met Zaynab's gaze, and for the first time, the doctor looked worried. That was alarming considering how calm Subha had seemed while discussing ghouls and magical plagues. "Who he's claiming he saw at the palace."

"Who's he claiming he saw?"

Subha hesitated. "He's very young and might be confused. Let's see if he tells you the same name and then we'll go from there."

That wasn't a comforting answer. Zaynab steeled herself and approached the little boy.

"Peace be upon you," she said kindly as she took a seat beside him and pulled away her veil. "I'm Zaynab. What's your name?"

He blinked at her, his eyes red-rimmed from crying. "Botros," he whispered, clutching an empty copper cup.

"Why don't we get you some more water, Botros?" she suggested, taking the cup and beckoning Aqisa. "Are you all right? Does anything hurt?"

He shivered. "I hurt my fingers trying to climb the wall, but the doctor bandaged them."

The little boy held up his hands. Zaynab blanched at the blood seeping through the linen at his fingertips. He must have literally tried to claw his way up the wall. What had scared him so badly? Who?

She cleared her throat. "Botros, can you tell me what you saw at the palace?"

"Monsters," he said haltingly. "Giant monsters of smoke and fire."

Giant monsters of smoke and fire? Over Botros's shoulder, Zaynab met Aqisa's eyes as she returned with his cup of water. The warrior woman merely shrugged. Zaynab couldn't blame her. After tonight, giant monsters of smoke and fire certainly seemed in the realm of possibility.

She handed the cup to Botros. "Can you tell me about the attackers? Did you see any soldiers?"

He took a shaky sip of water. "Yes. Daeva ones."

Daevas again. There was no denying it. It had been Kaveh who'd killed the king and unleashed the poison, and Daeva soldiers were accompanying the ifrit on the beach. This was the kind of sectarian violence that had been her father's worst fear. The catastrophe he warned was the single largest threat to Daevabad's peace: one that could lead to a bloodletting not even the Royal Guard would be able to quell and a body count to rival what happened when the Nahid Council fell during the war.

A catastrophe Zaynab would now need to prevent.

Subha touched the boy's shoulder. "Can you tell her what you saw in the library?"

Botros's eyes immediately filled with fresh tears. "I don't want to talk about it."

"I know, little one, but it's important." The doctor adjusted his blanket. "Just try. You're safe here, I promise."

He shivered again but kept speaking. "After the earthquake, the soldiers said we had to go to the library. Everyone was screaming. They were killing anyone who tried to fight or run away. And then— and then . . . when they brought us up to the library . . ." He was trembling so badly that some of the water sloshed onto his lap. "I saw him."

Zaynab steadied his hands. "Saw who?"

His eyes locked on hers, wide and terrified. "The Scourge."

She dropped his hands and sat back with a start. "You must be mistaken. The Afshin is dead. Prince Alizayd killed him, years ago."

The little boy shrank beneath his blanket. "I'm sorry, my lady. I didn't mean to upset you."

Shame swept her. By God, if Zaynab couldn't comfort a single child, how was she supposed to reassure and keep the peace over an entire section of the city? "No, I'm sorry. I didn't mean to frighten you. But what you're saying . . ."

Subha cut in. "Botros told me the other Daevas were calling him Afshin." There was quiet horror in her voice. "He said the man had bright green eyes and an arrow tattooed on his face."

"He was yelling a lot," the little boy added, shuddering again. "It was all in Divasti, but he sounded so *angry*. He was fighting with the emir and—"

"The *emir*?" Zaynab gasped. "Emir Muntadhir?"

Botros nodded. "They were tying him up when we entered the library. He was yelling at the Scourge, and then the Scourge . . . he-he conjured some sort of flying beast." He dropped his gaze. "I'm sorry. I was so scared. I started to cry, and that's when one of the Daeva scholars grabbed me."

The Afshin is here. The Afshin has Dhiru. The image of her grinning older brother warped viciously in Zaynab's mind. Muntadhir begging for his life. Muntadhir being flayed alive by the Afshin's infamous scourge . . .

"That cannot be," she whispered. "It simply cannot be. Did you see the Banu Nahida?" she asked urgently. Muntadhir had been with his wife, after all. Where the hell was Nahri, their supposed Daeva ally, during all of this?

Botros shook his head.

"Zaynab." Aqisa was standing at the window box. Her voice was intense. "Come here."

Feeling ill, Zaynab rose unsteadily to her feet and joined Aqisa at the window.

"Look at the palace."

Zaynab peered through a diamond cutout in the window's screened panel. It was hard to get her bearings straight. She'd spent a lifetime on the other side of this view: looking down upon the city from the palace's towering walls.

But eventually she found it. The palace. Her home. The ancient Daeva ziggurat standing proudly on a hill, surrounded by walls crowned with shedu statues and framed by a pair of delicate minarets and a golden dome.

She gaped. "Are the walls . . . *moving*?"

"They're rising," Aqisa whispered. "I wasn't sure at first because it's slow, but they're definitely getting taller."

"B-but that's not possible," Zaynab sputtered. "We have no magic."

Then, as if yanked by a sea of invisible hands, every Qahtani banner adorning the palace fell.

They fluttered down in a rain of ebony cloth. Narrow standards that had flown from copper poles and wider banners that draped the wall. Her family's flag had always been starkly plain: no heralds or words or personal crests. Zaydi al Qahtani had been a commoner, after all, fighting for a more just, egalitarian world.

The new banners that were unfurling amongst bursts of light and delicate wisps of golden smoke were not plain. They were beautiful, made to catch the eye. Bright blue silk and a brass-colored winged lion snarling at a rising sun.

The flag of the Nahids.

Aqisa must have recognized the banner too. "I'm going to kill her," she swore. "I will put Lubayd's khanjar through her lying heart, carve it out, and present it to her Afshin on a plate."

There was little doubt who *her* referred to. But as Zaynab stared in shock at the Nahid banners, something about them didn't seem right. "I'm not sure Nahri is behind this."

Aqisa spun on her. "What *in the name of God* is wrong with your family when it comes to that girl? Of course she's behind this! That's *her* flag flying over the palace! *Her* Afshin slaughtering people in your home!"

Everything Zaynab knew about her reluctant Daeva sister-in-law ran through her head. Nahri was a survivor, a brilliant one. She'd outmatched Ghassan and fought to protect her people with a fierce pragmatism Zaynab had always quietly admired. She was cunning, she was capable.

But she didn't strike Zaynab as a killer. "I don't think it was Nahri," she said, more stubbornly this time. "I don't think she planned this."

Aqisa had a look on her face like she was now considering putting her khanjar through Zaynab's heart instead. "Then who?"

"I don't know." Zaynab returned her gaze to the Nahid banners fluttering in the pale sky above the palace. The rest of Daevabad stretched between them, the shuttered homes and shops and schools and temples of the tens of thousands of people who called this misty magical island with its violent history home. How many of them had seen the Qahtani flags come down? Would the sight strike fear in their hearts, uncertainty about who ruled them?

They're not going to care who rules them. What did *rule* even mean right now? Their magic was gone, thousands were dead, and their city was a bloody wreck. Her people were not likely to care which flag happened to be flying today. They'd be hiding with their children or rushing to grab food and supplies before the true chaos of being stranded on a conquered island landed. They'd be grieving their dead and plotting revenge.

Daevabad comes first. It was her father's constant mantra, his warning, and for the first time in her life, Zaynab understood what it truly meant. Daevabad's *people* came first. Zaynab didn't have time to worry about her brothers. To mourn her father or pray her mother and Wajed would come back to save them.

No one was coming to save them.

"All right," she said, more to herself than anyone. "All right." Zaynab stepped back from the window, her movements precise. "I want to speak to the soldiers we have left and make sure this supposed wall protecting us from the rest of the city is secure. Any Geziris aching for revenge can funnel that energy into searching what's left of the Citadel and the buildings that fell during the earthquake for survivors. They could be hurt, and we don't have much time. Anyone who has a problem with that can answer to us."

"To *us*?" Subha repeated.

"To us," Zaynab said firmly. "Come, Doctor. I'd like to speak to your Daeva patients."

Muntadhir

This scene takes place at the end of *The Empire of Gold*. Spoilers for all three books.

G od, that's a beautiful sight," Muntadhir said admiringly as his wedding contract burst into flames.

Nahri clunked her teacup against his. "To the end of the world's worst political marriage."

"You don't think the fire is too much, do you? Considering both Kartir and that imam patient of yours already dissolved things legally?"

"I think the fire is the exact level of appropriate for my feelings on our marriage."

"I'm glad we're finally in agreement on something then." Muntadhir shifted on his cushion to ease the ache in his back. Though he felt better than he had when he was first freed from the dungeons—when his brother and Jamshid had to literally carry him out—his body was still shockingly frail, and the small movement left him winded.

Nahri noticed. "Eat," she said, pushing the bowl of semolina gruel she'd been forcing on him all morning as if he were a picky toddler. "You look like a skeleton."

"That's very unkind. I'm at least a marginally attractive ghoul by now." Muntadhir waved a thin wrist. "I believe that was the requirement for being released."

"I wish you'd stay in the hospital for a few more days. You need your rest."

"Says the woman who passed out moving mountains less than two days ago and is already back at work." Nahri glared and Muntadhir raised his hands in a gesture of peace—his ex-wife would always slightly frighten him. "I am staying with Zaynab just around the corner. She will watch over me and force food into my mouth even more rudely than you, I swear."

"Good." Nahri's gaze—if one could call it a gaze, because Muntadhir was used to seeing in it only various levels of aggression, from wanting to burn the world down to wanting to specifically burn *him* down—finally moved away from his face and back to her teacup. "Is Ali staying with the two of you?"

"I haven't seen or heard from Zaydi since he left the hospital, nor do I expect to. I believe civil chaos in which he can drive himself to exhaustion rewriting the tax code and turning the throne room into a soup kitchen is my brother's paradise."

"Mmm." Nahri made a sound that was very carefully designed to evince neither pleasure nor discontent.

Muntadhir's lips quirked into what might have been a grin if he felt like he could ever smile again. "Zaynab says the two of you were holding hands in your hospital room."

Ah, there it was. The murderous glare was back on him again. But teasing the scariest person he'd ever slept with was preferable to discussing more dangerous topics like Muntadhir's broken health, sanity, and a future he couldn't see. "She says it was sweet. That it was the first thing you did when you woke up."

"Muntadhir." Nahri's voice was ice. "As you've said . . . I move mountains now. Don't get on my bad side."

"Nahri, don't be ridiculous. All your sides are equally hostile."

She smiled, an even more alarming reaction than anger as her gaze slid past his shoulder. "Jamshid . . . ," Nahri greeted, a note of cool triumph in her voice. "Oh, good. I'm so glad you were able to meet us before Muntadhir left. He was just saying he was worried he would miss you."

Muntadhir's heart dropped. He had hoped to miss Jamshid actually. He had no idea what to say to the man he loved and whose father he had gotten killed. Slipping away like a coward seemed the lesser offense.

Nahri was already rising to her feet. "Stay out of my romantic life," she hissed in his ear. "And if you hurt my brother, I *will* drop a mountain on you."

"Yes, Banu Nahida," Muntadhir said meekly as Jamshid took her place.

Standing tall in the hospital garden, the Daeva man looked every bit the Baga Nahid, so much so that Muntadhir wondered how he had ever missed it. Jamshid had Manizheh's eyes and long nose, his profile an elegant, eerie echo of the woman who'd overseen Muntadhir's torture. Their positions had flipped so fast that Muntadhir felt as if the world had turned over. Dressed in a healer's smock stuffed with instruments and covered in potions and ash, Jamshid was the true royal here, a Nahid in the city of his ancestors. He could now mend people with the bare press of his fingers, take away their pain, their anguish. Reunite families and friends and lovers who might otherwise be forever parted.

Jamshid was indeed the very opposite of Muntadhir. The emir's instincts to fight back had not been the bravery Zaynab had shown uniting her block of Geziris and shafit, nor Ali's self-sacrifice before the marid. No, Muntadhir had struck back at his enemies with lies and deceit and revenge and absolutely nothing that brought healing to anyone.

Jamshid gestured to the spot Nahri had vacated. "May I sit?"

Muntadhir flushed, a ridiculous reaction. "Of course."

Jamshid sat, his movements effortlessly graceful. Muntadhir might have been the diplomat, the politician whose every gesture had been schooled and deliberate, but Jamshid made his way through the world in a manner that had always struck Muntadhir as almost ethereal. "How are you feeling?" he asked Muntadhir.

"Fine," Muntadhir lied. "Never better."

The old Jamshid would have rolled his eyes and called his emir out on the obvious falsehood. This new one didn't so much as blink. "And your eye?" he asked, his professional tone that of a healer only. "I can check it again before you leave."

"No," Muntadhir said quickly. The very thought of Jamshid's fingers upon his face, gently examining the injury Muntadhir had yet to come to terms with was nearly enough to crack the collected facade Muntadhir was trying to keep up. If Jamshid actually touched him, he would be undone.

"I'm sorry," Jamshid said, remorse softening his expression. "I wish Nahri and I could have done more."

"Please don't apologize. You have nothing to apologize to me about. Ever. And I'm all right." He wasn't, of course. Though Muntadhir hadn't been hopeful, part of him was still crushed when he'd learned that all Nahri could do for his injury was stave off infection and provide a clean scar; his eye was gone for good. But he'd be damned if he burdened any of the brave people he loved with his grief, so he told Jamshid another truth. "Others paid a far worse price. Just forget about me. How are you?"

Jamshid let out a breath, appearing unsteady for the first time. "Well . . . I've recently been orphaned after meeting my mother, a tyrant I'll never know and cannot mourn. I'm the newest of a trio of healers tasked with caring for the seemingly unending number of casualties of the civil war said mother caused. And all this after spending months locked up and waiting to be executed as I grieved the supposed murder of the man I loved." He stared at his hands and gazed across the hospital garden, looking dazed. "I don't know how I'm supposed to feel. I'm a Nahid—that should be a dream. I'm fairly certain that's your wedding contract burning before my eyes, which should be another dream. And yet I feel like I'm walking through a nightmare, Muntadhir. I'm so angry. I'm so . . . *lost*. I have so many questions I'll never have answers to. I have things I want to yell and beg and plead and yet—and yet . . ." He turned to face Muntadhir. There were tears glistening in his eyes. "I'm just sad. Am I allowed to be sad? Because I shouldn't be, should I? It's a good thing, yes? That we have won?"

Muntadhir reached for Jamshid's hand and gripped it tight. "You're allowed to be sad. You've been through hell and back. Anyone in your position would feel like they were trapped in a nightmare. And you're still getting your bearings after waking from that darkness, still sweating and breathing hard and realizing the nightmare is over. Let yourself mourn and let yourself be angry or happy or sad or whatever you need."

But Jamshid only sounded more exhausted when he replied, "We are to return my mother to the flames tonight, and I don't know that I can even stand at her side. I did not know it was possible to feel this kind of love and disgust at the same time."

Muntadhir hesitated. "Do you want me to come with you?"

"I would not ask that of you."

"There is nothing you cannot ask of me."

Jamshid squeezed his eyes shut, obviously trying his best not to cry. It was everything Muntadhir had not to pull him into his arms. But he was the cause of at least part of Jamshid's pain and he so desperately didn't want to make it worse.

"Not this, emir-joon," Jamshid finally said.

Muntadhir's heart broke. "I'm not sure you can call me that anymore if I'm not the emir."

"You will always be emir-joon to me." Jamshid wiped his eyes. "Nahri says you're going to stay with Zaynab in the Geziri Quarter?"

"I can't go back to the palace," Muntadhir confessed. "I haven't told my brother and sister yet, but I don't ever want to go back. There is only death for me there."

"I will not pretend to be disappointed if you never step foot in that place again." Jamshid ran his thumb over Muntadhir's knuckles. "Do you feel up for a walk?"

"A walk?"

"We need to talk, and it's a conversation I don't anticipate being very composed for. I'm new to being a Nahid, but I don't believe bawling in front of my patients would be very inspiring."

Muntadhir's mouth went dry. He knew what conversation this

was. And God forgive him, but he wasn't ready. "I'm afraid I won't make for a very attractive strolling partner on your arm right now."

Jamshid's eyes flickered to his. "You don't have to do that, you know."

"Do what?"

"Joke about things that hurt you."

Oh, but this man was going to take him apart. Muntadhir tried and failed to force a smile. "I don't know any other way."

"You're clever. I believe you can learn." Jamshid hooked his arms underneath Muntadhir's shoulders. Tears pricked in his eye at the familiar press of Jamshid's body and the gentle way in which he eased Muntadhir fully to his feet.

"You don't have to do this," Muntadhir protested weakly. "I don't deserve your help."

"Muntadhir . . ." Jamshid briefly cupped his cheek. "Please shut up. Lean on my arm with your left hand and hold your cane in your right. You can do this. I can sense the muscles in your legs. They just need some exercise."

Muntadhir blinked fiercely, determined not to cry. He would not burden Jamshid. He would *not*. "Don't tell me not to make jokes and then say something like that. How am I to respond in any way that's appropriate?"

"Less stalling, more walking." Jamshid tightened his grip, and a surge of heat rushed through Muntadhir's arm. It crested over him like a warm wave, leaving strength in its wake as though he'd had a dozen cups of coffee.

He gasped, shivering all over.

"Didn't know I could do that, did you?" Jamshid asked lightly.

"I bow before the wisdom of the all-knowing Baga Nahid." And Jamshid was right. The more they walked, the stronger Muntadhir felt. "Let me try by myself."

Jamshid released his hold and they walked, Muntadhir striving to lean less and less on the cane. If he could be done with the damn thing by the time he left for Zaynab's, all the better. He didn't want her fussing over him when he knew his sister had more important work to do.

Everyone has more important work to do. Zaynab and Ali, Jamshid and Nahri. The random merchant or laborer down the street. It was so easy to see where they fit into this new world they wanted to create, a Daevabad built on equality and justice. Not the Daevabad that Muntadhir knew, the one that ran on lies, tricks, and the lethal brand of politics his father had long ago drilled into his head. Muntadhir might have survived the war, but the role he was raised for was dead and buried.

Jamshid led him to an airy room across from the apothecary. It appeared to be under construction, with lemon-yellow tiles stacked on the floor beside unfinished cedar shelves. Sunlight streamed into the curtainless room to illuminate a desk covered in books and the pale blue scrolls Muntadhir had noticed Nahri and the other healers using to record patient notes.

"My future office," Jamshid said, waving a hand to take in the room. "Do you like it?"

Muntadhir didn't miss the eager pride in his voice. "I love it," he replied sincerely. "I am glad to see you have a place to call your own here. You deserve it. You deserve every happiness."

"I don't know about that." Jamshid stared at him. "There's something I need to tell you."

"What?"

"Do you remember the banquet your father held to welcome Alizayd back? The night he was poisoned?"

There was a nervous energy in Jamshid's voice that Muntadhir couldn't parse out. "Yes . . ."

Jamshid swallowed loudly. Spots of color had blossomed in his cheeks. "I . . . It was me, Muntadhir. I was the one who poisoned your brother."

Muntadhir rocked back. That was the last thing he expected Jamshid to say right now. The banquet at which Ali had nearly been assassinated seemed like it belonged to another decade, another world, but it didn't take much to recall the details of the lavish feast that had ended in screams as his little brother clawed at his throat. At the time, Muntadhir had been stunned that someone could have struck so close. His family had seemed on top of the world, his father's presence making them all untouchable.

How naive they'd been.

"*Why?*" he found himself asking. Such an act was not that of the Jamshid he knew. "Why would you do such a thing?"

Jamshid exhaled. "Because I was afraid. I was so afraid for you, Muntadhir, that it drove me to insanity. I was convinced Alizayd had come back to steal your position, and that your father wasn't going to protect you. So I did. And it was wrong. *I* was wrong, and because of it, I'll have the blood of those who were punished in my stead on my hands for the rest of my life."

Apprehension swept Muntadhir. There was always a price for such secrets in Daevabad. "Does anyone—"

"Know? Yes. I confessed to both Nahri and your brother. But that's not why I'm telling you now. I'm telling you because I need to clear the air between us. Because I need you to speak to me without fear of judgment." Jamshid stepped closer, his black eyes pinning Muntadhir where he stood. "Is what they say about my father's death true? Did he die in the streets like . . . like they say he did? Was it at the hands of the Daeva nobles you commanded?"

Muntadhir had known Jamshid would put this question to him and known it would end what was between them. Still he answered truthfully, "Yes."

Jamshid's expression didn't waver; it was obvious to both of them he already knew. "Why?" he asked instead, mirroring Muntadhir's response to his earlier confession about Ali.

"Because I did not see another way." Muntadhir's legs briefly threatened to give out and he clutched the edge of Jamshid's desk. "Kaveh let loose the poison that slaughtered my people. My father. My cousins. Every Geziri I knew in the palace since I was a child, from my tutors to my cupbearer. Women. *Babies.*" He choked on the word. "Do you remember the extra travelers from southern Am Gezira that I was so proud to host? The camp and market we set up in the palace garden?" Speaking of the camp aloud made Muntadhir want to throw up. There'd been no way he could have predicted its awful fate, and yet the guilt still devoured him. "I saw what was left of it before they burned the bodies, Jamshid. People trampled one another trying to escape. There were these little kids still holding sweets and I . . ." A sob finally broke through his chest. "I'm sorry."

"So it was vengeance?" Jamshid asked softly.

Muntadhir shook his head, the motion ragged. "It wasn't only vengeance. The Afshin tried to get me on their side after the attack, you know? I think he and Kaveh even meant it, but I knew Manizheh too well." A lump rose in his throat. "I knew what Daevabad had done to her because it had done the same to me. It did the same to my father. The Geziris left alive in the city would always be a threat to her. My sister free on the other side was a threat. You don't leave threats to fester."

Now it was Jamshid who looked sick. "So you didn't."

"No. I didn't. She needed the Daeva nobles on her side. I lured them to mine. She needed her muscle, her Afshin. I arranged his assassination." Muntadhir closed his eye, avoiding Jamshid's gaze. "And she needed your father. In a way she needed no one else. She needed his political skills and his presence. So when I saw the opportunity . . ."

"You took it." Jamshid's voice was thick. "Daevabad comes first."

That lay between them for a long moment; the words that had haunted their relationship from the very beginning, the creed that had shaped Muntadhir's life.

Jamshid finally spoke again. "Did you not think there might be another way to resist? That Nahri and Ali might return? That I might be alive?"

"No," Muntadhir said honestly. And he hadn't. "Maybe at first, but when she put me in that cell . . ." He broke off, struggling for words. How was he supposed to tell Jamshid what had happened to him during those endless days in the lightless cage in which centuries of other prisoners had been left to rot? That, terrified he'd be tortured into giving up information that would endanger his people, Muntadhir had tried to kill himself, smashing his skull into the wall until he was shackled so he couldn't even move his neck. That after years of neglect, he'd finally returned to prayer—only to pray for his own death and for that of his enemies. That his prayers hadn't been answered by God, but by the demons buzzing in his head, whispering his worst paranoid beliefs back to him. That Ali and Nahri had more likely been thrown to their deaths in the lake by a Manizheh who needed them gone but her Afshin still loyal. That Wajed—devoted to the king he loved like a brother and the prince he'd raised as a son—would have killed Jamshid in revenge the moment he learned what Kaveh had done. That Muntadhir hadn't fought hard enough, hadn't acted swiftly enough to save the thousands of Geziris in the palace who died an excruciating death.

Zaynab, though, Zaynab had been alive—he'd seen that truth in Manizheh's frenzy to hunt her down. Alive as well were the rest of Daevabad's citizens who had survived the initial invasion. And so Muntadhir hadn't grieved. He'd *planned*. He'd let himself be broken into the ruthless weapon his father could only have dreamed of. And by the time Darayavahoush had sprung him free, his only thought was how to best burn them all down.

How did he tell that to a man put on this earth to heal? "It was the only way I knew how to fight back, Jamshid. The only way I could protect the people I loved who were left, the city I was supposed to serve . . . was to get rid of everything that might hurt them, however viciously it needed to be done. I know . . . I know what that makes me."

"And what does it make you?"

A monster. A murderer. "My father," Muntadhir whispered.

Jamshid rose to his feet, pacing away. Muntadhir couldn't blame the other man for putting distance between them, but in the most selfish part of his heart, it made him want to weep. To throw himself at Jamshid's feet and sob apologies until his tongue could no longer speak.

"You don't have to be, you know." Muntadhir glanced up, but Jamshid wasn't looking at him, the Baga Nahid's words seemingly directed at the wall. "Not if you don't want to. Neither of us do."

There was a strange urgency in Jamshid's voice he couldn't understand. "What do you mean?"

Jamshid turned back around. "I want you to come home with me."

Muntadhir blinked rapidly. "I don't understand."

"Come *home* with me, emir-joon. You yourself said you did not wish to return to the palace. That you didn't know what life had in store for you. So make one with me."

Muntadhir felt like he'd been struck. To make a life with Jamshid was what he wanted more than anything. What he had wanted for years. And yet he couldn't take it. Not now. Not like this.

"I can't," he choked out. "I cannot ask such forgiveness from you."

Jamshid crossed the space separating them to take Muntadhir's face in his hands, and Muntadhir finally lost the battle with his tears.

"You're not the one asking for anything. *I* am." Jamshid wiped the tears from his eye. "I love you. Maybe that makes me the worst son in the world, but I still love you. I have always loved you. Come home with me."

Muntadhir's heart was racing so fast he could barely breathe. This was impossible. Impossible. "People will talk."

"I don't give a damn. We aren't the first, we aren't the last, and if I am to spend a life serving this city, I will have the man I love at my side."

Muntadhir stared at Jamshid, longing and despair tearing him apart. "I don't deserve you."

"And I don't deserve to lose *you* because of my parents' choices." He ran a hand through Muntadhir's hair. "Did you mean what you said to Nahri that night? That you loved me? That you wished you had stood up for me sooner?"

Muntadhir had pressed a hand to Jamshid's chest without even being aware of doing so. Whether to draw him closer or keep him back, he honestly could not say. "Yes," he replied hoarsely.

"Then stand up for me now. Stand up for us. At least . . ." Jamshid faltered. "At least let us try. We can try, can't we? Have we not earned that?"

There was heartfelt pleading in his wet black eyes. The eyes Muntadhir had lost himself in over a decade ago. The eyes he'd feared would never open again when Jamshid took six arrows for him without a moment's hesitation.

You're mine, Jamshid had said groggily when he'd finally woken up from the attack on the boat after months of hovering near death. Muntadhir had begged to know what in God's name he'd been thinking. Delirious, Jamshid hadn't said it was because Muntadhir was his emir or his duty.

He was simply Jamshid's, body and soul.

And his Baga Nahid had earned this. Maybe Muntadhir couldn't pick himself up for his own benefit, but for Jamshid he could try. He would try.

He pressed his brow to Jamshid's, breathing in the scent of his skin. "I will stand up for you, my love.

"Take me home."

An Alternative Epilogue to
The Empire of Gold

Spoilers for all three books.

Darayavahoush e-Afshin had led battles and masterminded a resistance movement. He had traveled the winds as no daeva had in millennia and defeated Banu Manizheh e-Nahid. He had walked away from Paradise itself, determined to earn its peace and pay penance for his crimes.

None of those feats seemed as intimidating as entering this Creator-damned tavern.

Dara stalked across the arched ceiling of the ruined mudhif. The cleverly constructed reed building must have been a sight to behold during the time of its human inhabitants. Massive, tightly packed columns of reeds had been bound and curved to create a large airy chamber. Delicate screens of woven grass served as windows, and though the eastern wall had been burned away, the mudhif seemed sound enough that humans probably could have rebuilt it—had the djinn not moved in first. In fact, right now Dara would bet on there not being a single human within three days' travel.

For this was no ordinary section of marshland along the Euphrates: this was Babili, the loose confederation of haunted ruins, criminal outposts, hidden villages, pop-up night markets, and raucous taverns that had long been considered the heart of the border between Daevastana and Am Gezira. It got loud. It got wild. And in Dara's experience, humans tended to run screaming from places whose nights were filled with the howling arguments and laughter of unseen spirits.

Dara was currently remaining his own version of an unseen spirit. He had stayed formless since arriving in Babili, preferring to sweep over the mudhif and spy on the tavern dwellers as a hot wind. More than one djinn had shuddered as he passed, and he'd accidentally knocked over a chess set with a forceful gust—the player marshaling the white pieces should thank him.

He crept to the edge of the roof now and gazed enviously upon a trio of traders laughing and gossiping over smoking clay cups as they passed around their wares on canvas mats. Dara desperately wanted that freedom for himself. He wanted the courage to walk into a tavern, a town, a village. He wanted to order a drink and make conversation without the Afshin mark on his face driving people away.

That was one of the reasons you left Daevabad, wasn't it? Dara remembered the confidence with which he had assured Nahri that he wouldn't need to hide anymore. In choosing to hunt the ifrit and serve his people, he would eventually be able to rejoin them. And in some small ways, Dara had. During his travels through the far reaches of Daevastana, he'd stopped by and aided a number of tiny settlements: chasing out the rukh nesting in the cabbage field of a farming village (for which he'd been paid handsomely—if unfortunately—in their home-brewed cabbage liquor) and killing a wolf-faced giant who been devouring shepherds in an isolated mountain town.

But there were no monsters here to hunt—well, maybe one, depending on who you asked. And Babili wasn't a small Daeva village on the edge of the world, untouched by the war he'd brought to Daevabad. In contrast, Babili hosted djinn and Daevas from all over the magical realm. It was a place people came to exchange news and ideas, to barter and ally and fight. They *did* have opinions on the war and many had been caught up in the violence. Travelers openly drank or prayed in the memory of those they'd lost and cursed the rulers who'd brought them such misery.

Dara would know—he'd been spying on the tavern and stalking its inhabitants for five days. By now he knew the Daeva bartender's name was Rudabeh, and she deserved to spend her third century with someone better than her wastrel husband. He knew the porter who carried traders' goods to the storehouse had a problem with drink and dreamed of earning enough money to return home to the Sahrayn coast. The old Agnivanshi oryx handler who stared mournfully at the stars had only enough coin for two more meals unless he was hired by a caravan, and Rudabeh's young grandson arrived early to sweep so he could flirt with the Geziri girl who brought bread from her village downriver in the morning.

They spoke of the war and the tumultuous rebuilding back in Daevabad, and Dara quietly thanked the Creator every time he heard no major new violence had broken out. Nahri was mostly praised, with more than one shafit traveler proudly claiming her as their own, and he'd overheard a salt merchant with a horrific gaping wound in his midsection advised to make haste immediately for Daevabad, where "at least the hospital is running well." A hushed group of sand sailors had spent an afternoon conspiring about how to avoid the new import taxes set by the "marid-eyed zealot" that Dara assumed was Alizayd, and a pair of Daeva pilgrims gushed about seeing the Nahid's shedu throne moved to the Temple.

Of himself, Dara heard little. Which perhaps wasn't surprising in an outpost that needed to straddle the line of tense peace between the Geziris and Daevas. Instead of long diatribes, his name evoked a grim whisper that seemed to instantly kill any mood. "Damn tragedy," he heard once. "Scourge," he heard far more often.

It might have been wise to wait a few years for emotions to calm down before Dara attempted to reenter society. A few decades. But Dara was learning the hard way he didn't have that kind of time, not if he wanted to find Vizaresh and the stolen vessels. He needed rumors to chase down: sightings of unnatural lightning and tales of humans with unusual abilities. Dara might be more powerful, but the ifrit had millennia on him when it came to hiding his tracks. It had been Vizaresh and Aeshma who had taught Dara the little he knew of the daevas' original enchantments. How to wield such magic against them was a feat he could not even imagine.

And you will have no better clues about where to find Vizaresh if all you do is pace this rooftop for another five days. Dara took a deep breath. He could always take to the wind again if things went poorly, could he not? That would not make for the most inspiring impression, but his reputation could not get much worse.

Gathering his courage, he flew down and re-formed, pulling a cloak of midnight blue over the trousers and boots a normal Daeva man might don. Resisting the urge to cover his face—it never worked—Dara summoned a flat-topped cap and placed it upon his head, tilting it to shadow his Afshin mark.

His heart was racing as he rounded the mudhif. Too late, Dara realized normal travelers carried at least some luggage—they didn't just use ancient magic to summon supplies. But he was already stepping through the entryway, and that seemed like the least of his problems.

Dara paused to do a sweep, carefully assessing the tavern for potential hostility. Its inhabitants did not seem to realize they were being assessed for potential hostility. Or that they were being assessed at all. Or were currently capable of spelling *assessed.* The majority were drunk. A man with a long, shockingly silver beard was swaying and singing to a puff of smoke cradled in his hands. Across from him, a trio of Geziri scavengers were arguing over a worn map whose markings shifted and changed, rearranging the borders of some unknown land. A larger group of both djinn and Daevas were crowded around a pair of men throwing jeweled dice that burst into vivid purple and bronze sparks when they were released, like miniature fireworks.

What this tableau amounted to was that no one even looked up at his arrival, so Dara continued, keeping his gaze down as he approached the tall counter where Rudabeh slung her drinks. It appeared to be constructed of a stolen human boat, the hull turned over and placed on two squat tree trunks to create a sturdy surface.

"I've told you a dozen times: you need to actually *scrub* the cups, not just rely on alcohol to clean them." The Daeva barkeep ambled up to Dara. "May the fires burn brightly for you, stranger. What would you like?"

Dara ran through his options. He'd been told more than once that his drink of choice—date wine—was considered a sickly sweet relic of gossiping old aunties with an alcohol problem, an opinion that thoroughly offended him, but one he was guessing didn't make date wine popular at a rough-around-the-edges watering hole on the dusty route between Daevastana and Am Gezira.

"Whatever wine you have open," he replied stiffly, trying to mask his accent. Another relic of a long-gone age.

"Easy enough." She retrieved a battered ceramic cup from a cupboard whose cheerful pink paint had seen better days and ladled out some wine from the large clay amphora half buried in the dirt floor. She met his gaze. "Where are you coming—*oh!*"

Rudabeh jerked back with a yelp and dropped the cup. Dara's hand shot out to catch it.

"Daevabad," he answered plainly. There was little point in lying. Dara could read her horrified shock for the recognition it was.

The wooden ladle trembled madly in her fist. "By the Creator," she whispered. "You're him. You're the *Afshin*."

If her yelp hadn't already attracted attention, that single word did, silencing the tavern of drunken laughter and heated business negotiations with a speed Dara wouldn't have thought possible. One of the gamblers dropped his dice, and they erupted into merry sparkles that crackled in the dead, shocked quiet.

Dara nervously cleared his throat. "Hello," he greeted awkwardly, trying to take advantage of the stunned moment before the djinn around him reached for weapons. He started to raise his hand in a wave and then immediately stopped when the motion made several people jump. "I am just passing through and mean no one any harm." He forced a smile. "That is all right?"

There was a long moment of silence, and then the Geziri trio rose wordlessly to their feet. One woman shoved the map in a bag while another threw a handful of coins at their unfinished cups.

But none drew a weapon and they settled for shooting him hate-filled glares as they stalked out of the tavern, rather than something more deadly. Dara tried not to react, hot shame washing over him. He could not judge the Geziris their enmity. Not after what Manizheh had done to their kin back in Daevabad.

What you let her do.

What you did yourself.

His face burned hotter, and flames flickered to life at his fingertips. Dara quickly tamped them down. Creator, he wanted to get drunk. Reluctantly, he put the cup down and pretended to fumble in a pocket, conjuring a few gold coins. "For your trouble, Rudabeh. Whatever anyone wants is on me."

The barkeep didn't move. "How do you know my name?"

I have been stalking you for five days. "I . . . ah . . . must have heard it in passing." Dara pushed the coins forward. "Please."

Rudabeh eyed the money a bit more ruthlessly. "Double that and I'll make sure no one bothers you."

Well, didn't someone recover from their fright quickly? "Done," Dara agreed, summoning another handful of gold.

The barkeep inclined her head in a nod of respect and then swept the money into her skirts. "The Afshin says order whatever you like," she announced, removing several glass bottles from the cabinet. One was painted with silver, and another was blue porcelain, studded with gems. "It is his gift."

She began making rounds of the tavern and Dara lowered his gaze, hunching over his cup. He took a sip of the wine, and though it left a sour aftertaste on the back of his tongue, it wasn't awful. His ears burned with gossip and he could feel every eye in the tavern boring into his back, but at least no blood had been shed. Yet.

You can do this, Dara told himself, drinking down his wine and then leaning over the counter to retrieve Rudabeh's ladle to pour himself another cup. It was like any sort of training, no? Small steps and all that. Perhaps he wouldn't be learning any useful information about mysterious ifrit sightings tonight, but he could at least finish his drink, get a brief taste of society, and leave in peace.

It wasn't as though he needed to make polite conversation with a *true* enemy.

ZAYNAB AL QAHTANI WOULD HAVE LED ANOTHER REBEL-lion for a break.

Every part of her aching, she shifted in her saddle to reduce the cramping in her lower back and nearly slipped off when her legs were too numb to properly grip the horse. With a grunt, she readjusted herself and spat out a mouthful of sand. How the sand kept getting past the cloth covering her lower face, Zaynab didn't know. She'd given up that battle at about the same time her head began pounding so terribly she could hear it in her ears.

By God, what I would do for a bath and a proper bed right now. Zaynab glanced up to see if Aqisa was faring any better. Just ahead, the warrior rode bareback on an oryx half the size of Zaynab's horse, a single hand lazily holding onto a horn. Swathed in a storm of dust from the oryx's hooves, her body rocking gracefully, her companion looked every part the mysterious supernatural warrior of human nightmares. Her scavenged robes rippled in the wind, her messy braids streaming behind her. Sunlight glimmered against the two curved swords strapped to her back, setting them alight.

Nothing about Aqisa suggested she needed a break, now or ever, and Zaynab tried not to despair. It couldn't be that much farther to Babili, could it? Aqisa had sworn they'd reach the outpost by sundown, and the sun was barely above the horizon now. Eager to impress the other woman, Zaynab had wanted to make it through at least *one* day of traveling without needing extra rest.

This is what you get for choosing adventure over your family. If Zaynab had been a good daughter, she would have gone the opposite direction and headed toward Am Gezira's western coast, where she could have boarded a ship for Ta Ntry to visit her mother and their homeland. She would have met the distant relatives she'd grown up hearing stories about and wandered the halls of their ancestral castle in Shefala. She no doubt would have greatly lightened her mother's heart and her burdens by taking up court duties and some of the work reorienting the Ayaanle's delicate relationship to a Daevabad in the flux of revolution.

But Zaynab hadn't done that. She couldn't, not yet. The prospect of returning to politics, to a world where everything from her jewelry to her hair to her smile would be carefully scrutinized, made her want to scream. A lot lately made her want to scream: Her blood-soaked nightmares of the battle in Daevabad's streets and the howls of prisoners being tortured in the dungeon where she had waited to die. The pounding of carpets and zing of blacksmith's tools that threw her back into her memories of buildings collapsing on top of families and blades slicing through flesh.

So she had fled, writing a rambling letter to her mother and praying Aqisa meant what she said back in Daevabad about wanting to travel together after they visited Bir Nabat. Ali hadn't exaggerated when he gushed about the warmth and peace of the oasis town that had once sheltered him. It was a wonderfully close-knit community that treated Zaynab more like a returning daughter than a distant princess. And Aqisa actually *was* one of its daughters, with a whole host of relatives clucking over her.

But they'd been in Bir Nabat barely a month when her friend had started itching to leave as well. "Lubayd is everywhere here," Aqisa had quietly confessed one night when she and Zaynab were alone, high upon one of the towering human tombs. It was an astonishing place, a carved rock facade as tall as a tower with a series of steps that seemed to climb to the heavens. "Our mothers were the closest of friends, and he was my shadow from the time we were born. I cannot stay here without constantly seeing him."

Zaynab remembered gazing at the other woman's expression, the harsh lines of her face softened by moonlight. It had been the first time they were alone together in weeks, and the realization filled her with a jittery uncertainty she didn't understand. "Did you love him?" she had blurted out.

Aqisa had rolled to her side to face Zaynab. "Yes. He was a brother to me." Her gray eyes were unreadable. "Why do you ask?"

Zaynab—the princess raised to hone her words as a weapon, who always had a clever response, a cutting retort, a charismatic tease—had flustered at the question. "I, well . . . you seemed like a good match."

Aqisa's gaze had stayed so inscrutable that Zaynab's entire face went hot. After an excruciatingly long moment, she had replied. "You know you don't have to think like that anymore. About matches. About love as some sort of contract."

She had been right, of course. But destined for a political marriage, Zaynab hadn't been raised with romantic notions. Love was owed to her family and people before it was owed to whatever foreign nobleman with whom she'd one day be required to navigate the most intimate of alliances. She had not let herself contemplate another option, seeing only heartache if she tried.

"I do not know another way," Zaynab confessed. "That is not the sort of life I've lived."

At that, Aqisa's lips curved into what might have been a smile. "Your life did not give you much opportunity for weapons training, either, and yet we rectified that quickly enough." She had lifted her hand then, and Zaynab remembered wondering what she would do with it. If Aqisa might touch her face, might cross the narrow space that divided them.

But instead Aqisa had let her hand fall, a hint of reluctance in her gray eyes. "Give it time, Zaynab," she said, a bit gruffly, as though she were reminding herself as well. "You'll learn."

They had left the conversation there, but the very next morning, Aqisa had started packing, and then the two of them were off. They didn't even have a proper destination in mind, just "away." Zaynab had quietly sworn to herself that she would not be a burden. Aqisa had left her home to accompany her, and Zaynab would pull her weight. She would learn to hunt and fight, to read the stars and wake early enough to brew coffee for them both.

However, right now, she wasn't sure how much longer she could even remain upright in this saddle. Mercifully, just when the ground was looming closer, Aqisa slowed her oryx.

"Babili," Aqisa announced, motioning for Zaynab to stop.

Zaynab blinked to clear the dust from her eyes and the fog from her mind. The sun had finally set and the bare crimson glow that remained did little to illuminate the spread of dark marshes and glistening water. It made for a forbidding sight, and Zaynab didn't spot anything that looked like a settlement, only spiky trees and bushes jutting into the sky like grasping claws.

"That's a town?" Zaynab rasped.

Aqisa handed over her still-full water canteen. "Drink. And no, not quite. Babili isn't a town. Think of it more as a place where a bunch of djinn and Daevas lay claim to various ruins and fight over the right to ferry travelers across the river—or depending on the mood, rob them."

Zaynab's mouth went dry again. "And this is where you wish to rest?"

"More places are like Babili than Bir Nabat, princess. Might as well get used to it. There's a tavern ahead, I remember. We can get something to eat, pray maghrib, and catch up on any news that might concern us."

"Can we make sure our arrival isn't part of that news?" Zaynab pulled off her grimy turban and shook it out.

"We can try." Aqisa was watching her, but when their eyes caught, the warrior quickly glanced away. "You're rather memorable."

Zaynab's fingers fumbled on the turban. *I'm rather what?* But Aqisa had already dismounted and started walking toward a hulking reed structure on the riverbank.

"Keep that zulfiqar close," Aqisa called over her shoulder. "This is a 'stab first, ask questions later' sort of place."

"You bring me to all the best places," Zaynab muttered, but did as she was told, pressing the hilt of her zulfiqar. The handle was cold. She and Ali had crammed in as many lessons as possible before her departure, but Zaynab had yet to successfully summon flames from their family's blade. She followed Aqisa, her sandals crunching on the gritty dirt and crushed grass. The air smelled of murky water and a hint of smoke.

"Odd," Aqisa mused as they headed for the tavern. "I remember it being livelier. Louder."

A trio of djinn separated from the shadows of the tavern, leading oryxes as though they meant to depart. Upon spotting Aqisa, one of the men broke off in their direction. Zaynab stilled. Was this a "stab first" situation?

But the man only touched his heart and brow in polite greeting. "Peace be upon you, sisters." His Djinnistani was rough, peppered with a northern Geziri accent similar to Aqisa's. "Might I suggest you visit elsewhere tonight? The company in this tavern leaves much to be desired."

Aqisa frowned. "What do you mean?"

The man let out a disgusted sound. "The Scourge is here. Guess he finally decided to crawl out from whatever foul pit he has been hiding in."

"The *Scourge*?" Zaynab repeated in disbelief. "Surely you don't mean—"

"The Afshin is here?" Aqisa asked. Her voice was low and lethal. "That Scourge? You're certain?"

"I wish I was not. He's inside having a drink like he doesn't have the blood of thousands on his hands." The other djinn shook his head, looking furious. "There is no justice in this world."

Aqisa drew the swords from her back in a single motion. "There can be."

Zaynab was still trying to wrap her head around the fact that Darayavahoush e-Afshin—the enemy she'd battled, the world's most notorious-if-not-entirely-fugitive former general—was in the forbidding, crumbling tavern just ahead of them. Too late she registered the intent in Aqisa's words.

"Aqisa, wait—"

But Aqisa was not waiting. She charged for the tavern and ripped away the faded curtain someone had hung in a halfhearted effort at a door. She stormed inside, Zaynab chasing after her.

The inside of the tavern was dim, but warm with a fire crackling merrily in a corner of the room exposed to the sky. Oil lamps burned at only a handful of tables, and "tables" might have been an exaggeration, for they were little more than a collection of turned-over crates, a cracked metal drum, and the emptied casks of some undoubtedly forbidden drink. The light wasn't enough to chase away the encroaching night, but it was enough to reveal a whole number of things Zaynab had never seen before. A man was having tea with a large tortoise who had candles set in its shell, while another pair of djinn were involved in what looked like a board game—a board game played with animated pieces of serrated teeth. Zaynab walked forward only to recoil: she'd stepped on the soft hand of a snoring man curled up in a pile of—of all things—shoes.

But however crowded the tavern was, Zaynab didn't miss that none of that activity touched the side of the room where a very large man sat alone, hunched over a cup with his back to the door. He was dressed simply in a dark blue coat and Daeva trousers, smoke curling out from under a woolen cap doing a poor job of containing his black hair. She saw no weapons. Not that it mattered.

You didn't need a weapon when you were one.

"Scourge," Aqisa hissed through her teeth. "Having a pleasant evening?"

Darayavahoush stiffened and then glanced back. Zaynab tensed. She'd seen the Afshin as a vengeful interloper in her father's court and as Manizheh's murderous general. She'd seen him as a broken slave, trying to cut his own throat, and as a chastened, uncomfortable guest at Nahri's bedside.

This Afshin just looked tired. Tired in a way that made Zaynab think he wasn't even surprised to see them, as if he'd already resigned himself to worse.

Darayavahoush drank back the rest of his cup and then set it down with a thud. "I *was*." He reached for the handle of a ladle sticking out of a half-buried clay amphora. "Care for a drink? It might help your disposition."

"The only thing I care for is putting a sword through your throat."

Now the tavern *did* react, the angry, armed Geziri warrior perhaps enough to pull even the most addled of minds from their stupor. The game pieces clashed against one another, snarling as their players backed away, and the man with the tortoise hefted the massive pet to his chest, clutching the shell protectively.

An older Daeva woman in a patchwork dress stepped out from behind the bar, seizing the ladle from the Afshin's hand. "Out. The both of you."

Zaynab moved for Aqisa and grabbed her friend's arm. "Come on." But Aqisa stood her ground, immovable as a rock.

Darayavahoush stayed put as well. "I mean you no harm," he said carefully. "I promise. I am merely . . ."—his bright eyes flickered away from Aqisa and locked on Zaynab, alarm blossoming through them—"Princess *Zaynab*?"

He said the words loud enough to carry, and Zaynab felt every head in the tavern swivel to her.

"Did I say leave?" The barkeep's expression changed so swiftly that she might have been replaced by another woman entirely. She quickly refilled Darayavahoush's cup and then pulled two more from a hidden cabinet with a beaming smile. "Stay! I insist."

Zaynab didn't respond. She was suddenly having trouble looking away from Darayavahoush's emerald gaze. How she could remember those burning eyes meeting hers from across the hospital as she surrendered herself. The long walk that had followed would haunt her for the rest of her life. A believer, Zaynab had held her head high and repeated the declaration of faith in her mind. She had expected to be executed in front of her people, a martyr in Daevabad's final fall.

But she hadn't died. Not there in the streets, nor in the dungeons. Neither had Darayavahoush. And here they were now.

He cautiously gestured to the cushions on his right. "Sit," he offered softly. "Please. We are at peace now, no?"

Aqisa hadn't lowered her swords. "I just buried my best friend's ashes." Her voice was trembling in a way Zaynab had never heard. "One of your ifrit put an axe through his back. Your 'peace' doesn't make him any less dead."

Darayavahoush flinched, and Zaynab stepped in. Her shock at

running into the Afshin was fading, replaced by a new determination to find out what the hell he was doing out here.

To say Darayavahoush had left Daevabad under contested circumstances would be an understatement. Depending on whom you asked, the Afshin was a monster who had fled justice or he was a tragic hero who had chosen a path of redemption. Zaynab knew what side of the curve she fell on. She had lost her father and dozens of loved ones in the attack on the palace and had seen with her own eyes the horror of the ruined Citadel. And that was before he'd carved a path of death through the infirmary. Before Manizheh's final assault to capture her, a carnage Zaynab would never unsee. Multifamily homes reduced to brick dust and bone. The academy in the Ayaanle district blown apart with its students inside. And while part of her could accept that he hadn't been entirely responsible for the last attack—he'd been enslaved by Manizheh—she could not help but wonder how many lives would have been saved if he'd turned on the Banu Nahida sooner.

But right now her personal feelings didn't matter. Darayavahoush hadn't been seen since he ran away, and Zaynab wasn't the type to turn down an opportunity to glean some useful intelligence about her family's ancestral enemy. She leaned closer to Aqisa. Zaynab's Geziriyya wasn't good, but she could handle a number of words and a few practiced phrases.

"*Information*," she whispered in their people's tongue. "For back home. Yes?"

Aqisa gave her a scalding glare but then sat down, keeping her weapons in her lap.

Zaynab sat as well and unleashed her most gracious smile on the Daeva barkeep. "Might I trouble you for coffee? My companion and I do not favor wine."

The woman bowed low. "Right away, Your Highness."

Darayavahoush had returned his attention to his wine. "What was his name?" he asked, not looking up from his cup. "Your friend who was killed by the ifrit."

Zaynab half expected Aqisa to stab him for the question. But instead Aqisa answered, gripping her swords so hard that her knuckles had paled. "Lubayd."

"Lubayd," Darayavahoush repeated. "I am sorry for your loss. Truly."

"Fuck you." But Aqisa sheathed one of the swords, and Zaynab decided to take it as a positive sign.

After another tense moment, Darayavahoush spoke again. "I must say . . . a princess of Daevabad is perhaps the last person I'd expect to see in a Babili tavern. What are you doing traveling into Daevastana?"

There was a hint of suspicion in his voice. Zaynab couldn't blame him. She probably looked mad, poorly disguised in this backwater place with only Aqisa for company. No, she probably looked like a spy, intent on nefarious deeds in his homeland.

"I needed to get away," Zaynab replied, seeing less damage in the truth than in a sarcastic response. "Somewhere fresh, with fewer memories, if you know what I mean."

"More than I would like to," he murmured.

The barkeep returned with two steaming cups. "On the house," she insisted. "Maybe you'll tell your brother to keep us in mind when it comes to setting new caravan fees, yes? We hear he's taking over as finance minister."

Darayavahoush scowled into his drink. Zaynab tried to give the other woman an enthusiastic nod. "I . . . I'll do that," she said, taking a sip of her coffee. It was wondrously bitter, the way Zaynab liked it, though she could not help but wonder if breaking the prohibition against alcohol might make this entire encounter less awkward.

The barkeep left again.

"Finance minister?" the Afshin repeated. "Is accounting how he's keeping himself occupied now?"

Aqisa snorted. "I'm sure he and Nahri are finding plenty of other ways to—"

Zaynab stomped on her foot. "Yes, finance minister. And the Nahids are doing well," she added, changing the subject to one she suspected he'd be more interested in. "They've been *busy*, incredibly so. But Nahri seems happy. She, Subha, and Jamshid have taken on their first class of medical students, which they were all quite excited about. And she has her own home, a little house near the hospital that she's been fixing up with her grandfather."

Darayavahoush started at that. "Nahri found her grandfather?" When Zaynab nodded, emotion swept his eyes. "The Creator be praised. I am . . . glad to hear that. All of it. She deserves every happiness. Thank you."

Zaynab merely nodded. "You're welcome."

He returned his gaze to his drink. "I owe you an apology. You were correct in the forest that night about Banu Manizheh, and I wish I had taken your advice sooner rather than later. I . . ." He seemed to fumble. "I will carry the price of that delay for the rest of my life."

"As you should," Aqisa muttered.

Zaynab hesitated. "People say you left Daevabad to make amends. To go after the ifrit. Is that true?"

Darayavahoush grimaced, swaying in his seat as he topped off his wine. "I am trying. It would be easier if my quarry did not have several millennia of knowledge on me when it comes to hiding, my own magic, and being general abominations."

"So no luck?"

The Afshin slammed his cup down and Zaynab noticed several tavern patrons jump. "I have lost every lead. I chased after Vizaresh by following what I could sense of his magic, but it is like following a trail that goes cold after a day, using eyes I cannot fully open."

Zaynab shivered. "Vizaresh is the one who stole the vessels from the Temple, correct?"

"Yes." Darayavahoush sounded haunted. "When I think of them being given over to human masters, masters who will control their every move like Manizheh did to me . . ." He squeezed his eyes shut. "And all I can do is blow around in the wind, hoping one day I finally run into him."

"I suppose actually *hunting* them is a new vocation for us. Any djinn or Daeva with sense runs the other way." Zaynab took another sip of her coffee. "Do you know how to contact any of the peris or marid? Perhaps they've seen him."

Darayavahoush scowled again. "My efforts to summon a marid resulted in a tidal wave being sent after me. And the peris have vanished. I suspect they are still nursing their wounds after Nahri humiliated them."

"Can you not set fire to their realms and slaughter their inhabitants until they respond?" Aqisa asked. "I thought that was how you typically got things done."

"I am trying to find less murderous ways to achieve my goals." Darayavahoush waved a hand around the tavern. "It is why I came here. I thought perhaps I could ask around trading posts to discover if people had seen any strange magic in their travels."

Zaynab glanced at the man still cradling his tortoise—which had turned a vivid cobalt blue. "I think it takes a lot for djinn to consider magic 'strange.'" But an idea struck her. "Though if you're after vessels and the ifrit enslaving them . . . shouldn't it be *humans* you're asking about magic? After all, if Vizaresh releases the vessels to human masters, they're hardly discreet. Go find out which put-upon servants suddenly replaced their kings and who's got a new smile that makes people fall head over heels in love with them."

Darayavahoush stilled. "That . . . is not a terrible idea." His face fell. "But I cannot manifest myself before humans, let alone speak to them. I would have no way of directing the conversations I need."

Ah. "Then I suppose it's a pity you've entirely alienated the shafit," Zaynab could not help but point out. "One could probably help you."

"You don't need to be shafit to appear before a human," Aqisa said. Her voice was suddenly less sarcastic.

Zaynab glanced at her in surprise. "I know, but it's still an incredibly rare talent, is it not? I don't know anyone who can do it."

"I certainly cannot." The Afshin attempted to retrieve more wine and then made a sour face when the ladle came up empty. "And now the wine is gone. Alas, I am going to take this as a sign to end my conversation with you two on this slightly less barbed note than how we began." He rose to his feet, far less gracefully than Zaynab remembered him and attempted a bow. "Good luck on your travels."

Zaynab watched as he staggered out of the tavern. She felt a strange duty to try and stop him, but to what avail? He could turn into the wind. With a sigh, she returned to her coffee.

"I can appear before humans," Aqisa said quietly.

Zaynab choked on the hot liquid. "You can do *what*?"

"Appear before humans. Speak to them. Not for long, but . . ." Aqisa cleared her throat. "Enough. Enough for short conversations."

Zaynab's mind whirled. "I had no idea." She was strangely stung. Not that she had any right to be. Aqisa didn't owe her any secrets. It's not as though they were . . . "How?" she asked, swiftly redirecting her thoughts.

Aqisa shook her head. "It's not a thing I can teach. You need a certain nearness to the human world from birth. The older one gets, the more they are exposed to true magic . . . the opportunity is gone." She paused and when she spoke again, her words seemed carefully chosen. "A centuries-old Daeva who turns into fire and flies on the wind is never going to be able to talk to a human."

"Aqisa . . . ," Zaynab said softly. "What are you suggesting?"

Aqisa was trembling. "I swore, Zaynab. I swore to avenge Lubayd. He would do it for me."

Zaynab hesitated and then took one of Aqisa's hands in hers. Her palm was rough and warm. "You heard what Darayavahoush said. His quest is nearly impossible. You hate each other. And the ifrit are dangerous. Are you sure—*truly* sure—you want to pursue this?"

"No. But not because I'm afraid of the ifrit or that abominable man." Aqisa gazed down at their entwined fingers. "It's . . . it's just that—well, it's you."

"*Me?*"

"You." Aqisa met her eyes. They were anguished, the warrior woman looking more vulnerable than Zaynab had ever seen her. "I do not want to leave your side. But I cannot ask you to follow me into this."

Zaynab stared at her. At the woman who had scared the hell out of her when they first met and the woman she'd thought might genuinely be insane when she brought training blades into Zaynab's soft, sumptuous royal apartment, dumped them on the bed, and insisted the princess who spent her life surrounded by armed guards needed to learn how to protect herself. The woman whose confidence in Zaynab hadn't seemed to waver once, not even when Zaynab herself had doubted her ability to rule, her ability to hold her people together and survive Manizheh's crushing war.

The woman who made her think there might just be more to life than politics and family duty. That maybe, just maybe, Zaynab could explore. She could get lost.

She could learn to fall in love.

Zaynab stood up, dropping some coins next to her coffee cup. She pulled Aqisa to her feet. "Come. We have an Afshin to catch up to."

"Zaynab—"

Zaynab hushed her, briefly cupping her hand around the other woman's cheek. "Aqisa, I owe you my life and my freedom. You're not asking me anything."

The sky was now completely black and studded with stars, the sun's crimson warmth gone from the horizon and the chilly air. There didn't appear to be anyone outside the tavern, and the only sound was a breeze rustling through the marshes. Zaynab searched the sky, but it was empty save a few wispy clouds reflecting the moonlight.

Was one of them Darayavahoush? Is that how this worked? "Afshin!" Zaynab cried, shouting into the sky. "*AFSHIN—*"

There was a rustling behind the tavern, and then a visibly annoyed Darayavahoush emerged from the shadows, his hands over his ears. "Please stop that."

Zaynab frowned. "What were you doing in the bushes?"

He gave her an incredulous look. "May I give you a lesson in visiting taverns? Do not ask where people go when they drink too much." She flushed, glad for the darkness, and the Afshin continued, "More important, why are you following me and shrieking my name to the sky?"

Zaynab drew herself up, adjusting her filthy traveling clothes into the best approximation of royal imperiousness she could. "We are joining you on the hunt for the ifrit," she declared.

Darayavahoush stared at her for a long, inscrutable moment.

"No." Then he turned and walked away.

Zaynab raced to catch up. "What do you mean, no?"

"Does the word *no* confuse you, Your Highness? I am certain you did not hear it a lot growing up. But to clarify, no, you are not coming with me. We are not in Daevabad, and even if we were, I do not take orders from Qahtanis."

"Give it another generation," Aqisa murmured. "They'll be Nahids."

Darayavahoush whirled on her. "You know what—"

Zaynab stepped between them. "She can speak to humans."

He glared back. "You are lying."

"I'm not." Zaynab stayed where she was, keeping herself between the two warriors, a situation she suspected she was about to find herself in very frequently. "She's lived alongside them her entire life."

"There are benefits when you don't view human blood as a contaminant," Aqisa said archly. "I can appear before them. Speak to them. All the things you cannot do."

"You yourself said you had no leads," Zaynab persisted before Darayavahoush could argue. "You want information? You want to be able to hunt down creatures with a thousand years of knowledge on you? Then you need help and a plan that isn't hoping you'll one day crash into Vizaresh while pretending to be a breeze."

He crossed his arms over his chest. "You despise me," he said flatly. "Now you want to go hunting together? We would murder one another in a week."

"We won't," Zaynab insisted. "Do you have any idea how many frightened, traumatized people I kept together during Manizheh's war? I can deal with you. Besides, we all want the same thing: the vessels returned."

"And Vizaresh dead," Aqisa added vehemently. "That was the

ifrit who killed my friend. If it means avenging him, I can put up with even you."

Darayavahoush pressed his lips in a grim line. "This is madness." He returned his attention to Zaynab. "If your brothers found out I took you with me . . ."

"I do not need my *brothers'* permission to do anything," Zaynab snapped. "You said you wanted to make amends, Afshin, didn't you? Let us help you find Vizaresh. Unless of course that was all just a ruse to escape Daevabad."

He drew up so fast that Zaynab stepped back. His eyes flashed, fire swirling into the green and making her wonder if perhaps she should have reconsidered royal proclamations before the man who'd gone to war twice in hopes of overturning her family.

But he didn't draw a conjured bow or disappear in a plume of smoke. Instead, he spoke a single word: "Dara."

"What?" Zaynab asked, baffled.

"If we are to spend every waking moment in one another's company hunting for monsters—and then likely being killed by them—I don't wish to be reminded of that title. *Or* the other title," he said before Aqisa could open her mouth. "You will call me Dara. And this is only the one time, understand?" he insisted, wagging a finger. "We find Vizaresh and then we go our separate ways."

"Dara it is," Zaynab agreed magnanimously. She glanced at Aqisa. "Does that work for you?"

Aqisa scowled. "I won't call you Afshin. Or Scourge."

"Good." Zaynab reached out to take Aqisa's hand again and gave it a squeeze, a thrill running through her. "Then let's go find some humans."

Nahri

This scene takes place about a year and a half after *The Empire of Gold*. Spoilers for all three books.

Finished with her day, Nahri pushed back from the desk.

"And check on Yusef, the surgical patient from this morning. I extracted the wing fragments from his back, but they were close enough to the spine that I want to take extra care infection doesn't set in. Have one of the students examine his bandages and apply an anti-scaling solution." She handed the patient's scroll to Jamshid. "That should be it."

Across from her, Jamshid, his arms already piled with other such scrolls, looked skeptical. "Are you sure that's something a student can do?"

"Jamshid, our students have been here nearly a year. Yes, I think them all capable of looking underneath a bandage and spraying an otherwise harmless solution." Nahri rose to her feet. The late afternoon sun streamed through the wooden screens covering the window, the air in her office sweet and fragrant with the rich earthy aroma of the papyrus and Egyptian water lilies growing in the fountain. She retrieved a small velvet bag from one of the desk drawers. "Let them help you when I'm not working. And don't you dare bother Subha. It's her day off."

Jamshid shot her a wounded look. "I would never bother Subha.

You, however, are family, and thus I feel far more comfortable accusing you of abandoning me with the children. Students. Whatever."

"You know many of those 'children' are older than you, right?" Nahri came around the desk and stood on her toes to kiss his forehead. "Learn to delegate, brother. It's a critical part of being a doctor."

Jamshid made a noncommittal grunt. "What's that?" he asked, gesturing to her bag.

"A gift."

"A gift?" He tilted his head, a little mirth stealing into his expression. "One that can't be given later? In front of everyone else?"

"One that is very much not your business," she replied tartly. "Now . . . anything else *hospital*-related before I leave?"

Jamshid eyed the bag a moment longer with a trace of amused curiosity. "No. But you'll be back in time for the party?"

"Along with the unsuspecting guest of honor." Nahri wrapped a hand-knit shawl a patient had given her around her shoulders and headed for the door.

The library next to her office was mostly empty this afternoon, with only a few students buried in books. Nahri nodded to the ones who noticed her but didn't interrupt—she knew well the dazed look of people who'd been studying for so long they would have struggled to recognize their own faces. She made her way to Mishmish, who was in his nest on the sun-drenched balcony, a nest he'd made by shredding a priceless antique rug that had been on loan from the Temple.

Nahri knelt and buried her hands in her shedu's thick mane, scratching behind his ears. "Hello, my brave little rainbow kitty," she crooned in Arabic, keeping her voice low to maintain a semblance of dignity in front of her students. Mishmish purred in response, loud enough to make the floor vibrate. He stretched out his massive wings and rolled so she could rub his belly. Nahri obliged for a moment, then said, "Want to go for a ride?"

NAHRI SUSPECTED SHE WOULD ALWAYS HAVE THE SOUL OF A city dweller. From Cairo's constant hustle to wandering the seemingly never-ending streets of Daevabad, Nahri delighted in the ceaseless energy of her urban homes. There was always someone new to meet or someplace new to discover. No longer Ghassan's prisoner, Nahri had thrown herself into exploring the city she had shoved an ice dagger into her heart to save, and it had repaid her with more joy than she could have imagined. She took Ali and Fiza to iftars held in the crowded apartments of her grandfather's garrulous community of Egyptian shafit to experience the food and traditions of her childhood, and she went with Subha for puja at her temple, meeting a people and faith she had barely known existed. On rare evenings off, she let Jamshid and Muntadhir drag her to the homes of nobles in various tribal quarters for recitals and poetry readings.

That didn't mean, however, that she didn't enjoy the occasional escape to the wilderness beyond Daevabad's walls.

Mishmish soared over the emerald expanse of mountains. Sitting on his back, Nahri closed her eyes, enjoying the fresh spring air and the sound of nothing but wind. Although several sections of the city's brass walls had been opened up, the parks and homes being built outside still clung close to Daevabad proper. The majority of djinn and Daevas were wary of the dripping forests and overgrown ruins that covered the former island—to say nothing of the mysterious new river that divided them from the mist-shrouded marid lake. By the time Nahri had urged her shedu to land in a patch of deep woods, any sign of the city was long gone. Ahead, the bare lines of a sandy path glowed faintly as it wound through the dark trees.

They walked, the sound of their padding footsteps melding with the twittering birds. Nahri wasn't sure what Daevabad's woods had looked like before she'd taken Suleiman's ring into her heart and rearranged the landscape, but between the curious mix of trees—like frost-limned pines sharing space with banana palms—and bizarre animals, such as tiny winged serpents and jewel-teethed mongooses, everything about this wilderness felt steeped in magic. Years ago, that might have alarmed her. Now it was like walking through her own soul. The vines parted to let her pass, and even the shyest of smoky-eyed gazelles didn't dart away. Her people might be forming a political system where everyone was equal, but it seemed the island itself remained a traditionalist, holding tight to its Nahid.

That connection faded as she got closer to the river. Though she could hear the crashing of rapids in the distance, this stretch looked calm today. But Nahri knew that didn't mean much: Ali's river was notoriously tumultuous, its currents changing direction from day to day. The first time she had visited, this very spot had hosted an enormous waterspout that had lifted from the surface to spin in a neat loop. Porpoises the color of dawn with spiraling horns had been leaping playfully through the loop while Ali pulled at his beard and fretted aloud over whether he was supposed to interfere. Apparently Sobek had told him that newborn rivers had their own wild youths to get through—advice that had left even Nahri lost for words.

But there was no gravity-defying enchantment now. Beyond a tangle of grasses—papyrus and cattails, lily pads and golden lotus—the river's surface was placid. Ali was nowhere to be seen, but his sandals and a neatly folded shirt had been left on a rock near a circle of scattered bricks. As Nahri passed by, she spotted the remains of a fire alongside the flint Ali must have used to light it. Her stomach turned at the sight. She hated that he needed such a thing.

Mishmish broke away from her side to nose through Ali's belongings.

"I don't think he's brought any fruit for you today, Mishmishi. We're unexpected guests." Nahri kicked off her shoes, slipped off her shawl and bag, and then approached the water. "Alizayd al Qahtani, you are far less sly than you think," she called across the silent river. "You can't get out of today by hiding here."

There was no response. Ali might have been floating in the next bend or he could be swimming in an ocean on the other side of the world. But Nahri had learned he seemed to sense if she was in the river, so she took a step into the water, pushing through the reeds. It shivered at her touch, rippling out from her ankles. The water was so clear she could look straight down to the shimmering pebbles and mossy rocks that made up the bottom. Here and there she saw one of Tiamat's glittering scales, dragged up from the lake. Ali threw them into the bushes when he spotted them. "Tiamat is not a river guardian," he'd say stubbornly, sounding like Sobek. "This place is not hers."

No, it was his, in the same way Daevabad was Nahri's. She and Ali had tried to uncover the source of his river several times, reaching out with their magic as they hiked and explored the boundaries of their altered world to little avail. They would always find themselves returned to the same spot in the woods where they had started, as though creation itself were reminding them of the limits of their knowledge.

Nahri waded a bit deeper, startling a school of tiny silver fish with blue striped fins. She stopped when the river was at her knees and lifted her face to the sunshine filtering through the trees, enjoying the rare peace. Nahri had once loved swimming, no matter how unladylike and, later, how un-*Daeva*-like such a hobby might be. She had loved the feeling of weightlessness that accompanied floating, the way everything went silent under the surface. During her worst years in Daevabad, she used to lock herself in the hammam to weep and float in the bath alone, closing her eyes and imagining she was elsewhere.

But swimming was a love Qandisha had stolen from her when she tried to drown Nahri in the Nile. Nahri couldn't even submerge her head in a tub anymore, let alone consider bathing in a river going through a "wild youth." Her new fear of water was mortifying, a weakness she despised and couldn't seem to get past.

And yet . . . the water was so calm today, the current barely more than a caress. Nahri was the Banu Nahida, for Creator's sake. She'd taken on peris, ifrit, and her murderous aunt. Surely she could get over this.

She took another step and then another, until the water was at her knees. Her waist. Nahri traced patterns over the surface in an effort to stay calm. The bottom was slippery and uneven, and it was a struggle to keep her footing steady. She stopped for a moment to take a deep breath, distracting herself with the rich smell of silty air and the sweet birdsong from the nearby woods. This wasn't so bad.

She kept going, the water soaking through her dress and then up and over her chest. It lapped at her shoulders . . . and then it was suddenly too much. Nahri quickly stepped back—too quickly. She disturbed a few of the rocks making up the riverbed, and a muscular, serpentine body shot past her legs, lashing her ankles.

It was only a water snake. She knew it; Nahri could *see* it swimming away. But memories were already rushing over her. Their boat burning as it sank and the Nile closing over her head. The dead fingers of ghouls dragging her down and the burning in her lungs as she fought for just one more breath, one more moment before the darkness closed in.

Nahri flailed backward, desperate to get out of the water. She slipped. The river's surface rushed up to claim her . . .

A pair of arms caught her. "You're all right," Ali said softly.

She squeezed her eyes against the prick of tears, embarrassed and furious. "I'm a coward."

"You're not a coward. You're the bravest person I know." Ali stroked back the hair from her face, letting Nahri rest against his chest. "Just breathe."

His voice was a soothing murmur, mingling with the sound of the current, and so cradled in his arms, Nahri tried to do just that, breathing steadily in and out. She was safe. There were no ifrit, no ghouls. No soldiers to dodge or wars to fight.

Eventually her heart stopped racing. Ali wordlessly eased her back to her feet, keeping one hand on her waist as she found her footing. "Better?" he asked.

She turned to face him and was promptly lost for any coherent response. Ali had bent to remain eye level with her, the river coursing over his shoulders like a liquid cape. The water's gleam reflected in his eyes, a silvery haze stealing over the black-dappled gold. Nahri had long ago gotten used to his changed appearance, but in his river, Ali was downright otherworldly, and there was no getting accustomed to it. Mist roiled off his frame, curling to surround them, and she was suddenly very aware of the press of his hands through her wet dress. He was close, so close she could have tasted the beads of water on his lips, wrapped her legs around his waist, and then . . .

Suleiman's eye, this is what led to a bunch of your ancestors drowning in the Nile after an encounter with Sobek.

Nahri shivered, trying to shake off the fog of desire that had replaced her panic. Neither was helpful, and she had yet to inform Ali how alluring he was in his river. He would probably do something annoying and overly honorable, like insist again Mishmish was not a proper chaperone.

Or you could let yourself have him. But Nahri knew that Ali didn't want a simple tryst in the water. He wanted more, so much more. And there were times Nahri thought she did too—if fantasizing about having someone to come home to, someone who would make her bad tea and read books in bed on a lazy day, didn't send her into a spiral envisioning all the dreadful ways she could lose just that. Nahri still cajoled her grandfather into a Nahid examination once a month, half convinced the very act of meeting her had shortened his lifespan. What she might dare to build with Ali . . . it seemed too fragile to hope for, let alone speak aloud.

But you don't need to speak it aloud. Not today. That was the point of the velvet bag waiting back at the riverbank. It was to be a small step, a stand-in for the words her still-healing heart would not yet let her say.

"Better," she finally replied, trying to bring a casual smile to her face. "How long have you been spying on me?"

Ali looked like he knew she was lying, but he didn't press it. "No spying, I swear. I was in the lake, and I felt you enter the water, but I was having a hard time pulling free of the currents. Then . . . there was sort of a jolt—your distress, I guess? And suddenly I was here." He shook his head. "I will never understand marid magic. I'm probably just lucky thinking of you didn't send me straight to the Nile."

"I'm sure Sobek would have been thrilled."

He rolled his eyes. "Sobek is the reason I was in the lake to begin with. He says if I spend more time with my 'kin,' I'll be able to better control my abilities."

"And how's that going?"

Ali's mouth twisted into an abashed grin. "I think a frog tried to break into my mind. There were all these memories of hopping around and eating flies . . ." He made a gagging sound. "Let's just say I didn't mind being summoned to your side."

Nahri burst into laughter. "Do you think the council members you're forced to abandon once a week to 'maintain our relationship with the marid' have any idea it involves getting in the mind of a frog?"

"I hope to God not. They'd probably take my ideas less seriously." His eyes twinkled. "Are you up to walking back to shore?"

With the heady river magic still swirling around them, Nahri was far more interested in re-creating the situation that had led to him shirtless beneath her back in Ta Ntry—minus the bloody surgery and marid ultimatum. But Ali had made himself clear back then how he felt about a physical relationship outside marriage and Nahri was trying to respect it. Mostly.

"Sure," she said, forcing a false cheer into her voice.

They made their way back to the riverbank. Nahri was trying extremely hard not to look at him—she had not missed that Ali wasn't wearing the reptilian armor that typically covered his torso—but by the time they were pushing through the reeds, he was shivering so badly, she could not help but notice.

"Cold?" she asked as he dashed for his shirt.

"Always," he replied, pulling it over his head. "Ever since . . . well, you know."

Nahri's gaze again fell upon the flint he'd used to light a fire, and her heart twisted. "I don't understand how you don't hate the marid for what they took from you."

"Because I am tired of hate, and I understand why they did it. Besides . . ." He scratched Mishmish behind his ears and then returned to her side. "I cannot deny the abilities the marid granted me in return don't carry their own blessings."

Nahri wasn't as forgiving, but today wasn't the day to make Ali dwell on his sacrifice. Instead she handed over her shawl. "Take it . . . no, *take* it," she insisted, wrapping the garment around his shoulders before he could argue. "Stop being stubborn. I don't need it, and we have a long walk back to Daevabad. Surely you know I've been sent to fetch you."

Alarm flashed in his golden eyes. "Fetch me?"

"Did you really think we wouldn't find out?"

"Yes." Ali groaned. "I begged Dhiru to keep it to himself. He promised."

"Oh, Ali, have you met your brother? He lied." Nahri grinned. "Happy quarter century, my friend." When Ali merely looked more crestfallen, she lightly swatted his arm. "What is wrong with you? Don't tell me you wanted to spend your birthday swapping minds with a fly-eating frog instead of celebrating with friends?"

Ali shuddered. "I'm not a birthday person. I don't like everyone making a fuss over me; it's so very awkward and undeserved. *Especially* for my quarter century. You know the kind of jokes people make about marriage and—oh my God." Horror lit his expression. "You said *fetch* me. Muntadhir is throwing a party, isn't he?"

"He's decorating my house as we speak. He's been planning it for weeks, and you will act surprised and happy and attempt to enjoy yourself." When Ali appeared even more stricken, Nahri reached out to take his face in her hands. "Alizayd al Qahtani, you have confronted deadlier foes than a party with people who love you and some inappropriate jokes. You can survive this, trust me." She brushed the back of her knuckles down his beard, and the protest she saw brewing in his expression turned flustered.

He caught her hand. "Your house? I hope we're not intruding."

"I insisted. I knew it would keep the guest list small—a favor for which you owe me. Add it to the debt." Nahri tucked his arm under hers to prevent any escape and then beckoned Mishmish to follow. "Come. The walk back will give you time to steel yourself."

They returned to the narrow path, leaving the river behind. "How did your case go this morning?" Ali asked.

"Pretty good. I still don't know how Yusef managed to make wings sprout from his back, but a few of my students are chasing down theories." Nahri shook her head, thinking fondly of her physicians-in-training. "Every day I thank the Creator we took them on when we did instead of waiting longer. They're such a great group. Hani and Rufaida are already talking about building clinics in other parts of the city when they graduate."

"That would be wonderful. It would certainly ease pressure on the hospital anyway." Ali glanced down at her, concern crossing his face. "And hopefully lessen your own burden. I worry about you, Nahri. Your grandfather told me you've taken to sleeping in your office some nights."

"Says the man who passes out in council meetings."

"That's different. I would challenge even the most alert person alive to stay awake during those interminable meetings."

Ali said the words lightly, but she could hear the weariness in his voice. They weren't fools; they had always known rebuilding Daevabad would be difficult, the work of a lifetime. But there were some days when that work was truly grueling, when the promise of peace, let alone political stability, seemed so very far away.

Nahri squeezed his hand. "It will get better," she promised. "For both of us. It already has. And you don't have to worry about any of that tonight."

They kept walking. The sun was low in the sky, filtering straight through the trees to cast a warm glow upon the forest. Nahri traced her fingers along a mossy outcropping of rock as they passed, and tiny blue flowers erupted in the wake of her touch.

A gift from the father she would never know. Nahri was still struggling to make peace with what she'd learned of her parents' loss—the life together of which they'd all been robbed. It seemed like so many promising starts stomped out. Their fragile love. Her father's dream of returning to Daevabad and raising Nahri as his own. The little home and life Duriya had cobbled together back in Egypt. Her parents had worked so hard to build something, only to see it all crumble down. Or, rather, be torn apart.

But at least they had the courage to try—a courage Nahri now attempted to summon, gripping the strap of her bag.

"So . . . ," she started. "Your mother must be very excited for today. She's probably been making lists and vetting candidates for months."

Ali gave her a baffled look. *"Candidates?"*

Oh, Creator . . . between his obliviousness and her anxiety, Nahri could not imagine this conversation proceeding effectively. "Well, you can marry now, can't you?" she asked, approaching the topic more directly. "Considering that Zaynab seems more content to adventure with Aqisa around the world, you're Hatset's best hope for grandchildren."

He snorted. "You must be reading my mail. Her letters have gone from hinting to openly reminding me of her age, my age, and the years I'm depriving her of such grandchildren. No candidates, though. I think I've made my wishes clear to her."

"Oh?"

"I have no time for marriage."

Wait, what? Nahri jerked to a halt. "Just to clarify . . . you think *I* spend too much time working, and now you're ready commit to eternal bachelordom so you can die alone adjusting tax rates?"

"Your dismissal of economics offends me." But Ali had stopped as well. "And no, I hope not to delay marriage forever. It's just that right now, I prefer to spend the little free time I have swapping minds with frogs and balancing the books of a very particular Banu Nahida." His voice softened. "I wouldn't want to lose that."

Tears pricked at her eyes. Maybe he wasn't so oblivious. "And what if the books were really unbalanced?" she whispered. "What if they took years to sort out?"

Ali smiled, and Nahri felt herself fall. She wanted to wrap herself in the sweetness of that smile and stay in it forever.

"I'm very good at accounting, and I have the patience of a Nile lord." Ali stepped closer. "Nahri, there's no deadline to heal by. To get over your fear of water or to make . . . other decisions. Truly. This is only the beginning of our story. *Your* story. And you can make it whatever you want it to be."

It was about the most promising answer she could hope for, and yet for a moment, Nahri hesitated, still uncertain. Right now, they were both still dancing around the subject. If she handed over her bag—

Have the courage your parents did.

"Then I have a gift for you."

"A gift?"

Nahri nodded and took Ali's hand, pulling him to sit beside her on a large, flat rock just beyond the path. "It's for your birthday, but I didn't want to give it to you in front of everyone. In case you don't like it. Or don't spill to use it."

"I can't imagine not liking any gift you picked out for me," Ali replied. "Though you didn't need to go to the trouble. I know how busy you are."

"You tracked down half the Egyptians in the city to design my office while *you* were busy restoring the hospital."

Ali grinned again. "That was different. I'm in your debt."

Nahri returned his smile but it faded as her heart rose to her throat. She normally never had a problem with her words; she could tease and curse, command and con the most silver-tongued tricksters and menacing tyrants. But this spilling of her heart was still so hard.

But you have spilled your heart to him before. That's why you're here now. "It was actually the office that gave me the idea," she said. "Do you remember what you told me that night at the hospital, when I was making a fool of myself pining for Egypt?"

A somber expression clouded across his face. So much violence had followed that last peaceful night when they celebrated the hospital's opening. "That you weren't being a fool to miss your human homeland," he said softly. "That those were your roots and they made you who you are."

"It was the first time anyone in Daevabad said anything like that to me. The only time really. You were the first person to actually see me, see *all* of me, and find the parts I couldn't reconcile with one another—Egyptian and Daeva, shafit and Nahid, thief and healer— stronger together." Nahri took a deep breath, forcing herself to hold Ali's gaze. "I would like to do the same for you."

Ali swallowed loudly. Both of them knew what she was talking about. If Ali had felt torn between his parents' peoples, it was nothing compared to the situation he was in now. The situation he would be in for the rest of his life as the ambassador between the marid and the djinn.

"All right," he breathed, his voice shaky. "That must be an astonishingly powerful bag."

Nahri could not help a nervous laugh, the knot of anxiety in her chest loosening just a bit. "It's what's *in* the bag. I had a patient a while back, an artist from Ta Ntry who sculpts all sorts of talismans and jewelry from rock salt. The pieces are stunning; she gave me a beautiful necklace but warned me to keep it away from water. Too much moisture, too much heat, and it would dissolve. I . . . well, I had her make something for you."

Ali gave her a quizzical look. "I can see the Ayaanle connection, but I'm not sure I should be handling anything that dissolves in water."

"It's meant to dissolve," Nahri explained, her heart racing as she handed over the bag. "That's the Geziri part."

Still frowning in confusion, Ali took the bag. It seemed to take an eternity for him to unlace the ties holding it closed, but then he was pulling out the silk-wrapped package that had been nestled inside. He unwound the cloth.

He went completely still.

It was a mask, masterfully carved of solid pink salt. It glittered wildly in the sunlight, like a jewel with a thousand facets. A swirling pattern of stars and diamonds, apples and iris blossoms twinkled over the arched cutouts meant for eyes and the graceful slope to accommodate a nose.

Ali's throat audibly caught. "Is this . . ."

"It's a marriage mask," she stammered out. "Or at least—it could be. It won't burn to ash like the wooden ones, but I figured if you used your marid abilities, you could make it dissolve." Her face was burning with mortification, but she pressed on. "It didn't seem fair that you would miss out on such an important Geziri wedding tradition because you gave up your fire magic."

"You got me a marriage mask," Ali repeated, sounding shocked. His eyes had locked on the gift. "I . . . did you have someone in mind who would wear it?"

Yes! her heart seemed to sing even as sheer terror tore through it at the prospect of such a blunt declaration.

"Someone who still needs time," Nahri said instead. "Someone who's trying—really trying—to build a life here despite this constant fear that the moment she's happy, it will all be torn apart." Tears stung in her eyes, and she quickly wiped them away, embarrassed. "But someone who hopes her feelings are clear, even if she can't say them yet."

"Oh, Nahri." Ali reached for her hand. "I don't know whether to weep or to kiss you. One would probably be a rather alarming response and the other is forbidden." He finally met her gaze and no matter what he said, his eyes were already wet and Nahri did not miss the desire burning there. "Your feelings are clear, my light," he said in Arabic. "I hope mine are too."

A weight seemed to slip—slip, not fall entirely—from her shoulders. "Are you sure? If you don't want to wait, I would understand. There are no names carved . . ."

"There is only one name I want carved next to mine on this mask." Clearly unable to resist bending the rules a little, Ali brought her hand to his mouth and lightly, so lightly it might have been a brush of the wind, kissed her knuckles.

The brief graze of his lips sent an unfair amount of heat unspooling in her belly. "Thank the Creator," she breathed. "I was so nervous."

"You don't need to be nervous." With his other hand, Ali traced the edge of the mask. "This is the kindest, most thoughtful gift anyone has ever given me. I will find a safe place for it. Take your time. And when you're ready . . ." The small clouds of fog that tended to drift around his feet had been roiling like thunderstorms, but they steadied now, misting against her skin. "We'll write our story."

Nahri waited for the panic to steal over her. The forest, typically full of birdsong and the chitter of various magical animals flitting from branch to branch, had gone quiet and soft. This moment was too sweet, too promising. But the urge to distance herself from it, to wall off her heart and protect herself from any future hurt, didn't come, and that itself seemed a hopeful sign.

Still she could not help but ask, half teasing, "Do you think it will be a happy one?"

Ali smiled at her. "I do."

ACKNOWLEDGMENTS

I could never have gotten this far if it wasn't for the excitement and enthusiasm of my wonderful readers. Thank you for indulging me, and I hope you enjoyed this expanded farewell to Nahri, Ali, Dara, and the rest of the Daevabad crew. Jen, if I haven't said it lately, I'm extremely lucky that you're my agent and had the sense to see in my ramblings a project that could be shared.

Roshani, thank you for the early encouragement to actually try and give my characters some nontragic romantic endings. Tasha, Rowenna, and Sam . . . I cannot tell you how much I appreciate your assistance through a last-minute panic read. Bunker friends, you continue to be the very best, and I hope your books take over the world.

And for Shamik and Alia, all my love as always.

Read an excerpt of

The Adventures of Amina Al-Sirafi

❉ ❉ ❉

A Word on What Is to Come

In the name of God, the Most Merciful, the Most Compassionate. Blessings upon His honored Prophet Muhammad, his family, and his followers. Praise be to God, who in His glory created the earth and its diversity of lands and languages, peoples and tongues. In these vast marvels, so numerous a human eye cannot gaze upon more than a sliver, is there not proof of His Magnificence?

And when it comes to marvels . . . let us delight in the adventures of the nakhudha Amina al-Sirafi.

Yes! *That* Captain Amina al-Sirafi. The smuggler, the pirate. The blasphemer that men of letters accuse of serving up human hearts for her sea-beast husband, and the sorceress—for she *must* be a sorceress, because no female could sail a ship so deftly without the use of forbidden magics—whose appearance somehow both beguiles and repulses. Traders along our fair shores warn against speaking her name as though she is a djinn that might be summoned as such—though, strangely, they have little compunction when it comes to spreading vicious rumors about her body and her sexuality: these things that men obsess over when they hate what they desire and desire what they cannot possess.

I am certain you have heard talk of her. After all, it is tradition for the traveled men of our ummah to share the wonders of the world by creating accounts of their voyages—particularly when those voyages are enlivened by gossip of fearsome female rogues. Many such travelers will swear their accounts are not written to tantalize or entertain—God forbid!—but are intended first and foremost to strengthen the hearts of the faithful and provide evidence of the promised splendor of God's creation. And yet, as Muslims, are we not told to speak honestly? To ascertain what is truth and beware spreading falsehoods?

And dear sisters . . . what falsehoods.

For this scribe has read a great many of these accounts and taken away another lesson: that to be a woman is to have your story misremembered. Discarded. *Twisted.* In courtyard tales, women are the adulterous wives whose treachery begins a husband's descent into murderous madness or the long-suffering mothers who give birth to proper heroes. Biographers polish away the jagged edges of capable, ruthless queens so they may be remembered as saints, and geographers warn believing men away from such and such a place with scandalous tales of lewd local females who cavort in the sea and ravish foreign interlopers. Women are the forgotten spouses and unnamed daughters. Wet nurses and handmaidens; thieves and harlots. Witches. A titillating anecdote to tell your friends back home or a warning.

There are plenty of slanderous stories like *that* about Amina al-Sirafi. She was too relentless, they say. Too ambitious, too violent, utterly inappropriate, and well . . . old! A *mother,* if you can believe it! Ah yes, a certain degree of rebelliousness is expected from youth. It is why we have stories of treasure-seeking princesses and warrior women that end with the occasional happiness. But they are expected to *end*—with the boy, the prince, the sailor, the adventurer. The man that will take her maidenhood, grant her children, make her a wife. The man who defines her. *He* may continue his epic—he may indeed take new wives and make new children!—but women's stories are expected to dissolve into a fog of domesticity . . . if they're told at all.

Amina's story did not end. Verily, no woman's story does. This humble scribe—ah, I should introduce myself: there is a bit more to my name, but for now you may call me Jamal. Jamal al-Hilli. And I have met grandmothers launching new businesses, elderly queens fighting wars of conquest, and young mothers taking up a drawing pen for the first time. Indeed, we may only have Amina's story *because* she was a mother. In our time together, she spoke constantly of her daughter. And though it may be a bold assumption . . . she spoke *to* her daughter. So that her child might come to understand the choices her mother had made. For when Amina chose to leave her home and return to a life at sea, she became more than a pirate. More than a witch.

She became a legend.

This tale will sound unbelievable. What proofs and documents could be collected are reproduced, but when it came to the nakhudha, this scribe felt it best to let Amina speak for herself. To resist the urge to shape and couch her words. But for the sake of honesty, another truth will be confessed. Her adventures are not only being told as evidence of God's marvels.

They are being told to entertain.

◆

God as my witness, none of this would have ever happened if it were not for those two fools back in Salalah. Them and their map.

—What? What do you mean, that is "not how you start a story"? A *biography*? You wish for a biography? Who do you think you are chronicling, the Grand Mufti of Mecca? My people do not wax poetic about lineage like yours do. We are not even true Sirafis. My father's father—an orphan turned pirate from Oman—simply found the name romantic.

—Don't you think so?

As I was saying. The idiots and their map. Now, I understand the appeal of treasure-hunting, I do. After all, we build our homes upon the ruins of lost cities and sail our ships over the drowned palaces of forgotten kings. Everyone has heard a tale of how so-and-so dug up a jar of Sasanian coins while sowing his fields or met a pearl diver who glimpsed hordes of emeralds glittering on the seabed. It was related to me that in Egypt, treasure-hunting is so popular its participants have organized into professional guilds, each holding their particular tricks close . . . though for the right price, someone *might* be willing to give you some advice. They may even offer to sell you a map! A guide to such fortunes you could scarcely imagine.

The maps are—and I cannot emphasize this enough—remarkably easy to forge. I can even tell you how it is done: You merely need a scrap of parchment and a bit of time. Tonics are applied to darken and yellow the paper, though regrettably, the majority require urine and the best derive from the bile of a bat. The map itself should be drawn with care, with enough details that some geographic locations will be recognizable (ideally directing the mark in the opposite direction of which the mapmaker intends to flee). Symbols can be lifted from any number of alphabets. Many forgers prefer Hebrew for its mystical connotations, but in my opinion, the text off an old Sabaean tomb makes for more mysterious letters. Wrinkle the whole thing up; fray the edges, burn a few holes, apply a thin layer of sandarac to fade the script—and that is that. Your "treasure" map is ready to be sold to the highest bidder.

The map my clients possessed that night did not look like it had been sold to the highest bidder. Though they had been trying to conceal the document along with their purpose—as though midnight excursions to ancient ruins were a common request—a glimpse had been enough to reveal the map was of middling work, perhaps the practice manuscript of an earnest criminal youngster.

But I kept such opinions to myself. That they had hired me to row them out here was a blessing, a chance job I had snagged while fishing. I must have seemed a prime candidate for their mission: a lone local woman a bit long in the tooth and almost certainly too dim to care what they were doing. I made the appropriate noises, warning them that the ruins were said to be haunted by ghouls and the surrounding lagoon cursed by djinn, but the young men assured me they could handle themselves. And as I had spent many a night fishing in the area without encountering even a whiff of the supernatural, I was not truly concerned.

—Excuse me? That "seems sort of naïve"? Do you not recall how we met, hypocrite? Stop talking and eat your stew. The saltah is excellent here and you are barely thicker than that pen you are holding. Another interruption, Jamal, and you can find some other nakhudha to harass for stories.

Anyway. Back to that night. It was an otherwise enchanting evening. The stars were out, a rare sight during the khareef, the summer monsoon that typically mires us in fog. The moon shone brightly upon the ruined fort across the lagoon, its crumbling bricks all that remained of a long-abandoned city locals said had once been a bustling trading port. This part of the world has always been rich; the Romans once called us Arabia Felix, "Blessed Arabia," for our access to the sea, reliable trade routes, and lucrative frankincense groves. Locals *also* say that the lost city's treasury—still bursting with gold—lays hidden beneath the ruins, buried during an earthquake. It was that story I assumed had lured out the youths until one of them loudly clucked their tongue at me in the manner of a man calling a mule to halt while we were still in the lagoon.

"Stop here," the boy ordered.

I gave the black water surrounding us, the beach still some distance away, a dubious glance. During the day, this was a lovely place that attracted flamingos and dolphins. When the wind and tide were just right, water would burst from the rocks in geysers to the delight of children and picnicking families. But during low tide on a calm night such as this, the breakers against the surf were mild, a steady soothing crash and glittering white spray that did little to differentiate between sea and shore. If my clients thought they could swim all the way to the barely visible beach, they were even more foolish than I thought. And I think I've been clear how foolish I considered them.

"We are not yet at the ruins," I pointed out.

"This is far enough." The pair were huddled together at the other end of my small boat, the map spread across their knees. One boy held an oil lamp for illumination, the other a burning bunch of dried jasmine.

"I do not understand," one of the youths muttered. They had been arguing in hushed whispers all night. Though their accents sounded Adeni to my ear, I did not know their names. They had rather dramatically declared that in lieu of offering their names, they would pay me an additional dirham for my discretion, and since I did not actually care, the extra payment was a delightful surprise. "The map says this is the spot . . ." He gestured to the heavens above, and my heart went out to him, for what was written on that map had nothing to do with any star chart I have ever seen.

"You said you wished to go to the old city." I gestured toward the hill—or at least I tried to. But a thick bank of fog had rolled down from the wadi, the monsoon-swollen stream that fed the lagoon, to surround us, and neither the ruins nor the hill were visible. Instead, as I watched, the shore entirely vanished so that we appeared to be floating on an endless, mist-shrouded plain.

The youths ignored me. "We have said the words," the one holding the oil lamp argued. "We have her payment. She should appear."

"And yet she has not," the other boy argued. "I am *telling* you, we were supposed to . . ."

But whatever they were supposed to do stopped concerning me. In the space of a breath, the breeze that had been blowing in from the sea all night abruptly halted, the air turning dead and flat. I stilled, a bead of sweat chasing down my spine. I am a sailor, and there is little I watch more closely than the weather. I lifted a fraying strand from my cloak, but no wind stirred the thread. The fog drew closer, accompanied by a smothering quiet that made thunderous every knock of water against the boat's hull.

There are places in the world where such signs might herald a vicious, dangerous storm, but the typhoons that occasionally struck here typically did not manifest so unexpectedly. The water remained gentle, the tide and current unchanged, but even so . . . there was an ill feeling in my belly.

I reached for my oars. "I think we should leave."

"Wait!" One of the young men stood, waving excitedly at the fog. "Do you see that shadow above the sea-foam?"

It *was* sea-foam, I realized, squinting in the dark. Years of the sun's glare upon the ocean had begun to take their toll on my vision, and I struggled to see clearly at night. But the boy was correct. It wasn't only fog drifting closer. It was sea-foam piled high enough to swallow my boat. As it approached, one could see a reddish-yellow hue to the substance and smell the awful aroma of rotting flesh and gutted fish.

"Give over her payment," Oil-Lamp Boy urged. "Quickly!"

"Forget my payment and sit back down," I ordered as the second youth reached into his robe. "We are—"

The boy pulled free his hand, revealing a large chunk of red carnelian, and two things happened very quickly:

One, I realized that was not *my* payment.

Two, the thing whose payment it was dragged us into the fog.

The boy holding the carnelian barely had time to cry out before the froth rushed to consume him, licking down his neck and chest and winding around his hips like an eager lover. A howl ripped from his throat, but it was not a scream any mortal mouth should have been able to let loose. Rather, it was more the roar of a tidal wave and the death cries of gulls.

"Khalid!" The other boy dropped the lamp in shock, extinguishing our only light.

But fortunately—fortunately?—the seemingly alive and possibly malevolent sea-foam was glowing. Its light was faint, but enough to illuminate Khalid as he bared his teeth like a wolf and threw himself on his companion.

"*You shall not have me,*" he hissed, groping for the other boy's neck. "We will curse you! We will devour you! We will cast you into the flames!"

The other boy struggled to free himself. "Khalid, please!" he choked as more sea-foam—now the crimson of blood—spread over them both. Fanged suckers were blossoming across its surface like the tentacles of a monstrous squid.

I would like to say I did not hesitate. That at the sight of two youths in mortal peril, I flew into action and did not briefly wonder if the malevolent sea-foam might be sated with eating them and leave me and my boat alone. That would be a lie. I did hesitate. But then I cursed them profusely, rose to my feet, and went for my knife.

Now, I am fond of blades. The khanjar that was my grandfather's and the wickedly beautiful Damascene scimitar I stole off an undeserving noble. The small straight knife that hides in an ankle holster and a truly excellent bladed disc from my second husband, who learned to regret teaching me to throw it.

But there's only one weapon for situations like this, one I commissioned myself and never leaves my presence. Made of pure iron, it isn't my sharpest blade and its weight can make it unwieldly. Spots of rust from the sacred Zamzam water I sprinkle over it in nightly blessings pepper the metal, the red flakes making it difficult to discern the knife's inscribed holy verses. But I didn't need the knife to be pretty.

I needed it to be effective when more earthly weapons failed.

I seized Khalid by the collar and ripped him off the other boy. Before he could make a grab for *my* throat, I put my blessed blade to his. "Be gone," I demanded.

He wriggled wildly, sea-foam flying. "You shall not have me. *You shall not have me!*"

"I do not want you! Now, in the name of God, be gone!"

I pressed the knife harder as the bismillah left my lips. His flesh sizzled in response, and then he crumpled. The sea-foam that had wrapped his body hovered in the air a moment then hurled itself at me. I fell as though struck by a battering ram, my head slamming into the boat's bottom.

Icy fingers with bone-sharp tips were digging into my ears, a great weight pinning me in place. But by the grace of God, I was still holding my blessed blade. I struck out madly, and the knife *stuck* in the air. There was a shriek—an evil, unnatural sound like claws scraping over seashells—and then the scaled monstrosity squatting on my chest rippled into sight. Its glittering eyes were the color of bilgewater, its filthy straw-like hair matted with barnacles.

It screamed again, revealing four needlelike teeth. Its bony hands scrabbled on my own as it tried to wrest away the dagger sunk into its wine-dark breast. Silver blood bubbled and dripped from the wound, drenching us both.

The youths were sobbing and begging God for mercy. The demon was shrieking and wailing in an unknown tongue. I shoved the blade deeper, thundering to be heard over all of them.

"God!" I shouted. "There is no god worthy of worship except Him, the Ever-Living, All-Sustaining!" Holding the dagger tight, I launched into ayat al-kursi, the passage from the Quran I had been taught all my life would protect me.

The demon on my chest howled and writhed in pain, its skeletal hands flying to cover scaled ears.

"Neither drowsiness nor sleep overtakes Him! To Him belongs whatever is in the heavens and whatever is on the earth—*will you get off of me?*" I elbowed the creature hard, and it spit in my face. "Who could possibly intercede with Him without His permission? He knows what is ahead of them and what is behind them, but no one can grasp any of His knowledge—except what He wills!"

Its skin smoking, the demon must have decided it had had enough. A pair of bat-like wings sprouted from its back, and with a gusty flap, it pulled itself off the blade and was gone, vanished into the night.

Gasping, I sat up. The mists were already receding, the youths still clutching each other on the other side of the boat. I held the dagger tight, searching the retreating fog for anything else. Fear coursed through me, thick and choking, as I waited for that familiar laugh. For fiery black eyes and a too-silky voice.

But there was nothing. Nothing but the star-splashed lagoon and the gentle murmur of the tide.

I spun on the youths. "You said you were after treasure."

Oil-Lamp Boy flushed, spots of color appearing in his chalky skin. "Treasure is a concept open to—no, wait!" he cried as I snatched their map and lump of carnelian, thrusting them over the water. "Do not do that!"

I tossed and caught the glittering red gem in one hand. "Do not pretend with me, boy," I warned. "Lie again and I will throw you both overboard. You mentioned payment and a name. What were you trying to summon?"

"We were not trying—Bidukh!" he confessed when I dipped the map into the sea. "My cousin told me about her. She is . . ." He swallowed loudly. "She is one of the daughters of Iblis."

I gaped. "You were trying to summon a daughter of the lord of hell? On *my* boat?"

"We did not mean any harm!" The moonlight had returned, and I could see him cowering. "It is said that if you please her, she will whisper the secrets of love into your ear."

Khalid swayed in his friend's arms. "I am going to be sick."

"Throw up in my boat, and you swim back to shore. A daughter of Iblis . . . may you both be cursed." I hurled the map and carnelian into the lagoon. They vanished with loud splashes amidst the protest of my passengers.

"Hey!" the boy cried. "We paid a lot of money for that!"

"You should be thanking God you did not pay with your lives." I thrust an extra oar in his arms. "Row. Perhaps some labor will knock a bit of sense into you."

He nearly dropped the oar, his eyes going wide as I shifted positions, the movement revealing the other weapons concealed beneath my cloak. I wiped the iron knife clean, placing it back into its sheath before taking up my own set of oars.

Both boys were staring at me with expressions of shock. I could not blame them. I'd fought off a demon, given up the slouch I'd been affecting to reveal my true height, and now rowed with my full strength—a far cry from the quiet, hunched-over old fisherwoman who'd reluctantly agreed to take them out here.

"Who are you?" Khalid asked hoarsely.

The other one gawked. "*What* are you?"

The lagoon was receding, but I would swear I still felt a heaviness in the air. For a moment the water splashing at the rocky beach looked like the yellow-hued crimson of the now-vanished sea-foam, the shadows dancing on the cliffs like tentacles.

"Someone who knows too well the price of magic."

I said nothing else, and they did not ask. But they did not need to. For stories carry, and even if the youths were ashamed to confess their own schemes, the tale of an unassuming fisherwoman who fought a demon like a warrior of God? Who threw off her tattered cloak to reveal an armory at her waist and a form like an Amazon?

Exaggerations, but the truth scarcely matters when it comes to a good tale. The kind of story that spreads in taverns and shipyards. To wealthy women's harems and the kitchens of their servants.

To the ear of a very desperate grandmother in Aden.

ABOUT THE AUTHOR

S. A. CHAKRABORTY is the author of the critically acclaimed and internationally bestselling Daevabad Trilogy. Her work has been translated into more than a dozen languages and nominated for the Hugo, Locus, World Fantasy, Crawford, and Astounding awards. When not buried in books about thirteenth-century con artists and Abbasid political intrigue, she enjoys hiking, knitting, and re-creating unnecessarily complicated medieval meals. You can find her online at sachakraborty.com or on Twitter and Instagram @SAChakrabooks, where she likes to talk about history, politics, and Islamic art. She currently lives in New Jersey with her husband, daughter, and an ever-increasing number of cats.